OTHER BOOKS YOU MAY ENJOY

Althea & Oliver	Cristina Moracho
The Disenchantments	Nina LaCour
Grasshopper Jungle	Andrew Smith
Highly Illogical Behavior	John Corey Whaley
I'll Give You the Sun	Jandy Nelson
Let It Snow	John Green, Maureen Johnson, Lauren Myracle
Mosquitoland	David Arnold
Still Life with Tornado	A. S. King
There Is No Dog	Meg Rosoff
Will Grayson, Will Grayson	John Green & David Levithan

KIDS

OF

APPETITE

DAVID
ARNOLD

speak

SPEAK
An imprint of Penguin Random House LLC
375 Hudson Street
New York, New York 10014

First published in the United States of America by Viking,
an imprint of Penguin Random House LLC, 2016
Published by Speak, an imprint of Penguin Random House LLC, 2017

THE LIBRARY OF CONGRESS HAS CATALOGED THE VIKING EDITION AS FOLLOWS:
Names: Arnold, David, date– author.
Title: Kids of appetite / David Arnold.
Description: New York : Viking Children's Books, [2016] | Summary: Teens
Victor Benucci and Madeline Falco sit in separate police interrogation
rooms telling about the misfits who brought them together and their
journey sparked by a message in an urn.
Identifiers: LCCN 2015042375 | ISBN 9780451470782 (hardback)
Subjects: | CYAC: Friendship—Fiction. | Voyages and travels—Fiction.
| Death—Fiction. | Love—Fiction. | Facial paralysis—Fiction. | People
with disabilities—Fiction. | Congolese (Democratic Republic)—United
States—Fiction. | BISAC: JUVENILE FICTION / Social Issues / Adolescence.
| JUVENILE FICTION / Social Issues / Friendship.
| JUVENILE FICTION / Social Issues / Death & Dying.
Classification: LCC PZ7.A7349 Kid 2016 | DDC [Fic]—dc23
LC record available at https://lccn.loc.gov/2015042375

Speak ISBN 9780147513663

Printed in U.S.A.   Set in Chaparral Pro   Book design by Kate Renner

1 3 5 7 9 10 8 6 4 2

For my brothers, Jeremy and AJ, the original KOA.

* * *

And in memory of my two grandfathers,
a couple of real Super Racehorses.

Cast of Characters

* * *

The Kids of Appetite

BRUNO VICTOR BENUCCI III, sixteen (VIC): Current Chapter. Opera, Matisse, Mad. Super Racehorse.

MADELINE FALCO, seventeen (MAD): New Year's darling. Punk cut, Elliott Smith, Venn diagrams, realness.

MBEMBA BAHIZIRE KABONGO, twenty-seven (BAZ): Collector of stories & tattoos. Anti-bread. Praise God.

NZUZI KABONGO, twenty (ZUZ): Baz's little brother. Jigs & Journey & snaps. Speaks in other ways.

COCO BLYTHE, eleven: Songwriter. Redhead. Ice cream & Queens & faux cussing. Frak yeah.

The Hackensack Police

SERGEANT S. MENDES: Coffee addict. Reluctant girlfriend. Clever & weary. More than meets the eye.

DETECTIVE H. BUNDLE: Atomic cloud. Paperwork & forms. Proud member of the bountiful bourgeoisie.

DETECTIVE RONALD: Weasley doppelgänger. Eager boyfriend. Sitting skills. Lost poodle.

The Family, Etc.

DORIS JACOBY BENUCCI: Vic's mother. Widow. Baking & family & moving on. Trying her best.

BRUNO VICTOR BENUCCI JR.: Vic's father. Heart-thinker. Mets fan. Wearer of sweatpants. Deceased.

THE SELF-PORTRAIT MAN (UNCLE LESTER): Mad's uncle. Whiskey & yelling & crying. Owner of guns.

JAMMA: Mad's grandmother. Dementia sufferer. Slippers & pj's & double-fisted Coca-Cola.

FRANK THE BOYFRIEND: Lawyer. Widower. Green-bean eater & literary novice. Wearer of suits.

KLINT & KORY: Frank's sons. Hot Topic & Batman. The Orchestra of Lost Soulz. Kids of No Appetite.

FATHER RAINES: Priest, sage, good-deed doer. Married Vic's parents. Iron Maiden superfan.

RACHEL GRIMES: Baz's current girlfriend. Daring nurse. Thunder & running & pancakes.

The Early Chapters

CHRISTOPHER (TOPHER): Tattoo artist. *Battlestar Galactica* & sobriety & resourcefulness. Bald.

MARGO BONAPARTE: Waitress, smuggler, flirt. Cheese fries. Rum. *Bonjour, mes petits gourmands!*

NORM: Russian butcher. Misunderstood. Meat. Bloody pigs. Not KGB. *Nyet.*

GUNTHER MAYWOOD: Hermit. Landlord. Owner of the Maywood Orchard.

The Goldfish

HARRY CONNICK JR., JR.: Survivor. Swimmer. Cold-weather enthusiast. Will not quit. But hey.

* * *

* * *

"*It seemed funny to me that the sunset she saw from her patio and the one I saw from the back steps was the same one. Maybe the two different worlds we lived in weren't so different. We saw the same sunset.*"

— THE OUTSIDERS, S. E. HINTON

* * *

ONE

THE MOMENTOUS MULTITUDES
(or, Gird Thy Silly, Futile Selves)

Consider this: billions of people in the world, each with billions of *I am*s. I am a quiet observer, a champion wallflower. I am a lover of art, the Mets, the memory of Dad. I represent approximately one seven-billionth of the population; these are my momentous multitudes, and that's just for starters.

"It begins with my friends."

"What does?"

"My story," I say.

Only that's not quite right. I have to go back further than that, before we were friends, back when it was just . . .

. . .

Okay, got it.

"I've fallen in love something like a thousand times."

Mendes smiles a little, nudges the digital recorder closer. "I'm sorry—you said . . . you've fallen in love?"

"A thousand times," I say, running both hands through my hair.

I used to think love was bound by numbers: first kisses, second dances, infinite heartbreaks. I used to think numbers outlasted the love itself, surviving in the dark corners of the demolished heart. I used to think love was heavy and hard.

I don't think those things anymore.

"I am a Super Racehorse."

"You're a *what*?" asks Mendes, her eyes at once tough and tired.

"Nothing. Where's your uniform?"

She wears a tweed skirt with a fitted jacket and flowy blouse. I quietly observe her brown eyes, very intense, and—were it not for the baggy pillows, and the crow's feet framing her features like facial parentheses—quite pretty. I quietly observe the slight creases on her hands and neck, indicative of premature aging. I quietly observe the absence of a wedding ring. I quietly observe her dark hair, shoulder-length with just a lingering shadow of shape and style.

Parenthetical, slight, absence, lingering: the momentous multitudes of Mendes, it seems, are found in the hushed footnote.

"Technically I'm off duty," she says. "Plus, I'm a sergeant, so I don't always have to wear a uniform."

"So you're the one in charge, right?"

"I report to Lieutenant Bell, but this is my case if that's what you're asking."

I reach under my chair, pull my Visine out of the front pocket of my backpack, and apply a quick drop in each eye.

"Victor, you've been missing eight days. Then this morning you and"—she shuffles through papers until finding the one she's looking for—"Madeline Falco march in here, practically holding hands with Mbemba Bahizire Kabongo, aka Baz, the primary suspect in our murder investigation."

"I wasn't holding hands with Baz. And he's no murderer."

"You don't think so?"

"I know so."

Mendes gives me a pity-smile, the kind of smile that frowns. "He just turned himself in, Vic. That, plus his DNA is on the murder weapon. We have more than enough to put Kabongo behind bars for a very long time. What I'm hoping you might shed some light on is how you go from running out the front door of your own home eight days ago to walking in *here* this morning. You said you have a story to tell. So tell it."

This morning's memory is fresh, Baz's voice ingrained in my brain. *Diversion tactics, Vic. They will need time. And we must give it to them.*

"Every girl who wears eyeliner," I say.

. . .

. . .

Sergeant Mendes squints. "What?"

"Every girl who plays an instrument, except—maybe not bassoon."

"I'm sorry, I don't unders—"

"Every girl who wears old Nikes. Every girl who draws on them. Every girl who shrugs or bakes or reads." *Tell them about all the girls you thought you loved, the ones from before.* I smile on the inside, the only place I can. "Every girl who rides a bike."

I pull out my handkerchief and dab the drool from the corner of my mouth. Dad called it my "leaky mug." I used to hate that. Now I miss it.

Sometimes . . . yes, I think I miss the hated things most.

Mendes leans back in her chair. "Shortly after you left, your mom reported you missing. I've been in your room, Vic. It's all Whitman and Salinger and Matisse. You're smart. And kind of a nerd, if you don't mind my saying."

"What's your point?"

"My point is, you're no hard-ass. So why are you acting like one?"

Under the metal table, I pick at the fabric of my KOA wristband. "*I am large, I contain multitudes.*"

Mendes picks up: "*I concentrate toward them that are nigh, I wait on the door-slab. Who has done his day's work? Who will soonest be through with his supper? Who wishes to walk with me?*"

. . .

I try to hide my shock, but I can't be sure my eyes didn't just give me away.

"Whitman balanced out the criminal justice classes," says Mendes. "You know what the next line is, don't you?"

I don't. So I say nothing at all.

"*Will you speak before I am gone?*" she says quietly. "*Will you prove already too late?*"

. . .

"Due respect, Miss Mendes. You don't know me."

She looks back at the file in front of her. "Bruno Victor Benucci III, sixteen, son of Doris Jacoby Benucci and the late Bruno Benucci Jr., deceased two years. Only child. Five foot six. Dark hair. Suffers from the rare Moebius syndrome. Obsession with abstract art—"

"Do you know what that is?"

"Oh, I've had my share of Picasso-obsessed crooks, lemme tell you, it's no picnic."

"That's not what I meant."

"I know what you meant." Mendes flips the file shut. "And yeah, I did some research. Moebius is a rare neurological disorder affecting the sixth and seventh cranial nerves, present from birth, causing facial paralysis. I understand it's been difficult for you."

Mendes's tone suggests a hint of self-satisfaction, as if she's been sitting on this definition, just waiting for me to ask if she knew what was wrong with my face. I've had Moebius syndrome my whole life, and here is what I've learned: the only people arrogant enough to use the words *I understand* are the ones who can't possibly understand. People who truly get it never say much of anything.

"You did some research," I say, barely above a whisper.

"A little."

"So you know what it feels like to have sand shoved up your eyelids."

. . .

"What?"

"That's what it's like sometimes, not being able to blink," I say. "Dry eye doesn't begin to describe it. More like desert eye."

"Vic—"

"Did your research offer insight into the night terrors that come from sleeping with your eyes half shut? Or how drinking from a cup feels about as possible as lassoing the moon? Or how the best I can hope for is that kids just leave me alone? Or how certain teachers slow down when talking to me because they assume I'm stupid?"

Mendes shifts uncomfortably in her chair.

"Don't get me wrong," I say. "I'm not complaining. Lots of people with Moebius have it worse than me. I used to wish I was someone else, but then . . ."

But then Dad introduced me to Henri Matisse, an artist who believed each face had its own rhythm. Matisse looked for what he called "particular asymmetry" in his portraits. I liked that. I wondered about the rhythm of my own face, and about my particular asymmetry. I told Dad this once. He said

there was beauty in my asymmetry. This made me feel better. Not un-alone, just less alone.

Accompanied by art, at least.

"But then . . . ?" says Mendes.

I almost forgot I'd started a sentence. "Nothing."

"Vic, I know you've had it tough."

I point both index fingers at my unflinching face. "You mean my . . . 'affliction'?"

"I never used the word *afflicted*."

"Oh right. *Suffers from*. You're a humanitarian."

Underneath my KOA wristband, I feel my tiny paths going nowhere. My fingers have always been a force to be reckoned with, scratching and clawing and pinching. The wristband is an effective reminder, but it's no match for my fingers, with their tiny little fingerbrains, determined to test my pain threshold.

I ask, "You ever hear that a person has to go through fire to become who they're meant to be?"

Mendes sips her coffee, nods. "Sure."

"I've always wanted to be strong, Miss Mendes. I just wish there wasn't so much fire."

. . .

"Victor." It's a whisper, barely even there. Mendes leans in, her entire presence shifting from defense to offense. "Vic, look at me."

I can't.

"Look at me," she repeats.

I do.

"Did Baz Kabongo put you up to this?" She nods slowly. "It's okay. He did, right?"

Still, nothing.

"Let me tell you what I think happened," she says.

"Kabongo gets nervous, sees his face posted all over town, decides he's done hiding. He talks you and your girlfriend into lying to us, saying you were in places you weren't, at times you weren't, with people you weren't. He knows his only chance is an alibi, or an eyewitness saying someone else did it. And who better than two innocent kids? Am I warm?"

I say nothing. I am an absolute ace at nonverbals, and every minute that passes is a win, a victory, no matter how small.

"I'm pretty good at my job," she continues, "and while I don't know where you *were* on the night of December seventeenth, I know where you *weren't*. You weren't in that house. You didn't see that pool of blood. You didn't see that man's eyes go out, Victor. You know how I know this is true? If you'd seen all that, there's no way in hell you'd be sitting in that chair right now, dicking around with me. You'd piss your pants, is what you'd do. You'd be fucking terrified."

. . .

. . .

Those fingerbrains are ruthless animals, munching on my multitudes.

"Kabongo is counting on you to lie, Vic. But do you know what he forgot? He forgot about Matisse. He forgot about Whitman. He forgot about art. And you know what all good art has in common, right? Honesty. It's the part of you that knows what's what. And that's the part that's gonna tell me the truth."

I count to ten in my head, where Baz's voice plays over and over like a scratched record. *Let them think what they want. But do not lie.*

"We'll protect you," says Mendes. "You don't have to be afraid. Just tell me what happened."

Diversion tactics, Vic. They will need time. And we must give it to them.

. . .

. . .

I lean in to the digital recorder and clear my throat. "Every girl who drinks tea."

Mendes calmly shuts the file. "All right, we're done here."

"Every girl who eats raspberry scones."

She scoots her chair out from under the table, stands with an air of finality, and speaks loud and clear. "Interview between Bruno Victor Benucci III and Sergeant Sarah Mendes terminated at three twenty-eight p.m." She pushes stop, grabs her coffee and folder off the table, and heads for the door. "Your mom should be here soon to pick you up. In the meantime, feel free to get coffee down the hall." She shakes her head, opens the door, and mumbles, "Fucking raspberry scones."

The Hackensack Police Department, Interrogation Room Three, dissolves into the Maywood Orchard, Greenhouse Eleven. I imagine: Baz Kabongo, with his borderline paternal instincts and sleeve of tattoos; audacious Coco, loyal to the end; Zuz Kabongo, snapping, dancing in place; and I imagine Mad. I remember that moment—*my* moment of heartbreaking clarity when the clouds parted, and I saw everything as if I'd never seen anything at all. The truth is, I didn't know what love was until I saw it sitting in a greenhouse, unfolding like a map before me, revealing its many uncharted territories.

As Sergeant Mendes opens the door to leave, I pull my hand from under the table, raise it up until the wristband is at eye level, admire those three block letters, white against the black fabric: KOA.

Walt Whitman was right. We do contain multitudes. Most are hard and heavy, and what a headache. But some multitudes are wondrous.

Like this one . . .

I am a Kid of Appetite.

"I *was* in that house, Miss Mendes." I focus on the snow-white *K* and *O* and *A* as the blurry image of Mendes freezes in the doorframe. She does not turn around.

"I was there," I say. "I saw his eyes go out."

(EIGHT days ago)

VIC

"The Flower Duet" ended.

"The Flower Duet" began again.

The magic of repeat.

I missed Dad. Ergo, I stood on the edge of the pier. It was the thing to do when I missed Dad like this.

I stood on the edge of the pier a lot.

Hands in pockets, jacket collar flipped up against the Jersey cold (which bit like an angry dragon with long icy teeth), I let my hair whip around in the wind. I didn't care that it got messed up. Not even a bit.

Hair wasn't momentous.

Two things that were momentous:

 1. This song, "The Flower Duet." It used to be
    Dad's favorite. Now it was mine.

2. This dormant submarine, the USS *Ling*. A once great and seaworthy vessel, it had been laid to rest in the Hackensack River long before I was born. The *Ling* reminded me of this: a retired racehorse sent to one of those sex farms where all they do is procreate with other racehorses in hopes that all the best genetics will win out and produce one Super Racehorse. (Dad took me to one of these places for a tour once; when our guide started in on "breeding phantoms" and various methods of artificial insemination, I decided it was best I wait in the car.)

Unfortunately, there were no other subs in the river with which the *Ling* could procreate.

Ergo, there would be no sub sex.

Ergo, no Super Sub.

This portion of the riverside had been sectioned off as an official navy museum, with guided tours and the like. It was only open on Saturdays and Sundays, which meant I had the place to myself during the week. Most days I stopped here on my walk home from school, which made me wonder what the USS *Ling* looked like at nighttime. I couldn't say exactly what drew me to it. Maybe the fact that the sub's real life was over, yet here it was. I felt I could relate.

My cell phone vibrated in my pocket. I pulled it out and swiped to read Mom's text.

Hey. can u stop @ babushka's, grab prosciutto? Pls? :) :)

The shorthand killed me. Mom still had this ancient flip phone where each button had to be pushed approximately one dozen times to reach the desired letter. On more than one occasion, I'd attempted to demonstrate the benefits of the miraculous QWERTY keyboard. It was beyond her.

I typed back the following:

> T'would be an honor and a privilege, good mother, for me to fulfill your Venetian salt-cured meat delivery requirements this fine evening. I shall return forthwith and posthaste. E'er your loving son, Victor. ☺☺☺

A second later, she responded:

> thnx, luv

. . .

Thnx, luv.

I slid the phone back into my pocket, looked out at the *Ling*. Not so long ago, Mom would have played along, called me out on my smartass response.

Things were different now.

. . .

. . .

"The Flower Duet" came to a heartrending chorus in my ears as the wind continued thrashing my hair. I didn't particularly like opera; I liked this particular opera. I pictured those two women, the soaring sopranos, absolutely killing it. They weren't singing; they were *flying*. Dad once said the reason some people didn't like opera was because they listened with their brains and not their hearts. He said most people's

brains were pretty stupid, but hearts could cut through bull-shit like an absolute ace. *Think with your heart, V,* he used to say. *It's where the music lives.* Dad used to talk that kind of shit all the time because he was a live-in-the-moment type guy, a genuine heart-thinker.

There aren't many of us left.

I kicked a nearby rock, aiming for the deck gun on the far side of the submarine, missing wide right. I spoke to Dad out loud, knowing full well he couldn't hear me. I couldn't hear me either, what with my headphones blasting the soaring sopranos, but it was nice, saying things without hearing them. Nice knowing my words were out there somewhere in the ether.

I kicked another rock. Bull's-eye. It clanked off the deck gun, and plopped into the dark water of the river. I smiled inside, imagined the rock sinking to the bottom of the riverbed, where it would exist forever, without anyone ever knowing about it.

Dormant. Like the *Ling.* Like my voice in the ether.

Like me.

I turned away from the pier, crossed River Street, one foot then the other, savoring the solitude of the street-hike to Babushka's Deli. It was cold out, the kind you could see, where your breath blossomed like a floating lotus in front of your face. It was the kind of cold where you couldn't tell if it was cloudy, or if the whole sky was just the color of clouds. The cold spoke in sentences, and here's what it said: *Snow is on the way, guys. Gird thy silly, futile selves.*

"The Flower Duet" ended.

"The Flower Duet" began again.

The magic of repeat.

God, I missed Dad.

* * *

I leaned over the glass case, trying to remember the difference between pancetta and prosciutto. Not that it mattered. The Benucci lasagna required prosciutto. It would run on nothing less.

"You are small boy, yez?"

I looked around, wondered if the butcher was addressing me. The only other person in the shop was a bulky teenager completely decked out in New York Jets paraphernalia: hat, scarf, gloves, coat. He sat at a small table in the corner, nursing a Coke and a sandwich, staring at me with a look of utter confusion, curiosity, and repulsion.

I knew this look well.

"*You*," said the butcher from behind the counter, pointing a beefy finger at me. "You are small boy. Yez?"

"I guess . . . um . . . I'm a little small for my age."

"What? Speak up!"

Behind me, the Jets fan snickered. I tucked my hair behind my ears and tried a shorter response this time. "Yes. I am small boy."

I am small boy.

The butcher, whose name tag read NORM, went back to the meat on his chopping block. "Okeydokey then. Small boys need meat. Strengthen bones. Make big 'n' strong." He smiled, flexing a bicep. "Like me! Ha!"

I never knew what to say to this guy. At least half lion, Norm was almost certainly Russian and had hair growing in ungodly places in ungodly amounts. He was fat, yes, but it wasn't just that. It was the *kind* of fat—firm, bulging, meaty—that betrayed a man who had dipped too many times into his own stock. The working theory was that Norm

was ex-KGB hiding out in North Jersey until the rise of a new Soviet regime.

. . .

A little bell jingled as the front door opened, and in they walked.

All four of them. Always together.

I'd seen these kids at least a half dozen times around town. Hackensack wasn't exactly a burgeoning metropolis—there were only so many places a person could go before bumping into familiar strangers. Usually it was incidental, more like déjà vu than fate.

"Hello, Norm," said the oldest kid. I'd heard the others call him Baz. Probably twenty-five or so, Baz was pretty muscular and six-foot-something at least. His shirtsleeves were cut off at the shoulder, revealing a slew of tattoos running the length of his left arm, a combination that defied more than society—it defied the weather itself. He had a slight accent of indeterminate origin, and always wore a Trenton Thunder baseball cap.

"Yez, Mister Baz," said Norm, eyes brightening as he wiped his bloody paws on his apron. "I was thinking I might be seeing you today. You give me one minute. I be right back." Norm disappeared into the back room while I stood off to the side, tucking my hair behind my ears again, feeling every bit a small boy.

For reasons not entirely clear, Norm transformed into a real Super Racehorse around these kids. Even the Jets fan, who just a minute ago couldn't stop staring at my face, had now been chewing the same bite of sandwich since the group had walked in the door. The kids had an air of reckless enthusiasm about them, like at any moment they might drop everything and run. For fun, for the hell of it, for whatever.

"The frak you staring at, kid?"

The littlest of the bunch, a girl of no more than ten or eleven years old, had curly red hair and freckles, wore an oversized coat and mismatched mittens, and could usually be found holding Baz's hand.

"Coco," said Baz. "Be polite." He offered me a quick smile, then turned and whispered something to a third kid, who listened, promptly shook his head, and snapped his fingers twice. In his late teens, maybe early twenties, this kid's arms were too long for the sleeves of his Journey sweatshirt, so you could see at least five inches above his wrists.

The last kid in the group was a girl with gray eyes, a fitted turquoise coat with rainbow stripes across the front, and a yellow knit cap; her hair was long and so blond you couldn't tell where the hat ended and the hair began. The yellow, the rainbow, the gray—she was an explosion of color, Matisse gone wild. She stood behind the others, her head in a book as if books had been created for the sole purpose of being read by her in a butcher shop. She was quite the Stoic Beauty.

This was the whatevereth time I'd seen these kids, but I was no more immune to this girl's charms now than I was the first time I'd seen her. Pancetta, prosciutto, *fucking ham loaf*, whatever. Being around these kids instilled a primal sense of excitement: a combination of wonder and fear.

"Okay, you know what?" said the little redhead, dropping Baz's hand and crossing her arms. "You have a serious staring problem, kid. Anyone ever tell you that? Anyway, *we* should be staring at *you*."

"Coco!" said Baz.

I let my hair fall in my face, and turned back toward the glass case of various salt-cured pork. I was used to those sorts of comments, especially from younger kids. But being used to something is not the same as being immune to it.

Norm returned from the back, carrying a bulky brown

paper sack. He hoisted it over the counter and into the arms of Baz, who smiled, said thanks, then turned and led the other kids out of the store, the four departing as one.

"Okeydokey," said Norm, turning back to me. "What will you have, small boy?"

Through the shop window, I watched the kids cross the street. Something about their cohesiveness made me wonder if the world wasn't at all what I thought it was.

"Pancetta," I mumbled, too busy staring out the window to know what I was saying.

"Okeydokey. How much?"

I watched the kids veer off Main Street, turn down Banta, and disappear around a corner.

. . .

. . .

"Hey, small boy. You okay?"

I did not answer.

Instead I tore out of Babushka's, without pancetta or prosciutto, practically knocking the bell off the door as I went, running across the street in a frenzied daze, down Main and around the corner onto Banta. My small boy brain was still processing things, but my heart cut through the bullshit like an absolute ace.

MAD

I flipped a page of *The Outsiders* and, once again, wished I could sink into the book. Sinking into fiction: the if-only of if-onlys.

"Häagen-Dazs coffee is good," said Coco. "Cookies and

cream, rocky road, Italian toffee tira . . . Mad, what's this word?"

I glanced up to find Coco, her nose pressed against the cold glass case, her frazzled hair like a red sun around which a thousand pints of ice cream rotated. "Tiramisu," I said. "It's like a soft cake. Only there's no actual cake, I don't think. But it has coffee and rum."

"Shut. *Up*," said Coco. "Rum, like what pirates drink? What miserable rock have I been living under, I don't know about tiramisu? Ooh, look, there's cookie dough! That's your favorite, right, Zuz?"

Zuz stared into the case of ice cream as if looking through it, and snapped his finger with a *pop!* that echoed down the aisle.

Foodville on Banta was just our speed, an ever-persistent brand of dull. Employees arranged, then rearranged, then re-rearranged boxes of generic cereals, chilled pickles, and ramen noodles. They mopped clean floors and tagged already-priced items and tapped their toes to feeble-rhythmic Muzak; they stacked soup can pyramids and hung out by shredded cheeses in the corners where fluorescent bulbs flickered. And in the center of Foodville, we stood in our own little town, the eleventh aisle, staring at frozen dairy desserts as if waiting for the ice cream to choose us.

Baz turned the corner, pushing a half-filled shopping cart, leaning over the top of it like a weary mother of four.

Every family has a normal, but some normal sure seems more normal than others.

"About time," said Coco, eagerly eyeing the ice cream. "Mad says tiramisu is a soft cake with real rum in it, like what pirates drink. Is that right? Tell the truth."

"I don't know." Baz removed his Thunder baseball cap and

ran his hand through his hair. I had seen this move before, knew what it meant. I prepared myself for the shit-storm of Coco's discontent.

"Okay, well, we have to try *that* obviously," said Coco, pulling open the freezer door. "But we'll need to get a second flavor, just in case soft cake ice cream sucks balls."

"Sorry, Coconut," said Baz. "It's not happening."

She sighed. "Well, if it's just the one, then—"

"No. I mean, no ice cream. Not this time."

Coco's ratty red hair flung as she spun. "Repeat that please."

"I don't get paid until tomorrow," he said. "So this is it for today. We have to come back in the morning for Gunther's stuff, so maybe then. Anyway . . . it's freezing outside."

"It's not freezing in my *stomach*," said Coco, turning back to the freezer. She reached for the handle, her voice slightly higher than before, laced with a thick tone of silvery virtue. "I could fit it in my jacket, Baz. No one would even know it was gone."

I couldn't help but admire how someone so small could swing such heavy bullshit. The thing about Coco was, she wasn't only skin and bones; she was survival and fight and ferocious loyalty that you just couldn't find anywhere anymore. When Coco spoke, no matter how high-pitched, you could almost hear a muted roar lining the underbelly of each word.

"*We* would know, Coco," said Baz. "You know my rule."

A towering crash sounded behind us.

There, at the end of the aisle, a kid stood in the middle of hundreds of soup cans, once a perfect pyramid, now scattered around his feet like a demolition zone.

"It's him," whispered Coco. "That kid from Babushka's. The one with a staring problem."

Coco was right. Before today I'd seen this kid around town maybe once or twice. He had long greasy hair and sharp blue eyes, but those weren't his defining characteristics. He wore a backpack, blue jeans, and lace-up boots, but those weren't his defining characteristics either. His defining characteristic was his face. For starters, it didn't move. Not a smile, not a frown, not a single visible reaction or emotion. Except his eyes. His eyes were lively and bright, but I'm not sure I would have noticed were it not for the fact that they were currently aimed directly at me.

A teenage girl in a hairnet approached the endcap where the soups had once been neatly stacked. "What the hell, dude? I just finished putting th—" She looked at him for the first time, and swallowed whatever words were next, instead letting out a feeble, "Oh."

For a second no one said anything. The employee in the hairnet bent down and started picking up the cans. "No worries, buddy. It happens, you know?"

The kid gripped his backpack, gave me one last look, then turned and ran.

"Told you," said Coco, refocusing her attention on the solar system of ice cream in front of us. "Frakking weirdo, that kid."

Zuz snapped once.

Baz walked over to help pick up the soup cans while I went back to my book, pretending to read, pretending the blue of those eyes wasn't quite so sharp, pretending not to wonder what the Foodville employee was about to say to that kid, what she surely would have said had his face not looked the way it did.

VIC

I shook the snow from my boots and placed them by the front door to dry. Two black guitar cases smothered in Bat-Signals and The Cure patches sat in the hallway with mighty aplomb.

Klint and Kory were here. Frank the Boyfriend's kids.

Since I'd knocked over a soup can pyramid in front of maybe the most beautiful girl I'd ever seen (or, if not the most beautiful girl, certainly the most striking, sweat-inducing one), the presence of Frank the Boyfriend—and his kids, who belonged in their own animated Tim Burton movie—was the last thing I needed.

It aplombed me. Mightily so.

Klint and Kory weren't twins, but hardly anyone could tell them apart. They wore the same Goth-style clothes, and their teeth were far too big for their heads. I liked to imagine the roots had dug deep into their skulls, firmly planted in the space usually reserved for normal-sized brains. Like me, Klint and Kory had lost a parent to cancer. Unlike me, they used that loss as a reason to wear black makeup and start a band called the Orchestra of Lost Soulz. (I used my loss for much more sensible things, like seeing how hard one must push the edge of a credit card into one's skin before one starts to bleed.) Mom offered them our basement as a rehearsal space, and just like that, they were regulars around the Benucci residence.

As I said: mighty aplombing.

I heard Mom now, in the kitchen with Frank and Klint and Kory. One happy family. With their happy family voices ringing like happy family bells from our happy family kitchen.

Ding-dong-how-was-your-ding-dong-day?

I set my backpack next to the guitar cases, hung up my coat, and started down the hallway. Mom, intent on not wasting another holiday, had begun baking and decorating the day after Thanksgiving. Pies, tarts, breads, cakes, puddings—"in the name of Christmas," Mom said, probably a hundred times. I wondered if maybe Christmas could go by a different name this year.

But hey.

I could hardly blame her.

Last Christmas was a bleak affair. The one-year anniversary(ish) of Dad's death. There were no lights. There were no pies. There was no tree. So if Mom wanted to string lights from every corner and crevice of our house this year, decking our halls like some wild-eyed holiday elf, I was fine with it. There was, however, one piece of furniture that remained untouched by my mother's voluminous cheer: the end table in the hallway.

The end table in the hallway was nothing special.

But what sat on the end table in the hallway was a thing of such momentous proportions, I could scarcely pass it without my knees buckling.

My socked feet inched forward, seemingly of their own volition, until I was close enough to nudge the table with my waist—close enough to reach out and touch my father's urn.

My phone buzzed. I pulled it out, glanced at a new message from Mom.

Where r u?

The happy family voices rang from the kitchen. *Ding-dong-how-was-your-ding-dong-day?* I set my phone on the end

table, and reached toward Dad's urn, fingers stopping only centimeters away.

Not being able to close my eyes made many things difficult: sleeping and blinking, primarily. But one thing people didn't consider was *envisioning*, and how frequently people closed their eyes—not for long, more like a prolonged blink—when picturing a place or thing.

It was a real problem for me. Until Dad taught me to go to my Land of Nothingness. He said the reason people closed their eyes when they tried to picture something was because they needed a blank place to start from. He explained what it looked like when he closed his eyes, how it wasn't darkness or blackness, exactly—just nothingness. *And only in a place of nothingness can somethingness be found, V.*

Now he was Nothingness personified.

Now he was in a jar.

I went to my Land of Nothingness, imagined the way Dad poked his head into my room before bed.

Hey, V. You need anything?

No, Dad.

You good?

Yeah, Dad.

All right then. Good night.

Night, Dad.

The whole thing, like he was such a nuisance.

Sock-footed in the oblivion of this dark hallway, one arm outstretched, I stood stuck between somethingness and nothingness, wondering how it was possible for this plain old urn to blaze like a desert heat.

Dad died two years ago. And I still couldn't touch the thing.

* * *

"Dynamite meal, Doris." Frank eyed his sons. "Boys? Isn't this meal something?"

Klint cleared his throat. "Sure is, Dad."

Kory chewed, chuckled, nodded.

"How do you get the little"—Frank poked at his potatoes, apparently unable to find his words—"crispy parts here . . . the sweet herbs . . . how do you get them so . . . ?"

"Crispy and sweet?" asked Mom.

Frank laughed, leaned over, and kissed her cheek. One arm shifted under the table in Mom's direction. I choked and miraculously didn't die on the spot.

"I literally did nothing to the potatoes," said Mom. "But I'd be happy to pass along your compliments to the chef down at the Ore-Ida frozen potato factory. I had been *planning* to make my world-famous lasagna, but someone forgot to pick up prosciutto."

Here, she aimed an eye at me.

"Right," I said, clearing my throat. "Sorry about that."

I pictured the face of the Stoic Beauty and knew I wasn't sorry, not even a little.

"I could have picked up prosciutto on my way home from court, sweetheart," said Frank, serving himself more green beans.

Frank loved to talk about court. Court this, court that. Talking about court made Frank the Boyfriend feel more like Frank the Racehorse.

In reality, Frank was more of a French poodle.

"In fact," said Frank, "I called earlier to see if you needed anything, but you didn't answer. I would have left a message, but—"

"I know, I know."

"*Someone*, for reasons passing understanding, refuses to clear out her freaking voice mail in-box."

"I *know*," said Mom, smiling ear to ear. "I'll do it tonight. Okay?"

Frank leaned in, whispered, "You'll *do it* tonight, all right."

"*Dad, gross*," said Klint.

Kory chewed, gagged, shook his head.

I took a sip of soda, wondering what would happen if I reached across the table right now and slapped Frank the Boyfriend across the face.

Frank was everything my dad wasn't: dainty, professionally successful, head full of hair. Subtlety completely eluded him. He was a loud-talking, green-bean-chomping lawyer who always wore suits. I'd never *not* seen the guy in a suit. He just really loved suits, I guess. And maybe it wasn't momentous, but it sure felt like it, because Dad was a wear-his-sweatpants-to-the-grocery-store type guy.

I was that type guy too.

"So, boys," said Mom. "How's the band coming along?"

"Oh," said Klint, his eyes shooting toward his dad. "Um. Good, Miss B. Really, umm . . . good. Right, Kory?" He elbowed his brother in the ribs. Kory stopped chewing momentarily, focused instead on his chuckling and nodding.

Frank scooped a third helping of green beans onto his plate.

I don't know. The man really liked his green beans.

"Well, that's just great," said Mom. "Maybe we can hear something soon. Like a concert. Wouldn't that be nice, Vic?"

I raised my favorite thin-brimmed glass in a sarcastic toast, carefully drained the last of my soda, and stood.

"Where are you going?" asked Mom.

"Refill."

Klint dropped his fork onto his plate, stood, and grabbed my empty glass. "I'll get it." He disappeared into the kitchen,

leaving us all to wonder what the hell had just happened. Klint rarely did anything nice, certainly not for me.

Mom beamed. "That is so sweet of him."

"He's a sweet kid," said Frank, mouth full of beans.

I did a mental checklist of undetectable poisons that might be found in our kitchen, things Klint could use to lace my drink. A minute later he returned, set a full glass in front of me, and sat down without a word. Mom continued talking, something about how happy she was to see us all getting along. I didn't really hear her. I was too preoccupied with the fact that Klint had traded out my original glass for Dad's favorite beer tumbler, the one with the Mets logo printed across the front. It had a thick brim, making it almost impossible for me to use without dripping liquid down my chin.

"Klint and Kory have a special relationship," said Frank. "Especially so close in age. They even share a wardrobe."

I grabbed the bottom of the glass but didn't lift it.

"Something wrong?" asked Klint, just the hint of a smile on his lips.

Kory chewed, chuckled, nodded.

Klint and Kory much preferred sneaky-mean to outright-mean. They didn't make fun of my face the way normal mean kids did. They understood that lasting pain could only be dealt at the root.

"Genetically speaking," droned Frank, "brothers are just as close in DNA to each other as they are to a parent." He took a bite of green beans as if it were a period at the end of his sentence.

"Frank, you are a wealth of knowledge," said Mom, either not noticing Dad's tumbler or choosing not to acknowledge it.

Ever since Mom got serious with Frank, ours had been a relationship of few: few words, few touches, few feelings. Much of her beauty had been spent during the Dark Days, but she still had an ample supply. Her hair, like her smile, was bright and young; the creases around her eyes had grown more severe, but what did people expect? From diagnosis to funeral, she'd waited on Dad hand and foot. The only three reasons Mom had left the house during the Dark Days:

1. Groceries.
2. Prescriptions.
3. Procedures.

Post-diagnosis, Dad lived another eighteen months. The doctors said that was rare. They said he was a fighter. They said he was lucky.

I said they should get their heads checked if they thought Dad was lucky. At least he had Mom to take care of him. For a year and a half, she sacrificed her life to give Dad some comfort at the end. So shouldn't I be happy for her now? Hadn't she earned it? Shouldn't I welcome Frank the Boyfriend with arms open wide? The answer was yes. To all of it. But part of me thought about all those sacrifices she'd made, and compared them to what she'd gotten in exchange.

"It's in literature, too," said Frank, right on cue. He took another bite of green beans, and it took everything in me not to ask him if he wanted a second fork, one for each hand. "Take that Russian novel with the four brothers," he said. "Whatchacallit . . . ? Gosh, I can never remember the name."

I looked at Mom, daring her to make eye contact with me. *Look at me. Just once tonight, really look at me. Just once, let's skip the shorthand and talk like we used to.*

"Well, this is just gonna bug me," said Frank, who, for the moment, had stopped shoveling green beans into his mouth. "*The Brothers* something-or-other. It's one of Tolstoy's more well-known works."

"*Karamazov*," I said quietly, still staring at Mom.

Her smile dissolved. Slowly, finally, she met my gaze. For a few seconds the dinner table dissolved. Frank, Klint, Kory—gone. It was just the two of us, living in the saddest house of happy memories. We stared at each other until she looked away. And just then, I knew I'd lost her.

I pushed my plate away, tucked my hair behind my ears, and shifted in my seat. "Frank, you're a fucking moron."

"Victor!" shouted Mom.

Frank, temporarily stunned, turned to help Klint, who had suddenly choked on the crispy part of his potato; Kory chewed, chuckled, nodded.

Mom stood from the table with authority. "Kitchen. *Now.*"

I took my time getting there, scooting my chair out from under the table with more defined force than necessary, following her through the swinging kitchen door. A strand of Christmas lights lay at the foot of the fridge, gravity having gotten the better of the three-week-old duct tape. The counter was a mess of flour and sugar and eggs, vestiges of Mom's recent romance with the baked good.

"Out with it," she said, arms crossed.

"Out with what?"

"That was *unbelievably* rude."

"I can't help it if your boyfriend knows everything about the fucking chromosomal similarities of siblings, yet somehow thinks Tolstoy wrote *The Brothers Karamazov*, which I'm fairly certain he pretended not to remember the title of so he wouldn't have to mispronounce it out loud."

"Honey," she said.

"Maybe if he'd give it a rest with the Churchill biographies, he could devote some time to—"

"Victor."

"What?"

"What is this really about?"

. . .

. . .

"The literary prowess of Fyodor Dostoyevsky."

Mom did not laugh. Not even a chuckle. "We don't like the same books, Vic. You can't base a relationship on literary preferences."

I felt myself try to smile, which happened sometimes. It was amazing—even though I'd never done it, not once in my whole life, the *urge* was there. Mom used to say she could tell by my eyes when I was laughing. She said they changed somehow. Said they got happy enough for my whole face.

"What's so funny?" asked Mom.

Traitorous eyes.

"Nothing is funny." I crossed my arms. "What could ever be funny?"

It was quiet for a moment. Mom put a hand on my shoulder. "I know it's hard. This hasn't been . . . *Nothing* has been easy. But you remember what we've been talking about? About moving on?"

I swallowed the knot down as she pulled me closer. I remembered. How could I forget? Lately she'd been going on about the importance of healing, of allowing ourselves time to wade in the grief pool, and of recognizing when the time came to get out and dry ourselves off.

Mom had been dry for a while, I guess.

I was sinking like a rock.

"Frank makes me happy, sweetheart," she said. "Or at least, *not* sad. I'd like to feel more of that, you know? I'd like for you to feel it too. Maybe not toward Frank, but toward something, somebody."

I imagined the knock on my bedroom door again. *Come in*, I would say. Frank the Boyfriend would open the door, poke his head full of hair inside. *Hey, Vic. You need anything?* I would nod. *Go jump off a bridge, Frank.*

Mom hugged me.

And it felt like a last meal. It felt like *thnx, luv*.

I tried to hug her back, but my arms hung like vines by my sides, awkward and too long for my body.

"He gave me dad's tumbler," I said quietly.

"What?"

"Klint. When he came in here to get my Coke." Suddenly the hug takes on a new sense of restraint, a hesitation that wasn't there seconds ago. "He switched out my glass and gave me Dad's. They're awful, Mom. They hate me."

. . .

. . .

"They don't hate you. They just don't know you yet."

Yet.

For such a tiny word, it sure could flip a sentence on its ass.

"I'll talk to Frank about it," she said. "Speaking of which, you owe him an apology."

I nodded and Mom let go, stepping toward the door, toward the dining room, toward her new family, away from me.

"It's not true, you know," I said, staring at the fallen strand of Christmas lights.

"What's not true?"

Just when I decided not to say it, the words came out. "You and Dad liked the same books."

Watching her eyes water offered a strange sense of relief. He still mattered to her. What we had still mattered. Mom could flirt and smile and bake a billion pies, but in the end, her eyes were traitorous too. They told me all I needed to know. Whatever this was with Frank, even *she* knew it was nothing like what she had with Dad.

She blinked away tears, forced a smile, and opened the door to the dining room. "After you, honey."

I stood frozen to the spot.

I stood staring into the dining room.

I am mighty aplombed.

"Vic?" said Mom, turning to look through the door. "What's—"

In the dining room, Klint and Kory were standing in their chairs, each one with a guitar strapped around their shoulders. *"Two! Three! Four!"* yelled Klint, his voice even raspier than normal.

The Orchestra of Lost Soulz plunged into song with that special enthusiasm reserved for people who had no idea they couldn't sing. It was awkward and sweaty and uncomfortable for everyone. Frank sat in his chair, staring at Mom through the whole thing, his face strangely constricted. After the song came to a close, he said, "I realize this is sort of . . . well, not ideal timing." His eyes shifted to me. "Vic, I hope you see this as proof of my love and commitment. To both you, and your mother."

Before I could ask what *this* meant, Frank cleared his throat and scooted out of his chair. I waited for him to stand, but it never happened.

Frank the Boyfriend took a knee.

Frank the Boyfriend reached into his pocket.

Frank the Boyfriend pulled out a ring.

Frank the Boyfriend wanted to be Frank the Husband.

Frank the New Dad.

Mom covered her mouth with both hands as I helplessly watched the scene play out before me.

"Doris Jacoby," said Frank.

I quietly observed the conspicuous absence of *Benucci*.

". . . make me the happiest man alive."

I quietly observed my mother, who, bizarrely, had yet to run screaming through the front door, racing down the street, pulling clumps of hair from her head, rending the clothes from her body, shrieking in havoc and mourning . . . or, at the very *least*, laughing, grabbing Dad's urn from its dark place of prominence in our hallway, shoving it in Frank's face, and saying, *I'm spoken for, bitch!*

She had yet to do any of these things.

Bizarrely.

"Marry me," said Frank.

Someone screamed.

Everyone looked at me.

The scream—which, in my estimation, had been the most sensible thing to happen in the last two or three minutes—had come from my own throat. Or gut. Or mouth. All of them, actually.

I did it again. It seemed the thing to do.

And again.

Yes, screaming at the highest of pitches was very sensible.

No words. Just animal screams as I exited my body.

From above, near the ceiling, I saw Vic run from the kitchen. In the hallway, he overcame his inability to touch his father's urn by simply picking it up. He felt the weight

of the urn in his hands, remarkably heavy. *I shouldn't be surprised,* he thought. *I am holding the whole of my father, the same bald heart-thinker who taught me to find beauty in asymmetry, led me to the Land of Nothingness, gave me the soaring sopranos. If anything, his ashes should be heavier!* Vic stuffed the urn into his backpack, slipped on his boots, threw on his coat, and bolted out the front door. He had to get his dad out of that place, away from all those disturbing *ding-dong-how-was-your-ding-dong-day*s, and the rest of the happy family voices. He needed to find a place where his father, the world's last and greatest Super Racehorse, might rest in peace.

He knew just the spot.

MAD

Being born on December 31 meant watching everyone in the world celebrate a thing on your birthday that wasn't you. Mom never saw it that way, though. She called me her New Year's darling, said I was special, meant for great things. I was a little younger than most in my class—Mom said this gave me an edge. I'd finish school sooner, discover the world first, and maybe find whatever great thing I was meant for.

I lit my cigarette and wished she were here now.

Drag.

Blow.

Calm.

The snow kept falling, the wind from the river kept coming, and I stared at the submarine, pondering the intricacies of my past, but mostly, wondering about my future. Three weeks from now, happy New Year would be my happy birth-

day, and the freedom of eighteen would be upon me with all the honors and benefits granted therein. One benefit was the legal opportunity to get myself, and Jamma, out from under the iron fist of Uncle Les. Sure, I could sneak off now for days at a time, and he either didn't notice or didn't care. But I had to go back. Even though Jamma rarely knew who I was anymore, I always went back. I'd been thinking a lot about love recently, and how it wasn't contingent on the person receiving it; it was contingent on the person giving it. Whether or not my grandmother recognized me didn't matter. I loved her too much to leave her stranded with Uncle Les.

Enter the freedom of eighteen, with all those pesky honors and benefits.

The problem was, eighteen or not, I had no idea where we should go or how we should get there. I couldn't choose a place too far away; the thought of being separated from Baz and Zuz and Coco was almost as difficult as the thought of losing Jamma.

Drag.

Blow.

Calm.

I often considered various situations as if they were sets of a Venn diagram. In this case, it was a supremely shitty Venn diagram where set A = {A Person Who Knows What Needs to Be Done}, and set B = {A Person Who Has No Idea *How to Do* What Needs to Be Done}, and the intersection = {Mad}.

I stomped out the last of the cigarette, pulled the edges of my knit cap over my ears, and blew warm air into my hands. There was something about sitting by the *Ling* at nighttime that helped me think, like the very heart and soul of the sub was here to keep me company. The black winter-water rip-

pled as thousands of snowflakes dissolved the second they hit the Hackensack River. And I couldn't help but wonder if it looked as beautiful in the daytime.

Just as I was about to stand and head back, I heard footsteps behind me.

The navy museum was currently closed, and though I'd never had trouble before, I wasn't entirely sure my being here after hours was allowed.

There, about twenty yards downriver, someone approached. I stayed low, watched as the figure walked up to the fence that separated land from water, laced one hand through the metal mesh. A second later he looked around, and in the snowy moonlight I saw a familiar, unforgettable face: the kid from Babushka's and Foodville.

Okay, look. I was no believer in a higher order of the cosmos. There was no evidence in my mind to suggest that fate interceded in our lives like some tragic demigod moving humans like pawns on a chessboard. So possibly it was the magic of the *Ling* that made me want to talk to this kid, or just the fact that I'd only seen him a total of maybe three times before today, and now three times today *alone*, or hell, maybe there was a tragic demigod moving me like a pawn, but whatever the case, I found myself approaching him.

The Madifesto dictates: *when the order of the cosmos sets the board, position yourself as Queen.*

I was feet away now, close enough to see white earbuds coiling up to his ears. He knelt on the ground and pulled something out of his backpack, a pot or a jar of some kind, then leaned over it.

"I hope you were right," he whispered. "I hope there's beauty in my asymmetry."

Okaaaaaaaaay.

"You weren't a nuisance," he continued, his words growing louder in the cold, snowy silence. "You were the Northern Dancer, sire of the century, the superest of all racehorses."

Without a doubt this was one of the more bizarre one-sided conversations I'd ever heard, and that was saying something, considering I lived with Coco.

I watched him pull back a piece of tape and open the lid of the jar. His body deflated, as if everything leading to this point had been full of air, energy, expectation—and now . . . not.

I turned quickly, quietly, suddenly feeling I shouldn't be here. And then . . .

"Hey."

Dead in my tracks.

I turned back around. "Hey."

The kid stood clumsily from the snow. "What are you doing here?"

It struck me as an odd first question. *What are you doing here?* presupposed that the person asking it knew the *you* to begin with. As opposed to *Who are you?*

"I like to come here at night," I said. Because that wasn't creepy at all.

He let out an "Oh," as if it really wasn't, then bent down, put the lid back on the jar, and stuffed it into his bag.

"What are *you* doing here?" I asked, shivering.

The kid pulled out a handkerchief and wiped his mouth. "I can't go home right now," he said.

Me either. I nodded, brushed my hair out of my face, and thought about what he'd said when he didn't know I was listening. *I hope there's beauty in my asymmetry.* Maybe that was it: a slight asymmetry, along with a complete frozenness of features. It wasn't ugly, or even unpleasant. Far from it, ac-

tually. His face was just wholly unique. And I couldn't help being a little curious.

I pulled out my pack of cigarettes, offered one to him, but he declined. I lit up.

Drag.

Blow.

Warm.

"I mean—I don't know where to go," he said. "But I can't go home."

"Okay."

"It's a long story."

"I have one of those too."

Drag.

Blow.

Warm.

I watched my smoke in the cold night air. "I may know a place, though."

* * *

I should really be dead.

The sentence basically lived on the tip of my tongue. Especially around strangers, which made sense, considering a person isn't invested in a stranger the way they are, say, in a family member or a close friend. Maybe that's why so many people ended up leaving their spouses for complete strangers they met online. It cost almost nothing to tell a stranger almost everything.

"So how about this," I said, turning down Mercer. "I'm not going to ask you your name, and I'm not going to ask you why you can't go home tonight. I'm not even going to ask you what's in that jar."

"Okay."

"But I am going to ask you about Northern Dancer, and supreme racehorse and all that."

"Super," he said.

"Great."

"Wait, what?"

"What, what?"

"No, I didn't mean"—he shook his head, pulled out his handkerchief again, and wiped his mouth—"I meant, it's not *supreme* racehorse. It's *Super* Racehorse."

"Okay then."

"My dad used to call himself an equestrian sport enthusiast. Basically, he was obsessed with horse racing. He didn't even bet on them, just loved the sport. At one point he got really interested in the actual horses and their lineage and stuff. Like, he could tell you all the fastest horses and who their sires and dams were."

"Sires and dams?"

"Fathers and mothers. He took me to this farm once, like an hour away. What they do is they take horses that are too old to race, or injured, and they put them on this farm in hopes that they can, you know, *produce* an even better racehorse. Or—some places, um, harvest the sire's *goods*, and then, um, inject them into the . . . dam."

"Gross."

He nodded, shifted his backpack as we walked. "Dad would fix a leaky faucet, or win a board game, or get a *Jeopardy!* question right, and then call himself a Super Racehorse. Anyway, to answer your question, Northern Dancer sired some of the most successful racehorses ever."

As we turned right on State Street, passing the police station on our left, I noted the use of past tense when he re-

ferred to his dad. I said nothing, though. I didn't much feel like talking about my past tenses either.

"So how about this," he said. "I'm not going to ask you your name, and I'm not going to ask you what you were doing alone by the river at night. I'm not even going to ask you about the other kids I always see you with. But I am going to ask you about your sire and dam."

"I don't have any," I said.

"I meant your parents."

"I know what you meant."

So much for not discussing past tenses.

"So the other kids you're always with . . ."

"You mean the ones you weren't going to ask about?" I smiled sideways at him. "It's fine, man. They're basically family. We're undesirables, so we desire each other." We were only two or three minutes away now—it would've been easy to leave it at that. But I didn't. I blew into my hands to warm them up, then said, "All right, you told a story about your dad, I'll tell one about my mom. She used to have this framed poster full of pithy inspirational sayings, which she'd ordered off some equally pithy website and hung in our hallway. She made it, like, her personal manifesto. *Start doing things you love. All emotions are beautiful. When you eat, appreciate every last bite.* That kind of shit. I used to come home from school and find Mom standing in the hallway by herself, reading the thing out loud." We crossed over Banta, one more block to Salem. "So I started reciting them too. Got to where I'd memorized them, so I could lie in bed at night and stare up at the ceiling and just go with it, you know? I figured if Mom believed in her manifesto that much, there must be something to it. Then one day, we're all in a car on our way to the mall when a drunk

driver hits us head on, killing both my parents. I should really be dead." There it was—the line, in all its glory, officially packed up and moved out. "But I only got this." I raised my hat above my ear, pointed to the scar on the side of my head. I kept that whole side shaved for just such occasions, to show I wasn't hiding it or ashamed of it, wasn't afraid of who I was or where I came from. My scar was a battle wound, my very life proof of the victory. "Anyway. Mom's manifesto was total bullshit."

I stopped there, though that was hardly the end. I didn't tell him about my Madifesto, the antithesis of Mom's pithy poster, a banner I marched under proudly, one that called for independence, self-sufficiency, and the incessant pursuit of survival.

Stranger or no, those things were for me.

Between Banta and Salem, I veered into a little alleyway known throughout town as the Chute. Famous for drug busts and muggings, the Chute was a narrow stretch that connected Main and State Street, so named because of its lack of any windows whatsoever. It was as if the architects had simply forgotten to draw them into the plans. There were a few doors—exits for shops to dump trash and whatnot—but they were all locked from the inside. With no windows, and such little street visibility, it had become a veritable breeding ground for all sorts of criminals.

I walked up to one of the locked doors. "We're here."

VIC

"What. *Here?*"

The Stoic Beauty pulled a key from her back pocket. "Please," she said. "I wouldn't wish an overnight in the Chute on my worst enemy. No, you're just inside."

It was dark out, the only light coming from a distant streetlamp reflected off the snow. I reached for my pocket to use the flashlight on my phone before remembering I had left it at home. As she fumbled with the lock, I pretended to watch the fumbling.

What I actually watched:

1. Her yellow hair dripping out from under her hat like a leaky sun.
2. Her pale cheeks, red from the cold.
3. The outline of her shoulders under her coat.
4. The outline of her waist under her coat.
5. The outline of her ass under her coat.
6. Her legs.
7. Her inked-up Nikes.

I was a mess.

"It's not the Hilton," she said, opening the door and flipping on a light. "But it's warmer than crashing down by the river if that sweetens the deal at all, which, you know, it should."

I took in the stench of the room as we stepped inside. It was no big mystery why the place smelled the way it did, thick and substantial and rotten. Six swine carcasses dangled from the ceiling like used piñatas. On the floor, little pools of watery blood gathered in tiny red reservoirs. It was all quite good and gross. I pulled the collar of my shirt up over my nose.

"This *has* to be against some sort of FDA regulation or something."

"Oh, it is," said the Stoic Beauty, slipping the key back into her pocket. "It gets cleaned up before inspections, then falls back into . . . well, what you see here. But again. *No* hypothermia. So, you know. Win."

In addition to dead hanging pigs, the room had an industrial oven, a dishwasher, and a large desk with papers and work orders strewn across it.

"All right then," she said, turning for the door. "We'll be back in the morning."

"We?"

"Don't worry. Norm doesn't usually show up for work till midmorning."

Suddenly things made sense. "This is the back of Babushka's."

The Stoic Beauty nodded. "Sleep tight."

"Wait a second."

I had serious questions. Big burning-a-hole-in-my-brain type questions. I started with the one that seemed most important.

"What's your name?"

. . .

"That's against the rules," she said.

"What rules? There were no rules."

"The rules of questioning. The rules we set forth during our prior conversation."

I couldn't tell if she was half joking or what. If yes, it was about the cutest thing I'd ever seen. If not—shit, it was cute anyway.

"I'm Madeline. I go by Mad."

She pulled a pack of cigarettes from her back pocket and lit up.

"I'm Vic," I said. *That's good. Keep that going.* "People call me Vic, I mean." *Okay, that's enough.* "Which is to say, my name is Victor." *You're done.* "But, um. No one calls me Victor, really." *Abort! Abort!* "Yeah, just Vic is good."

I was quickly becoming an absolute ace at face-palming myself. But then, miracle of miracles: Mad smiled a little.

And I died a little.

And she left.

* * *

The slaughtered pigs of the alleged KGB let loose an army of stink.

I left on my coat and boots, tucked my backpack under the metal desk, and slid in after it. In the world of backroom butcher shops, the corner farthest removed from dripping swine carcasses was prime real estate. More cramped than cozy, I pulled four things from my bag:

1. My Visine, which I applied and replaced.
2. My earbuds, which I inserted.
3. My iPod, which I turned on, turned up, and flipped to "The Flower Duet."
4. My dad. In an urn.

I kicked myself for leaving my phone at home, though I'm not sure who I would call, or for what reason exactly. There was a measure of comfort in knowing you were only a phone call away, exponentially true given my current locale. But I'd left in a hurry—according to the clock on my iPod, less than an hour ago if that was even possible—with only one idea in mind: get Dad out of that house. This

turned into quite the Shakespearean notion of me tossing his remains into the Hackensack River, where he would rest with the *Ling* forever and ever, sparing him whatever catastrophic events were sure to occur during the coming months (and years?) within the tragic remnants of the Benucci residence. But then, on the banks of the river, the soaring sopranos in my head, I opened the urn. And I saw things I had not expected to see.

Consider this: among the billions of people on Earth, there is one you care about, live with, and love; that one person dies and is burned into billions of microscopic pieces; those billions of pieces are placed in one receptacle. Billions to one, one to billions, billions to one. Sometimes I think love really is bound by numbers.

Now, in the shadows of dangling pig carcasses, I stared at Dad's urn, pulled back the tape, lifted the lid, and went to my Land of Nothingness . . .

Hey, Dad. You need anything in there?

No, V, my father's ashes would say.

You good?

Yeah, V.

All right then. Good night.

Night, V.

As far as I knew, the average urn contained only ashes, nothing more. By those standards, this was no average urn. Because: in addition to ashes, my father's urn contained a Ziploc bag, and in that bag, a photograph. An old Polaroid of my parents, fresh-faced, eager, young. They were high up somewhere, on the rooftop of a skyscraper, the New York City skyline behind them. Young Doris smiled at the camera. Young Bruno smiled at Young Doris.

Young Parents in young love.

It was the kind of happiness I barely remembered, the kind that felt foreign and far away, like Singapore. I knew people traveled to Singapore, and lots of people lived there. I'd seen Singapore on maps and globes and TV. I took this to mean that Singapore actually existed, even though I'd never been and had no idea how to get there.

This happiness was like Singapore.

In addition to the photo, there was one other thing that separated this urn from all the others. An open, blank envelope. It had no address, and no markings of any kind. From inside, I pulled out a single sheet of notebook paper, unfolded it, and read . . .

My Doris,

It hardly seems fair that the only ones expected to leave notes are those who end things themselves. I haven't chosen to die; death has been thrust upon me. As such, consider this my Terminal Note.

I think most people only have the capacity for one Great Thing in their lifetime. From the moment you and I jumped in that pool with all our clothes on (Emily Edwards's house, 11th grade, you'd had a few too many—I know you remember even though you always pretend not to) to five minutes ago, when you kissed my forehead, promised to bring Vic by on Saturday, then, in true Doris fashion,

tripped on your way out the door (and thought I didn't see you, but I totally did)—and every flawed, real moment in between—you have been my Great Thing.

So many memories.

By the time you read this, will there be more? Are you smiling now, thinking of some hilarious or awkward or sad thing that happened between your tripping out my hospital door and my dying? I hope so. I really do. But I feel it, Doris. I feel it coming. I'm not afraid. I may wish for more time, more memories, but I have no regrets. You and Victor are my North, South, East, and West. You are my Due Everywhere.

How could I ever be lost?

You know the places on this list. Take me there, won't you?

Till we're old-new,

—B

1. Hang me from the Parlour

2. Toss me off the Palisades

3. *Bury me in the smoking bricks of our first kiss*

4. *Drown me in our wishing well*

5. *Drop me from the top of our rock*

The soaring sopranos filled my head, and I knew what needed to be done.

And I would not return home until it was finished.

TWO

IMPROBABLE THINGS
*(or, The Sedative Properties
of Green Bean Casseroles
and Sideways Hugs)*

Detective Bundle is an atomic cloud personified. His feet are narrow, his ankles twiggy, his legs skinny; he wears a belt at the waist, and then—*BOOM*—stomach explosion like a mushroom cloud pouring over his belt so you can hardly see the buckle. His barrel chest, stubby neck, and sweaty red face only perpetuate the comparison.

"You left him where?" he asks.

"In Babushka's. Well, the back of Babushka's."

"Via this, what's it called . . ." Bundle shuffles through the files in front of him. "Chute."

I shift gently in my chair. The bruises on my back, hip, left arm, and face make themselves known way down deep, like my actual bones got tattooed.

"You're sure Jamma's okay?" I ask.

"Madeline, we've been through this."

"I know, but she gets confused."

"As we speak, your grandmother is receiving the best possible care over at Bergen Regional, okay?"

"And you promise it's not a complete shit hole?"

Bundle raises a hand as if swearing an oath. "Took my own mother there when she got shingles. Okay? Now. Tell me about the Chute."

"Honestly, how do you *not* know about the Chute?"

Detective Bundle eyes the digital recorder. "Well, how do *you* know about it, then?"

"I'm telling you, man, everyone knows about the Chute. Wait, did . . . did you just move here, or something?"

"Madeline."

"What?"

"Why even bother coming in if you're just gonna jerk us around?"

By now Baz is most likely praying in a nearby cell, his only hope resting on our ability to tell our story truthfully, while Zuz and Coco and Jamma are depending on our ability to tell our story slowly. Here's the thing: in a Venn diagram where set A = {Tell the Truth}, and set B = {Stall for Time}, the intersection is awfully cramped. But if things go according to plan, this is where Vic and I will live for much of the day.

"You're right," I say, sighing dramatically, regurgitating clichéd elements of suspects under harsh bare lightbulbs. "God, this is hard. Okay. The reason I'm here is . . ."

Detective Bundle folds his hands on the table and shifts to the edge of his seat, his chair creaking under such tremendous mass.

I lean in close to the recorder. "I wanted to see if you had any gum."

Bundle lets loose a roaring sigh, his face cherry red. "Madeline, this afternoon you and Victor walked in here with Baz Kabongo, the three of you smelling for all the world like you just stepped out of a shit tornado—"

"I told you, there's a good reason for that."

"—insistent on Kabongo's innocence, a man with means, motive, a history of violence, a man whose DNA was found *on* the murder weapon. Clearly, you feel some allegiance to

him, and I can respect that, misguided though it is. We know your uncle was abusive. You've got abrasions up and down your face, you've been squirming in pain since you sat down, so what was it—self-defense? Kabongo tried to stop your uncle from hitting you, they fought, and Baz killed the guy. Just say the word *self-defense*, and Kabongo will get a deal, I promise."

"Is *self-defense* one word, though?"

Bundle shakes his head. "You know what? I don't give a shit. If it were up to me, we'd have kicked the two of you kids out on your asses from the get-go. Sergeant Mendes tells me your boy Vic claims the two of you were there, in the house when Kabongo did the deed. Now if that's true, Madeline, you witnessed one of the grisliest murders I've ever heard of, read about, or seen the aftermath of. Not to mention it happened to your own uncle."

"I'm glad he's dead."

The words are out of my mouth before I can stop them.

"That may be," says Bundle. "But if Vic is telling the truth—if you saw it happen, and you don't tell us *exactly* what you saw—you're not facing a world of trouble, Madeline, you're facing a whole universe of it." He leans back in his chair, sticks his hand into his pocket, pulls something out, and tosses it across the table. "There's your fucking stick of gum."

I stare at the gum on the table for a full ten seconds. During that time it occurs to me that, until a few minutes ago, I'd been throwing the punches of the interview, little jabs here and there, either dodging or absorbing the meager returns of my opponent. But I'd misjudged him. Detective Bundle wasn't weak. He'd been biding his time, waiting for his moment to land the knockout punch.

I reach my hand around the stick of gum, pick up the glass of water I've ignored thus far. The liquid feels good against the cut on my lip, clean and soothing. I lower the glass and clear my throat gingerly. "What time is it?"

Bundle checks his watch. "A little after four."

In my head, Baz's voice has the same effect as the water on my lips: clean and soothing. *Let them think what they want. But do not lie.*

It's time to tell my story, cramped Venn diagram or no.

"The reason I took Vic to Babushka's is because the owner is an early Chapter."

(SEVEN days ago)

MAD

The late morning sun shone through the back door of Babushka's, its rays stretching like tentacles across the room. It could not reach underneath the table, however, where Vic lay fast asleep in the fetal position, curled around his backpack as if protecting it from a tidal wave.

"Is he dead?" asked Coco, who barely had to lean over to see under the desk. She scraped the bottom of her carton of ice cream with a spoon, having polished off the entire pint. It was a little before eleven a.m. "What's with all the blood?" she asked, her mouth full, a ring of chocolate around her lips. "I mean, he looks dead, right? Do you think he's dead? If he's not dead, he sure is a late-riser. Wait, why's he back here again?"

Coco asked questions the way most people took breaths.

"I told you," I said. "I ran into him by the river. He said he needed a place to stay."

Next to me, Zuz set down the bag of groceries we'd just purchased from Foodville. He was wiry but strong, and no one argued when he insisted on carrying the bag. I finished the last of my cranberry muffin, nursed my coffee while Baz approached Vic. He set a tray of coffee on the desk, bent down, and gently poked Vic in the arm.

"Rise and shine, little man."

Vic jerked awake, ramming his head on the underside of the desk.

"Why're you covered in blood, kid?" asked Coco. "And don't lie to me. I'm from Queens."

Vic looked down at himself, still rubbing his head. Blood had dried to the side of his jeans. Only then did we see it: the tiny red stream running directly from the floor under one of the pig carcasses to where he'd been sleeping.

"Motherfrakker," whispered Coco, tossing her empty pint in the trash can.

"Coco," said Baz.

"Hey, I'm sorry, but that is the grossest thing I have *ever* seen."

Vic pulled himself out from under the desk, dragging his backpack behind him. He coiled the cable from his earbuds around his iPod and stuck it into a side pocket.

I grabbed the last muffin from the top of the grocery bag and held it out. "Here. There's coffee too if you want."

On the other side of the room, a door opened and in walked Norm. "Don't mind me, don't mind me," he said, tossing unopened mail in a pile on his desk. "Aha! Small boy has met my friends, yez?"

Vic looked down at his boots.

Norm slapped him on the back. "You are the new Chapter, then?"

"The, um, what?"

Norm looked at us, pointed a thumb at Vic. "He does not know?"

Baz put an arm around the husky Russian and walked him back across the room. "Thank you for your hospitality, truly. You are a loyal friend."

Norm's chest inflated, his smile reaching from one ear to the other. He looked back at Vic, said, "These are good people, small boy. Very good people. You listen to them, yez? They will help you."

Norm disappeared with an *okeydokey*. Vic looked around, accepted the muffin, and when Baz offered a coffee from the tray, he took it with a quiet thanks.

"Guys," I said. "This is Vic. Vic"—I waved around at the others—"meet Baz . . . his brother, Nzuzi . . . and Coco."

Vic nodded at everyone, and when it became apparent he was going to wait for us to speak first, Baz dove in. "I apologize for rushing this, but I'm late for work already. Normally, I'd like to hear more about your situation, your goals, but all that will have to wait. I have two questions for you, and the only wrong answer is a lie. First question. Do you need help?"

Not so long ago Baz had asked me the very same question. Shortly after moving in with Uncle Les, I took to sneaking through the back door of the Cinema 5 in Bergenfield. It was an old-school setup, incredibly lax, perfect for what I needed: a hideout. Sometimes I did homework, sometimes I watched whatever movie was playing, but usually I just fell asleep in the back row. It was during just such a nap, I'd heard the words . . .

"Do you need help?" repeated Baz in the here and now.

Vic rubbed his head, the spot where he'd hit the metal desk, and nodded slowly as if still considering the question.

Baz squinted. "I need you to say it."

"Yes," said Vic. "I need help."

I remember how hot the Cinema 5 had been, how I used to push my sleeves up, and it always made me smile, because it was such a luxury being able to push up my sleeves, knowing it was too dark for anyone to see the bruises. Per usual, I had fallen asleep, and when I woke up, there he was, this employee carrying a sweeper and asking me if I needed help. I was still in the hazy fog of sleep, but I'm not sure it mattered. *Yes,* I'd responded. Then came the second question . . .

"Did you hurt anyone?" asked Baz.

Vic took a nervous sip of his coffee, and said the exact same thing I'd said when I was asked. . . .

What do you mean?

The employee had stood stock-still, sweeper in hand, and I'd wondered if I should be afraid. I honestly couldn't remember where I landed then, because where I ended up wasn't that far from fear: I grew to love Baz. It was an odd love, something between the love for a brother, a father, a priest, a childhood friend.

"What I mean," said Baz, "is . . . did you hurt anyone?"

Vic sipped his coffee, holding the cup with both hands, as if concentrating on not spilling it. "No," he said. It was quiet but resounding.

Baz nodded. "Good. You may stay with us if you like. We live on an orchard in New Milford. A bit of a walk, I know, but it's warm and we have food. It is your decision, of course, but I do need an answer now."

It was a rare offer, but when made, typically it was answered with a prompt yes. Most new Chapters were in such

dire straits, they didn't need much convincing, but with Vic it took a little longer. He looked around at all of us, his breath coming in long steady increments, his skull as good as transparent—those wheels were churning.

"Okay," he said finally.

"Wonderful," said Baz. "Nzuzi, Mad, Coco—can you take Vic back to the greenhouse? Get him settled in, cleaned up."

"Oh, I can't," I said. "I was . . . gonna go to the library."

Truth was, I'd been planning to go see Jamma, probably stay for a couple of days. Baz stood in the doorway and stared at me. He didn't even have to say anything.

"Fine," I said.

"Thank you. I get off at five. We can meet at Napoleon's then, and discuss our new Chapter." Then, to Vic: "The others will show you around. Please make yourself at home." Then, to Zuz: "Do not forget Gunther's bag." Then, to Coco: "No cursing. Best behavior."

And he was gone.

We stood in awkward silence for a few seconds until Zuz snapped twice, picked up the paper bag, and headed out the back door. "Hit the nail on the head, Zuz," said Coco, following him outside. "Frakking babysitters all day."

I looked at Vic, shook my head. "Don't mind them. They always take a while to warm up to newbies."

Vic redistributed the weight of his backpack to his other shoulder. "What's with the word *frak*?"

"Ha. Right. You ever seen the show *Battlestar Galactica*?"

Vic shook his head.

"We had this Chapter once who was obsessed with it. I guess on the show, they all say *frak* instead of *fuck*, and Coco used to have a swearing problem, and Baz is a bit of a

stickler. Anyway, this Chapter, he suggested Coco adopt the Galactican faux curse."

Vic nodded. "And what's a Chapter?"

It sounded like he'd been sitting on the question, pinning it down for the right moment to ask, only to have it pop out from under him like an overeager egg.

"I'll let Baz explain. It's a haul to New Milford, though. We should get going."

Together we traded in the wilds of the backroom butcher shop for the winter-white streets of Hackensack, and I tried to remember the last time I'd felt a person's thoughts so tangibly, floating and dancing and swirling through the air like the snow we walked through.

VIC

Both of my paternal grandparents died of heart attacks in April.

The same April.

People called on the phone to tell us they were praying for our family, or they were sending good thoughts our way. People brought green bean casseroles to the house. People squeezed our shoulders and gave us sideways hugs. (Sideways hugs are such bullshit. Hug me or don't. The indecisiveness is a real problem for me.) I don't know. When people think *comfort*, I suppose they think of these things. Either way, that April our house wasn't full of people. It wasn't full of love or heartfelt condolences or good thoughts. That April, our house was full of green bean casseroles and sideways hugs.

The whole thing really took its toll on Dad. But hey.

Both of his parents had just died in the same month, of the same thing. That shit's tough on anyone, especially a heart-thinker of his stature.

We used to visit my grandparents on the regular; being there was like being trapped in a house full of lovers. (Dad was never able to keep his hands off Mom, and it was no secret where he got it.) My grandparents would have blended in nicely in the science wing of my high school with all the other handsy teenagers. Which was really something, because my grandparents grew up in the day and age when husbands and wives slept in separate beds and called each other Mother and Father and the like.

My grandparents called each other Joe and Helen. And, despite the cultural milieu of the era, my grandparents slept in the same bed.

My grandparents were real Super Racehorses.

But yeah, it was pretty gross. And really, there wasn't much for me to do at their house other than the following:

1. Stare at a wall of photographs depicting my father from birth to age thirty. The pictures progressed chronologically, so I could actually watch Dad grow up before my eyes. They reminded me of those silhouette paintings that show the evolution of human beings from monkey to man.
2. Wait for the quarterly chimes of the cuckoo clock in the living room while watching my grandfather fall asleep in a full upright position in his favorite armchair.
3. Get my ass handed to me at the pool table downstairs. (Everyone in my family was an

absolute ace at billiards. I sucked balls at billiards.)

4. Count bowls of potpourri throughout the house. (Twenty-seven. There were twenty-seven. Twenty-seven bowls. Of potpourri.)
5. Watch everyone around me happily paw at one another. (Like handsy teenagers in the science wing of Hack High.)

My grandparents lived in a small town on the outskirts of Hackensack called New Milford. Just to get out of the house, away from all the heightened geriatric sexual impulses, I took long walks. Suburban excursions, I called them. And I got to know those streets pretty well. My favorite spot was this old stone wall across the street from a disheveled graveyard, which was kind of beautiful in an overgrown, cinematic sort of way. Big mossy trees stretched their limbs, vines and foliage dangled over scattershot tombstones. I used to sit on the stone wall and think, *Yeah. Okay. I could be buried here.*

And in the plot adjacent to the graveyard, there was an orchard. An acre of well-kept plants, flowers, and trees made all the more immaculate given their proximity to the neighboring mess of graveyard moss. A tapered stream ran the length of the orchard; a vine-covered wooden bridge crossed in the middle. There was a giant barn with a sign that read GIFT SHOP, an old colonial two-story with smoke rising from the chimney, and in the back, a row of greenhouses.

That momentous April, we buried both my grandparents in the graveyard next to that orchard. Grandma went second, and at her funeral, Dad stood next to his parents' joint tombstone, stared at the neighboring orchard, and swore he

would visit at least once a week. And for a couple of years, he did.

And then he got sick.

And then he died.

And that was the end of him visiting his parents who had both died of heart attacks that one momentous April. (It was the end of a lot of things. Pretty much everything, actually.)

It was highly likely that my following these kids was a very poor decision. Certainly, I hadn't planned on saying yes to Baz's odd question. Until . . .

We live on an orchard in New Milford.

In that moment—and it's quite possible I was wrong about this—I saw it as more than an opportunity to reunite my dad with his dead parents. I saw it as a sign. I saw it as Dad compassing me in the right direction.

As I walked down River Street, my backpack suddenly felt quite a bit lighter.

* * *

"You okay?"

I emerged from my Land of Nothingness to find Mad, her head turned, staring at me.

"What?" I asked.

What?

The most medium of words.

"I asked if you were okay."

"Oh," I said. "Yeah, thanks."

The kids had their own rhythm. Nzuzi led the way, using the grocery bag as a barricade between his face and the biting snow; just behind him, Mad held Coco's hand, carefully keeping her on the side opposite River Street traffic.

Together they reminded me of a flying gaggle of geese turning in blind cohesion, and you don't understand how those geese know the when or where of those turns, but they do. And you figure it must be a miracle.

I brought up the rear, wiping my leaky mug and trying not to feel like the straggler with the broken wing.

Mad's blond hair lashed around under that yellow knit cap, and in the white winter light, it looked like a fresh slice of lemon, or the tip of a sparkler at night. My poor heart-thinking brain brimmed with frothy thoughts of Mad. But there was no chance she saw me the way I saw her. Far more likely, she saw me the way I saw me.

I am small boy.

I drained the last of my now-lukewarm coffee, and before long we veered off the road toward the Hackensack River, where a little field opened up with a sign reading HISTORIC NEW BRIDGE LANDING. I'd been here before, years ago, on a school trip. The site of a Revolutionary War battleground, it had a few city-protected houses scattered here and there. I looked down at our tracks in the snow and thought of what that must have been like at the time, and how weird that it happened *here*.

On this step.

And this one.

This one too.

We made our way toward the short pedestrian bridge connecting Hackensack to New Milford; a group of kids launched snowballs at one another from either side. As we approached, one of them raised both hands in the air and yelled, "Game off!" I recognized him from school. Roland, I think, but he went by some odd nickname I couldn't remember. Roland always wore mismatched

shoes like he got dressed in the dark or something. He and his friends belonged to that particular faction of kids at Hack High who did not leave me alone. (Being left alone at Hack High was essentially the goal, though an occasional hallway hello from the student council president, Stephanie Dawn—who was too nice to know how pretty she was, and too pretty to go anywhere but up the social ladder—could literally fortify me against a week's worth of tongue-lashing.)

I kept my head down as we crossed the bridge, and thought about the war that had been waged in this exact spot hundreds of years earlier. From troops marching toward a bloody demise to Bruno Victor Benucci III marching toward, well, who could say really.

Land was weird. Unlike a person, it did not care who stepped on it.

. . .

Halfway across the bridge, it started. They were not words; they were wasps, stinging in all the soft, fleshy places. *Buzzzzzzzzzzzzzzz.*

A snowball hit my back.

Then my leg.

Then my face.

"Bull's-eye!" yelled one of the kids.

I heard Dad from my backpack. *Think with your heart, V.*

I scraped the snow off my cheeks, tried not to let them see my eyes. This was key. If they saw my eyes, they'd know they'd gotten to me. From the side pocket of my backpack I fumbled for my earbuds, my empty heart begging to be filled by the soaring sopranos. Scroll, scroll, scroll, *play*—now, to disappear completely into an entirely other world.

In that world: every faction left me alone.

In that world: I was not one seven-billionth of the planet's population.

In that world: I was one-fourth of the planet's population: it was Dad, the two sopranos, and me.

In that world: we soared through the sky and clouds, above it all, not a care in the world, the most miraculous of gaggles, catching the souls of those rare, lovely heart-thinkers.

In that world: my wing was mended.

MAD

I didn't know what Vic was listening to, but I sure hoped he had the volume turned up.

VIC

"Straight to the back," said Coco, lifting the bottom of the chain-link fence. Mad had already scrambled underneath and was currently reaching for the bag of groceries as Nzuzi handed it over the top. Across the street, I saw my old perch: the stone wall, the fig tree. I felt the presence of that little graveyard on the other side of the orchard, wondered how many times Dad had visited, and if he'd ever stopped by the orchard.

"Dude," said Coco. "You okay?"

"What?"

She motioned under the fence. "Shit or get off the pot, kid."

This little girl's vocabulary, it seemed, knew no bounds. "How old are you, exactly?"

"I'm eleven," she said. "But that's, like, twenty-six in Queens years."

"Right. Okay then."

I handed my backpack over the fence, wincing as Mad dropped it carelessly onto the ground. After crawling under the chain link, I dusted the snow off my chest and legs, took a quick look inside the bag (luckily the tape on the urn's lid held strong), and followed the kids down a path of thorny-dead rosebushes.

"What do you got in there?" asked Mad. "A cannonball?"

I let her words ring in the air, left them there.

"Well, whatever else," she said, pointing to my bloody jeans, "I hope you have a change of clothes."

I was about to ask what kind of kid carries around a change of clothes in their backpack when I realized I did, in fact, have my favorite sweatpants tucked away. During winter, the gym at Hack High grew incalculably drafty, ergo, our PE teacher allowed us to wear our own gym clothes instead of shorts.

"I do, actually."

"Cool. After we get settled in, I'll show you where you can change and get washed up."

Snow was piled high on either side of the path. Ridged grooves ran up and down the embankments where some-one had recently shoveled. It was bizarre walking through a place I'd only ever admired from a distance. I started across the wooden bridge, where a posted sign read: CHANNEL A LA GOLDFISH. Between the slats of two-by-fours under my feet, a giant goldfish swam idly in the narrow stream below.

Channel à la Goldfish was a very literal channel.

Once across, Nzuzi darted off toward the only house on the premises—the old colonial two-story. We waited by the bridge while he sat the bag of groceries on the porch, knocked on the door, and jogged back toward us.

"Let's go," said Mad in a shiver, leading the way down a row of greenhouses.

There was something Oz-like about the whole thing, as if I'd stepped into a portal and been transported to some bizarre world with an unexplained set of rules and a pack of reckless, parentless, wild kids. (So Oz with a dash of Neverland, I guess.) Even though these kids were effectively homeless, they had an air of pride about them, and I could see why. Like Oz, the orchard was beautiful and cozy in its strangeness. Most of the plant life was barren, but even so, it felt like a lush botanical garden, as if the outside of the orchard were incapable of reflecting its inside.

The orchard reminded me of this: an old man's youthful heart.

Mad stopped in front of the smallest greenhouse, tucked in the back like an afterthought, half the width of the one next to it. Less a greenhouse, more the footnote of a greenhouse. Less the entrée, more the leftovers.

I loved it from the word *go*.

"Welcome home," said Mad. A rush of warmth hit me in the face as she opened the door. The kids filed inside, took off their jackets, hung them on a coat rack, and walked down the center aisle.

I was wrong.

This place was stranger than Oz.

While the front half was full of typical greenhouse fare—rows of blossoming vegetation on waist-high tables, and potted plants hanging from the clear curved walls—the

back half reminded me of a postapocalyptic movie I once saw about a family who lived in a bomb shelter for something like seven years.

There were bookshelves, for starters. I counted five of them—stocked with canned fruits and vegetables, bags of nuts, chips, beef jerky, gallons of water, stacks of books and vinyl records, and an old turntable. A space heater hummed from the back wall; just underneath, four sleeping bags were spread on the ground, neatly made, a pillow at each head. A green couch sat in the opposite corner, a coffee table in front of it (as if this were a perfectly normal living room, thank-you-very-much). On the coffee table was a stack of cards and a lamp. I spotted an outlet under the space heater, and a power strip for the lamp and record player.

"What about the owner?" I asked. "Or . . . orchard keeper, or whoever? The guy who lives in the house."

Mad stuck her hands in front of the space heater. "Gunther doesn't mind, so long as we bring him groceries and supplies so he never has to leave the grounds. Apparently he hit the lottery decades ago, figured he could wave good-bye to customer service. People stopped venturing onto his orchard, and Gunther stopped venturing off of it."

"What about school?"

"Gunther's too old for school," said Coco, who burst out laughing. "Ha! Nailed it." She kept laughing as she pulled a cup of applesauce off the shelf, opened it, and used two fingers to scoop it into her mouth. "Anyway, Mad's done with school, Baz works at the Cinema Five until he and Zuz get their cab service up and running"—Nzuzi, who was debating which record to pull off the shelf, snapped his fingers once—"and that leaves me. And I'm an orphan."

"So?"

"So, orphans don't go to school. You gotta have moms and dads to sign shit. Plus, an address. What, I should write *Eleventh Greenhouse on the Right, Maywood Orchard, New Milford*? Might as well add *Cupboard under the Stairs* while I'm at it. It's a public school, not Hogwarts. I'd get laughed out of the building."

"Hogwarts is definitely the shit, though," said Mad.

Coco nodded. "Oh, Hogwarts is the shit."

"With the Cornish pasties and treacle tarts and all."

"I don't even know what the frak a Cornish pasty is, and I still want one."

Nzuzi snapped once, pulled a record off the Shelf of Improbable Things, placed it on the turntable, and lowered the stylus. After the initial hiss of white noise, the music started and Nzuzi broke into dance. Strikingly nimble, he pulled his elbows in, cocked his head to one side, snapped his fingers on every upbeat. It wasn't synchronized; it was authorized. As if each body part had given permission to the other body parts to go nuts as one.

Nzuzi was an absolute ace at jigging.

"'Don't Stop Believin','" said Coco, polishing off the applesauce. "His favorite. Hey, Zuz, you hungry?"

Still jigging, Nzuzi snapped a finger. Coco grabbed a plastic cup of peaches off the shelf, tossed it to him. He caught it mid-jig, tore back the lid, and dug in.

I was a real mythology-sucker-legacy-loving type guy. I needed history. I needed know-how. I needed *origin*. I had roughly one zillion questions, and planned on asking one after another until someone shut me down.

"What's with the finger snapping?" I asked, as good a place to start as any.

Coco said, "One snap means yes, two means no. Zuz has

plenty to say, you just gotta know how to listen." She tossed the plastic cup into a nearby trash can, leaned back, and spread her arms wide. "So, what do you think, kid? Pretty sweet setup, right?"

I was done being referred to as "kid" by an eleven-year-old.

"My name is Vic," I said. "Or *Victor* is fine."

"You mean like—to the victor belong the spoils?" Coco let out a raucous, juicy laugh, little bits of leftover applesauce flying from her mouth. "Maybe we'll just call you Spoils. How about that?"

Coco kept talking, but I really couldn't say what about. Mad had just removed her knit cap; ergo, my head had just removed its eyeballs.

She'd shown me the scar on the side of her head last night, but even so, I found myself almost completely incapacitated right now, as if I'd had a blown fuse my whole life and someone had only now replaced it. On one side, her hair was long, wavy, unruly, exactly as I imagined; the other side was shaved right up to the top of the temple. Not bald, but buzzed, a total West Coast punk cut. The hair led to the eyes, which led to the lips, which led to the skin, which led to, which led to, which led to . . .

Mad was a map.

And I was Magellan.

I plotted my course, dreamed of uncharted territories and the glories found in each valley and crevice. I dreamed of the sloping, sensual summit, and of mounting its zenith.

"You can sleep on that," said Coco quietly.

I am a Super Racehorse.

"What?" I said in a breath.

"The couch." She pointed toward Mad. I stood there like a sideways hug, wondering if the couch came with the girl.

"Chapters get the couch," said Coco, tossing a bag of beef jerky to Mad.

I took a deep breath. "And what exactly *is* a chapter?"

"Not chapter," said Coco. "Chapter. With a capital *C*."

"How do you know I didn't say it with a capital *C*?"

"I could hear it in your voice."

Nzuzi grabbed a metal watering can and danced up and down each aisle of plants, watering as he went.

"Okay, fine." I cleared my throat. "What exactly is . . . a Chapter?"

"*Patience*, cockroach," said Coco.

"Grasshopper," said Mad.

Coco raised an eyebrow. "You sure?"

"Pretty sure."

Coco shrugged. "*Patience*, grasshopper."

. . .

The kids were more than just a gaggle. They were puzzle pieces, a well-packed trunk, as improbably organized as the improbable shelves in their improbable habitat. I stood there, wiping my leaky mug, a circle-peg-square-hole type guy saying sideways-hug type things like *oh* and *what*. Less a puzzle piece, more the box it came in.

I unzipped my backpack and pulled out my Mets sweatpants. Dad called them my Metpants, which I used to hate.

Now? Shit. Missed it.

"You said there might be somewhere for me to change . . . ?"

"Right." Mad hopped off the couch. "Let's go. I could use a smoke anyway."

Metpants in one hand, I picked up my backpack with the other and was about to follow, when Coco said, "What d'you think, we're gonna steal your stuff? Poor loathsome urchins that we are."

I pulled my iPod and Visine out of the side pocket, put the bag back where it was, and tried not to imagine Coco stuffing her grimy little hands inside Dad's urn. "I'm sure it'll be fine."

Coco smiled theatrically, put her hand on her heart. "Your vote of confidence means the world to us. Truly, Spoils. Actually, hey, you got a phone in there? With games and stuff?"

"Sorry," I said. "Left it at home."

Mad waited by the front door, rainbow coat on, hands stuffed into pockets. The knit cap was back too, and I had a sudden desire to paint her. I wasn't an artist, so much as an admirer of art—just good enough to know I was no good at all.

She pulled a cigarette out of her pocket and stuck it behind her ear. Normally, I found smoking to be quite disgusting. However, it suddenly seemed sexy, though not in that sexy-smoker type sexiness. Mom and Dad used to watch *Casablanca* about once a week (which I used to hate, now I miss, etc., etc.), and the idea of Mad smoking felt more like that. Like a *Casablanca* type sexiness.

I don't know.

At that exact moment I wasn't really thinking with my heart *or* my brain. I was thinking with the deck gun of my USS *Ling*.

MAD

Drag.

   Blow.

   Calm.

"Hey, Harry Connick Jr., Jr. What's the word on the stream?" Honestly, had the bloated thing not been upright, I would have assumed it was dead. I dangled my legs off the edge of Channel à la Goldfish and waited for Vic to finish washing up and changing. He'd been pretty surprised by the available amenities, and I can't say I blame him. Unlike the greenhouse accommodations, though, these amenities were highly unauthorized. Gunther had no idea we'd figured out a way through the window and into the gift shop bathroom. Not that he had any reason to get upset; I couldn't remember the last time he'd had a customer.

The sky was still that cold gray, the color of a slow death, but at least it had stopped snowing for a beat. I lit another cigarette just as Harry Connick Jr., Jr., reappeared, floating the other way now. "You taking shortcuts, Junior?"

"Who are you talking to?"

"Shit!" I dropped my lighter in a narrow gap between two beams of the bridge, heard it plop into the stream below. *"Dude."*

"Sorry," said Vic, sitting next to me, his bloody jeans wadded in his lap. "You shouldn't smoke anyway. It gives you cancer."

I smoke-glared at him as I took the next drag. Hold, exhale, keep up the glare. "Lots of things give you cancer."

"True. But some things do so with a much higher rate of efficiency than others."

"What would you know about it?"

He looked down at the stream when I noticed what he'd changed into: blue sweatpants. They had a Mets logo on the right thigh and elastic bands around his ankles that made the fabric bunch up like a bouquet around his lace-up boots.

"They're my Metpants," he said.

I laughed a little puff of smoke. "Your what?"

"Metpants."

There was just something so patently awesome about Vic wearing these pants, as if he'd glimpsed the world's stockpile of ammunition against him, shrugged, and tossed an extra crossbow onto the heap for good measure.

Metpants. Vic's double-bird to the world. I loved it.

And just then I wished I'd given each of those kids on the bridge a swift kick in the junk.

He rolled his eyes around for a second, but only up and down, not side to side. I'd seen him do this a few times now, but it still took me off guard.

"Who's *Junior*?" he asked.

As if summoned by the god of goldfish himself, Harry Connick Jr., Jr., appeared below our feet.

"*That*," I said, "is Junior. He's our goldfish. I named him Harry Connick Jr., Jr."

"After the singer?"

"Yep. And actor. That guy does not quit. He's everywhere, especially during the holidays. Anyway, this summer there were dozens of goldfish, now this is the only one. Here, look." I pointed about twenty feet upstream to a red object that resembled an upside-down salad bowl floating in the water. "That's a de-icer. It keeps the water at a high enough temperature to not freeze over. The thing is Gunther only put in one de-icer this year, which isn't nearly enough. So one by one the fish started dying until it was less Channel à

la Goldfish and more Plague à la Goldfish. They just couldn't survive."

"Except Harry Connick Jr., Jr."

I nodded. "The fish who does not quit."

Drag.

Blow.

Calm.

"I like your greenhouse," said Vic.

"It's weird, I know."

"Not that weird."

I gave him a classic *Are you kidding me?* look.

"Okay." He nodded. "It's pretty weird. But cool."

"Anyway, it's not permanent—just until we can afford better."

Drag.

Blow.

Calm.

"I used to stare at this place," whispered Vic. He pointed across the street. "I sat right there on that stone wall and stared at this orchard."

"Really? You ever see us?"

He shook his head. "It was a while back. My grandparents used to live in this neighborhood, but they're—" He stopped abruptly, looked down at the stream. "Anyway. I thought it was kind of a weird bump."

"Bump?"

"Coincidence."

Vic pulled out his handkerchief, wiped the bottom corner of his mouth, and that was when I saw the scabs on his right wrist. There were five or six, varying in length, but all very thin. They weren't scars like the one on my head. And I had a friend in high school who cut herself regularly—

this wasn't that either. These seemed duller, more shallow or something.

He pulled his iPod from his jacket pocket, pushed his long hair behind both ears, and stuck in his earbuds.

Conversation over, I guess.

Drag.

Blow.

Calm.

"Here," said Vic, holding out an earbud.

"You're offering an earbud," I said.

"I am."

"I thought that was just something people did in movies."

"Are you suggesting we're in a movie?"

"I wish."

"Which one?"

"What?"

"Which movie do you wish we were in?" asked Vic.

I'd seen other people—usually in coffee shops, or that recently defunct outdoor café on Henley—speak to one another with this kind of fluid banter, as if the conversation had been all mapped out and memorized before the involved parties opened their mouths. I'd even been part of a few, but only with Coco—until now.

"*Apollo 13*," I said.

"*Apollo 13*."

"Sure. Tom Hanks in space. What, you're too good for Tom Hanks in space?"

"Things go horribly wrong for Tom Hanks in space if I remember correctly. Come to think of it, things go horribly wrong for Tom Hanks on deserted islands, too."

"Au contraire," I said, "Tom Hanks survives both space and islands."

"Survival. That's your aspiration?"

"You bet your ass. Anyway, I love space."

"What do you mean?" asked Vic.

"I mean, I love space. Black holes and dwarf planets and stars that faded to nothing decades ago but we can still see them—all that shit. Can't get enough."

Drag.

Blow.

Calm.

"That's actually a common misconception," said Vic.

"What is?"

"The idea that we're looking at stars in the sky that have already died and faded."

"No, I'm pretty sure it's true. Because of the light-years, I mean—if a star died, we wouldn't know for, like, decades I think."

Vic was quiet, but sort of shook his head in that way people do when they've got more to say—or worse, when they know they're right and you're wrong.

"Okay, *Spoils*," I said. "Out with it."

"It's just—most stars live for millions and millions of years. We live for eighty, give or take, and can only see around five thousand stars with the naked eye. The odds that one of them dies during my lifetime are pretty minuscule. Possible, I guess. But highly improbable."

Drag.

Blow.

Calm.

"So I'm trying to decide if you're a show-off or a nerd or both," I said.

"Nah, I just like numbers. Anyway, what do you think?"

"Honestly, I forget what we were even talking about."

He held up the earbud again. "Maybe it's something people do in real life too."

It was clear he wouldn't take no for an answer. I sighed, snuffed out my cigarette, and took the earbud. "What are we listening to?"

"You'll see."

And he was right. I did see.

To say the song was beautiful was like saying the sun was hot, or the fish was wet, or a billion was a lot. It was opera, I think, or something like it, a duet, two ladies, both singing their hearts out, and even though it was in a foreign language, I almost cried because there was just something so familiar about their voices, like they understood my own personal sorrow on a molecular level.

When it was over, I handed the earbud back and was about to ask him what the song was called when he said, "I think we're being watched."

A dozen yards away a pair of piercing eyes ducked behind a high snow embankment. A second later they reappeared, trained on Vic.

"That's just Zuz." I smiled a little, wondering how long he'd been lying on his stomach in the snow. "He does that."

"Does what?" asked Vic.

"He's just—very protective of his family."

"So Zuz is protecting you from . . . me?"

"He spies on all the Chapters for the first few days. And don't call him Zuz."

"Why not? You guys do."

"First off, Baz doesn't. I mean, he could if he wanted. He's earned the right. You haven't. Not yet, anyway."

Vic stared at the embankment. "Okay. So how will I know I've earned it?"

"You'll know."

It was quiet again, the two of us sitting in the echo of a song.

"What about money?" asked Vic.

"What about it?"

"I mean, you have to have money to live, right?"

"Not as much as they'd have you believe."

"Who's *they*?"

"You know. *They*. Like, the government and media and shit. The consumerist mentality and our propensity to price tag happiness." Honestly, I had no idea what bullshit I was spinning, but it sounded good saying it. "Anyway, we've got a few early Chapters around town who help out, and Baz's job at Cinema Five covers the rest. He's been saving for a while now. Plans on opening his own taxi service—Renaissance Cabs."

"Cool," said Vic. "Why a cab service?"

I pulled my hair around to one side as Harry Connick Jr., Jr., swam lazily under our feet.

"You sure have a lot of questions," I said.

"You don't have many answers."

"I'll let Baz tell you about it. It's his thing."

"Okay," said Vic. "What about your thing, then? Coco said you just graduated?"

I smiled at him, grabbed his bloodied-up jeans, then stood and dusted the snow off my backside. "We should probably head back. I'll take these for you."

"Mad."

"Yes?"

"What's a Chapter?"

I turned and started back toward the row of greenhouses, Zuz close behind. "Patience, cockroach."

It was a full ten minutes before Vic returned. During that time, I'd shoved his pants on the shelf next to the records, still unsure why I'd taken them in the first place. I then settled onto the couch, where I tried to immerse myself in *The Outsiders*, a feat that usually took very little prodding, but something about Vic's song had crept inside my brain, my veins, now pulsing through my body.

Zuz had "'Round About Midnight" by Miles Davis cranked on the turntable while Coco knelt over Vic's backpack, digging through his stuff.

"Coke, what are you doing?"

She pulled out some textbooks, set them on the coffee table. "Checking for contraband. I mean, we don't really know the guy. He seems nice, but what if he's one of those army-guys-turned-Taliban?"

"Coco, that's ridiculous." I set the book in my lap. "Vic is *not* Taliban, and whatever's in his bag isn't fucking *contraband*. Do you even know what that word means?"

She whipped her hair around. "Do *you*?"

Zuz snapped twice. He hated when we argued.

Coco went back to searching Vic's bag.

"Coke, I'm really not comfortable with you nosing through Vic's stuff. He could be back any min—"

"Aha!" she said, pulling out Vic's jar.

In the light of day, it was obvious what it was. Coco set the urn on the coffee table.

"*Contraband*."

"Sorry," said a small voice. It happened just as I imagined: none of us heard Vic come in. He stood by the door, staring at us. "Guess I need to stop sneaking up on people." In a daze

he walked to the coffee table and stood over the urn like a predator about to pounce on its prey.

"Well, I suppose you were right," said Coco. "I'm a no-good street urchin."

We all moved toward Vic as if a massive invisible magnet pulled us in, then stood around him and peered down at the urn.

"What is it?" asked Coco. "What's inside?"

Vic pulled out his handkerchief, wiped his mouth. "My dad."

It wasn't a whisper, but it might as well have been.

THREE

OUR PAST TENSES
(or, The Inevitability of Corresponding Units)

"Vic, you're not listening."

I stuff my handkerchief into my pocket, look around for a clock. As it turns out, time is hard to pass when you can't see it.

"Sorry," I say. "What was the question?"

"Did Baz ever mention why Nzuzi doesn't talk?"

Mendes taps the edge of her file with her pen. She rarely writes anything, which makes sense, considering the whole conversation is being recorded. The pen she uses like a tiny drumstick, clicking it against the table, the pad of paper, the bracelet on her left hand . . .

Rhythmically. Rhythmically. Rhythm, rhythm, rhythmically.
Rhythmically. Rhythmically. Rhythm, rhythm, rhythmically.

. . .

"He did," I say.

"And?"

Truth is, until the last twenty-four hours I didn't know many details about the Kabongo brothers' past life. But a lot has changed. And last night—or early this morning, I really couldn't say which—I'd learned plenty.

"The Kabongos were born in Brazzaville, in the Republic

of the Congo. Their whole family had to flee when Baz was ten, I think. Zuz would have been really young—and they had a little sister at the time too. They walked for months, ate and drank very little. People were dying all around them. Made it pretty far together until their father died of malnutrition."

"That's terrible. You said Baz was ten?"

I nod.

"About how old do you think Nzuzi and Nsimba were?" she asks.

"By then, probably three or—"

. . .

Shit.

. . .

. . .

"Vic, you okay?"

. . .

I stare into Mendes's eyes, second-guessing everything. "How did you know about Nsimba?"

"What?"

"Before. Just now. You said, 'Nzuzi and Nsimba.'"

Mendes flushes, flips through some papers in the file in front of her. "You mentioned a sister—"

"Not by name."

"It's common Congolese practice, naming twins Nzuzi and Nsimba. I just assumed."

"I never said they were twins."

It wouldn't be that difficult to learn information about the Kabongos' lives before resettlement in the States. Baz mentioned organizations like the United Nations High Commissioner for Refugees and the Red Cross—certainly, there were records, documentation outlining their experi-

ences. But it does make me wonder what else Mendes knows, and to what lengths she's gone to gather information.

She sips her coffee, checks her watch. "Anyway, you were about to say why Nzuzi doesn't talk."

I run my hands through my hair. "I don't really feel like talking specifics. The kid saw some pretty horrible things at a pretty young age, Miss Mendes. If he doesn't feel like talking, I don't blame him. To be perfectly honest, considering all he's been through, I'd say he's coping fairly well."

Rhythmically. Rhythmically. Rhythm, rhythm, rhythmically.

. . .

Mendes pulls a manila file out of nowhere, drops it onto the desk. Something about it is terrifyingly simple, like a lone stranger's face in your own family's portrait.

There's a knock on the door, quickly followed by the entrance of a guy in a suit, and a shock of red hair.

"Detective Ron," says Mendes. "This is Vic Benucci."

Detective Ron nods at me, his eyes landing on my face. In a matter of seconds, I see the forced casualness, the attempted internal explanation, followed by the nothing-to-see-here smile, and finally—the slow look-away.

If I had a nickel for every slow look-away . . .

"What's up?" says Mendes.

"It's not good," says Detective Ron, totally avoiding eye contact with me now.

"Ronald, what?"

Judging from Mendes's tone, I'm guessing Detective Ronald is the Hackensack Police Department's resident Frank. He does seem to have a certain French poodle quality about him.

"We keep calling," says Ron. "She doesn't answer."

Across the hall, I catch a glimpse of Mad's yellow hair in

the door window. It's crazy: you can miss just about anything when it belongs to the right person. Mad is my right person, ergo, I miss her hair and her shoes and her just-about-everything, pretty much.

"Leave a voice mail?" asks Mendes.

"Tried. Her in-box is full."

I feel a sudden dryness on the back of my tongue, a twitch in my ear, a mighty aplombness in my belly. I knew they were trying to get ahold of Mom, but the reality of seeing her here . . .

When she shows up, she'll just have to wait. I'm not stopping now.

"Okay, keep trying," says Mendes. "And let me know the minute you reach her."

On his way out the door, Detective Ron gives Mendes a peculiar smile. Over the years, I've become something of an expert smile-reader, as if my own inability to grin affords me a heightened awareness of others'.

. . .

. . .

"So," I say. "Detective Ronald."

"What about him?" asks Mendes.

"He's your bitch, isn't he?"

Mendes crosses her arms, says nothing.

"Question," I say. "Does he just relish being the dude outside the door? To be honest, I always thought it was a bit of a chump's errand, you know? *Hey, you know what you'd be* perfect *for? Sitting. In the hallway.*"

Mendes unclasps the manila folder in front of her, pulls out a few sheets of paper. She flips them upside down, folds her hands across the top.

"Vic, have you ever heard of touch DNA?"

. . .

"No."

She picks up her pen, holds it in the air. "We've been sitting here for just over an hour. During that time, my body has shed roughly thirty thousand skin cells. Now let's assume only a fraction of those cells transferred from my fingers to this pen—maybe .01 percent. So about three hundred dead skin cells. Or we could be extra conservative and cut that by a third. Let's say one hundred of my dead skin cells are on this pen. Do you know how many cells a lab needs to develop a person's DNA profile? Seven, maybe eight. That's touch DNA." She slides the envelope across the table. "We pulled DNA off the murder weapon, compared it to nuclear DNA also found at the scene, then ran the results through what's called the Combined DNA Index System—CODIS, for short. It's an FBI database that contains DNA samples of known felons."

She slides a photo of a man across the table. I don't know him, or at least I don't think I do. He's so badly beaten, it's hard to tell. The picture is a close-up of his face, his wounds and bruises so severe, you might think you were looking at a fresh corpse.

"Who is this?" I ask.

Mendes sips her coffee. "When they arrived in the States, Baz and Nzuzi were categorized as M4 refugee minors, meaning they had no relatives here and knew no one. They were placed in the foster care system almost immediately, with a family in Syracuse. Things go well for a number of years—Baz graduates high school, moves out, gets a job at a local electronics store. Eventually he meets some bad dudes who get him mixed up in their shit. The family says they're done. They have a biological son and don't feel they can trust Baz anymore."

"You said he moved out."

"He did, but Nzuzi was still there, so Baz was coming around all the time. So once the Syracuse family bows out"—Mendes nods at the photo in my hand—"Thomas Blythe steps in. Single father, decent home, decent job. Eventually the care is approved by Catholic Charities. By all accounts, Mr. Blythe did the Kabongos an incredible kindness, taking Nzuzi in." She reaches out, taps the photo. "And this is how Baz repaid that kindness. Beat him within an inch of his life."

. . .

"So he *is* alive, then?" I ask.

Mendes slides another photo across the table. In this one, Thomas Blythe is in a hospital bed, half a dozen machines around the room, tubes running along (and *into*) various parts of his body. His face appears to have healed for the most part, though there are some visible scars.

"This photo was taken a couple of months ago by a nurse who takes care of him. He's in a coma, Victor. On life support. If you call that living."

I am an eternal blank page.

"What makes you think it was Baz?" I ask. "This man—"

"Thomas Blythe."

"He's in a coma, you said. So we can't know what really happened."

Mendes slides the third and final sheet of paper across the table. This one is very different from the first two. Across the top, it states in bold lettering, CRIMINAL HISTORY REPORT. Below that, Baz's face stares up at me. It's him, but it's not. There are no smiles from his mouth or his eyes. It's a cold photo, gray and hard, hard and heavy, heavy and horrible. Baz-in-the-photo doesn't require the truth, or speak

of the provision of the Living God. Baz-in-the-photo doesn't take the bread off the burger, or quietly pass on soda. Baz-in-the-photo breaks my heart.

To the left of his picture, a list of descriptions includes sex, race, place and date of birth, height, weight, and identifying marks.

"This is what I meant when I said he fell in with some bad dudes," says Mendes, tapping a line halfway down the page. *Prior convictions*. There is only one: Grand larceny in the fourth degree (*"Suspect stole a Lexus LS 600 value est. over 150K . . ."*). "That's a Class E felony," says Mendes, "which accounts for his DNA landing in the CODIS database. As I understand it, there was a bit of leniency with sentencing, considering he had no priors, but he did serve the minimum of one year in prison."

Do you need help? Did you hurt anyone?

Baz's questions weren't conjured from thin air; they were pieces of his past. His no-stealing rule, too, now carried far more weight.

The document goes on to say Baz had been suspected of being involved in one case of assault and battery, and another case of kidnapping.

Mendes reaches over, picks up the picture of Thomas Blythe, stares at it while she talks. "There was no sign of forced entry into Blythe's apartment. Nothing was stolen. No instrument or weapon was used in the assault of Mr. Blythe, and the wounds were consistent with those of a fist. Repeated and forceful blows by someone who possessed great strength. And I would guess—plenty of rage."

Fingernails. Push. Deep into the skin of my right forearm.

Push and hold.

Harder now.

I am an old habit.

"Baz Kabongo is not who you think he is, Victor. And he's counting on you to be a follower. To be *his* follower. He's counting on you to be stupid. I'm counting on you to be smart."

Mendes's voice is dull, fuzzy, like she's speaking through a walkie-talkie from some far-off land.

A bad connection from Singapore.

I stare at Baz's rap sheet, my eyes focusing on a single word. "Kidnapping?" I say.

. . .

. . .

"Victor. Did Coco ever talk about her father?"

(SEVEN days ago)

MAD

"It's a tattoo shop," said Baz.

Vic sipped his soda intentionally, angling the rim a bit off-center. "What is?"

"*Hang me from the Parlour*. The Parlour is a tattoo shop—a friend of ours works there. It's not far. We can head over when we finish eating."

We sat in the back corner booth of Napoleon's Pub, wedged between a pool table and a dart board, talking about Vic's list and drinking sodas (except Baz, who always ordered water). Vic was nestled next to Coco and Zuz on one side of the booth, and I sat with Baz on the other.

"I still think we should have gone to White Manna," said Coco. A Hackensack institution, White Manna was famous for its sliders. Just hearing the name of the restaurant conjured a Pavlovian response in my salivary glands; unfortunately for us, White Manna management had little patience for shenanigans, especially ones involving a short redhead stealing fries off the plates of other customers. "Best sliders this side of the Mississippi."

I raised an eyebrow. "Have you ever been to the *other* side of the Mississippi, Coco?"

"I don't need to. White Manna is the best, and you know it."

"Well, you should have thought about that before you decided to go around jacking other people's fries off their—"

As if on cue, a plate of steaming cheese fries appeared on the table before us. "Okay, guys, here you go. My world famous pepper jack fries."

Margo Bonaparte was exactly as outlandish as her name suggested. She wore rain boots no matter the weather, tight-fitting bright-colored pants, and long pigtails (which looked more like flappy dog ears than hair), and seemed to have an endless supply of old Beatles T-shirts. Margo's father, Hubert Bonaparte, was the owner of Napoleon's Pub, so she could do pretty much what she wanted.

Except Baz. She couldn't do Baz no matter how bad she wanted to. Currently, Baz was seeing Rachel-something, a girl he worked with at Cinema 5. Apparently they had things in common—namely movies and baseball—making her different from the others. Baz usually had a girlfriend, though they rarely lasted, and they *never* came around. He and Rachel ate out a lot, stayed at her place sometimes, and occasionally went to Trenton to catch a Thunder game. I could hardly blame Baz for keeping

serious separation between his love life and Greenhouse Eleven.

"You lose my number again, Mbemba?" asked Margo Bonaparte. As far as I knew, Margo was the only one who used Baz's full name. She pulled a pen and a slip of paper from her apron, wrote her number down, and handed it to him. "I swear, you'd lose that beautiful head of yours if it weren't attached." Then, to the rest of us: "Burgers okay? I can bring salads, too. We got an overload of lettuce in the last shipment, it's all gonna go bad soon. But, oh! *Guys.* Listen. You *have* to save room, okay? I've got a special treat for dessert. Promise me."

We assured Margo that we would save room for her special treat, and off she went, pigtails flapping behind her.

"But *guys*," said Coco, in a singsong voice. "*Listen.* We simply *must* save *room*." She stuffed a forkful of cheese fries in her mouth, continued to talk with her mouth full. "Freak show, that girl. Still. What do you think, Zuz? She got some ice cream back there?"

Zuz snapped once.

Despite the name of the establishment, the only thing French about the place (other than its fries) was the trademark greeting of its waiters and waitresses. "*Bonjour, mes petits gourmands*," which translated to, "Hello, my small gluttons." In a Venn diagram where set A = {People Who Speak French}, and set B = {Regular Patrons of Napoleon's Pub}, the intersection = {Basically No One}. Napoleon's Pub was preposterousness personified, which probably explained why we liked it so much.

The fries were gone in no time, and a few minutes later Margo brought the salads. It had been a while since our last Chapter, so we ate in silence for the most part, each of us ac-

climating to the presence of another person at the table. Once done with the salads and cheese fries, we passed around the two items from the urn: the letter and the photograph.

I read a portion of it aloud. "'You and Victor are my North, South, East, and West. You are my Due Everywhere.'" What I wanted to say was, *This is the sweetest fucking thing I've ever read*, but all that came out was, "Doris is your mother?"

Vic nodded, and I read aloud the locations on the list. "'Hang me from the Parlour, toss me off the Palisades, bury me in the smoking bricks of our first kiss, drown me in our wishing well, drop me from the top of our rock.' Well, the Parlour we know. The Palisades are the cliffs, I assume."

Baz nodded. "That one should be easy enough. We can get there from Englewood." He looked across the table at Vic. "Do you have any idea about the other three places?"

"No," he said, staring into his empty glass.

I passed the letter across the table; Coco grabbed it with cheesy hands and read it out loud between bites. When she got to the closing, she paused. "'Till we're old-new.' What's that supposed to mean?"

"It's something they used to say," said Vic. "I don't really—I don't know what it means."

Vic's mannerisms, the tone of both language and body, suggested some deep embarrassment, as if we'd just broadcast his personal diary throughout the country. Though there was something intensely personal about the letter, his father's "Terminal Note."

Zuz passed the Polaroid to me.

"Who put these things in your father's urn?" asked Baz. "And why would they do such a thing?"

"Mom must have," he said. "The list, the photo, the ashes. She needed to keep all of him together, I think. Everything

in our house is different now. But those things are still him. Those things haven't changed."

In the photograph, Vic's parents are on a rooftop, the familiar skyline of New York City behind them. There was a fair resemblance between Vic and his parents, but I wondered how much stronger it might have been were it not for the wall of hair he hid behind like a shield, a divider between himself and the world around him.

"They look really happy," I said, looking back at the picture.

Vic pushed his glass away, reached across the table, took the Polaroid out of my hands. Just then Margo appeared with a tray full of burgers, setting a plate in front of each of us. She disappeared with an *"Au revoir, mes petits gourmands,"* but I barely heard her. I watched Vic as he stared at that Polaroid in his hands, and I wondered what he was thinking.

VIC

I bet Mom asked a complete stranger to take this picture. She was always doing that, asking strangers to take photos.

Strangers stared hardest.

It was a real problem for me.

"They *were* happy," I said. "We were happy."

I was happy.

Now? Shit. Singapore.

I put the photo down, stared at the burger in front of me. The weird waitress was gone, but no one was eating. I thought about what Baz had said, about the Parlour being a

tattoo shop, and in my Land of Nothingness I saw two compasses pointed at each other. *So we never get lost*, Dad used to say.

I knew Baz was right about it being a tattoo shop. It made so much sense. Which meant we would calmly finish our food and make our way to the Parlour, where I would begin a process whose end was *the* end. Dad's end.

And I felt like this: a shaken bottle of champagne; an angry volcano tired of humans building silly little houses on my arms and legs like I didn't exist, like I couldn't wipe them out whenever I wanted. I felt full of fiery things, and icy things too, things that bubbled and boiled and popped, things that begged for liberation.

"Mom and Dad started dating in high school," I said. "Got married in college."

I needed to be empty.

I needed someone to pour me out.

"They always said, 'We fell in love silly young.' And I really miss that, you know?"

I looked around the table. None of them seemed fazed, which made me want to give my bubbles and anger to these kids who would listen, kids who would finally fucking listen and see me for me, and not some statue on a street corner, holding a sign that says, *Look at me, don't look at me, look at me, don't look at me*, over and over, but it's never over; it goes on forever, this desire to be both seen and unseen.

"Mom and Dad had all these sayings, all these sentences only they understood. *Till we're old-new.* I have no idea what that means." I was crying now—rare, but not impossible. I relished the moisture, and thought, *Yes, this makes sense.* Get it out, get it all out with the lava and the champagne. Liberate all things. "There are times when I think I knew

him better than anybody, and then times when I feel I never knew him at all. And now it's too late. And he . . . *fucking promised* me"—I shook myself up until the cap popped off, *fizz, fizz, bubble, bubble, pop,* take a breath now—"when I was little, Dad promised he'd never leave. He taught me how to think with my heart, how to hear the whispers—the really mean ones—how to take those and make myself stronger, how to be a Super Racehorse, and not some silly sideways hug. Well, how is he supposed to do all that when he's dead?" I grabbed a nearby napkin, wiped the liberation from my face. "And now the whole stupid world has moved on, including my mom, who I barely even recognize."

. . .

. . .

. . .

Say it.

I am Northern Dancer, sire of the century, the superest of all racehorses.

. . .

Do it.

. . .

"Dad died of pancreatic cancer."

. . .

Five words I'd never said before.

The first two were the only ones that mattered.

. . .

"He died two years ago." Again, the first two words rendered the others pretty impotent. "Mom just got engaged. To someone who thinks Tolstoy wrote *The Brothers Karamazov.*"

. . .

. . .

"He didn't write it?" asked Coco.

The table breathed for the first time in what seemed like hours. I looked at Coco, tried to smile with my eyes, but I couldn't be sure it worked. "No, Coco. He didn't."

Coco nodded in a very serious manner.

I looked across the table at Baz. "Yesterday I took the urn and ran. I was going to scatter him in the river, but then I found the note and the photo. I can't go home. Not until I see this through."

. . .

"Do you remember my first question?" asked Baz.

"Yes."

"Do you remember your answer?"

"Yes."

"Say it again," he said.

"I need help."

"And again."

"I need help."

"And once more."

I hoped Baz could see the smile in my eyes; I certainly saw the one in his.

"I need help, Baz."

"And we will help you, friend."

Friend.

What a beautiful word.

Suddenly Singapore didn't feel so far away.

MAD

Baz carefully removed the top of the bun from his burger, then the bottom, setting them both on the side of his plate. He ate meat; he ate veggies; occasionally, if Coco fell asleep before finishing her ice cream (so *very* occasionally), he would eat her leftovers. But never bread.

"You watching your carbs?" asked Vic.

"Baz is anti-bread," I said, rolling my eyes.

"Anti-bread?"

I nodded. "He is against bread."

Vic looked back at Baz. "I don't understand."

Baz took a bite of ground beef and lettuce, swallowed. "You do not have to understand everything."

I couldn't help but laugh at this. Baz had a way of taking very simple words and putting them together in a way that people weren't accustomed to hearing. *You do not have to understand everything.* The problem was people didn't know what to do with such forthright simplicity, because they had no practice with it. People expected backroom agendas, conversational Trojan horses that sneaked behind enemy lines and burned you from the high ground of moral ambiguity.

God. The longer I was a person, the less I wanted to be one.

Coco scribbled on her napkin while she ate—songwriting was a sort of hobby of hers, though I'd yet to actually hear a final product. Zuz looked over her shoulder, occasionally nodding or shaking his head at what she wrote. He was the only one privy to her creative writings, the only one she let in her circle of trust.

Eventually Margo brought out another plate of cheese fries, and we all ate while Baz told a story about the time

the air conditioner went out at the Cinema 5. "People were yelling very loud," he said. "They wanted their money back, and all the rest. Later I was on break with a coworker named Russ. Russ remarked how hot it had been. I agreed it had been very hot. He said, 'Aren't you from the Congo?' I said, 'Well, I am an American citizen now, but yes—I was born in the Republic of the Congo. Why do you ask?' Russ said, 'Oh, nothing, I just figured you would be used to the heat, having lived in the jungle.' I looked Russ in his eyes, asked him, 'Are you from New Jersey?' 'Yes,' said Russ, 'born and raised.' I nodded. 'So I assume you strip down to your underwear and make out with very tan girls in hot tubs.' Russ raised an eyebrow and smiled. 'No,' he said, 'why would you think that?' I said, 'I have seen the television show *Jersey Shore*, so I am educated in the way all people from New Jersey live. Admit it. You strip down to your underwear and make out with very tan girls in hot tubs, do you not?'"

The table chuckled, but I couldn't. The day it happened, Baz had come back to the greenhouse in a mood, and when he told me what had happened, I really couldn't blame him. The shit he had to put up with.

"So, what did Russ say?" asked Vic.

"He had nothing more to say on the subject," said Baz, smiling sadly. "It was not the first time, it won't be the last. People see movies or TV shows, and they think they know us." He pointed to his brother across the table. "Nzuzi was too young to remember what we lost, praise God. I was also young, but I remember. Our mother was an English teacher, our father worked for the government. We had a nice house and nice things. It was a good life in Congo-Brazzaville.

"But war changes things. At nine, I did not understand oil or lust for power, or the measures countries would take to

have both. At nine, I only understood that the light had left my mother's eyes. I understood my father's fear, so thick, I could smell it on him. I understood the sound a bomb makes in the seconds before hitting the earth. I understood that when soldiers enter your home, tell you they are taking your table and chairs, your father's VCR and favorite movies, your mother's best dresses—and tell you to be grateful for this— you keep your eyes on the floor and say nothing. I understood the truth about nighttime, the urgency in my brother's and sister's cries. And when my own head hit the pillow and I drifted asleep to the violent lullaby—*pop! pop! pop!*—I understood I would not live to see the sun rise."

The table was quiet as we watched him recount his old life. I'd heard this much before, but it didn't make the hearing of it any easier. If anything, the story grew considerably harder with each telling.

"You have a sister?" asked Vic.

Zuz put a hand on Vic's shoulder, lifted his head high, and put his other hand on his own heart. Baz said, "My brother is telling you about his twin—our sister, Nsimba. When we were very young, Mother sometimes called me by both names, Mbemba Bahizire. When Nsimba tried to say it, all that came out was Baz." He smiled for a moment, but it soon became a frown. "I do not know if it is better or worse that I remember our lives from before the war. But I do—I remember our beautiful life in the Congo." He stopped, took a sip of water. "Anyway. No one was living in a jungle. Not where we come from."

"It's a shit job, the Cinema Five," I said. "Plenty of places you could work until Renaissance Cabs is ready."

Baz smiled again, but this one didn't need to turn into a frown; part of it already was. "My father loved movies. Being

there reminds me of him. And it's a good place to find new Chapters."

"Okay," said Vic. He'd been holding his burger, but he hadn't taken a bite for a while now. "So, what's a Chapter?"

Baz wiped his hands on a napkin, pushed away his empty plate. "I collect stories. For a book I'm writing. And books need Chapters."

"Okay."

"With your permission, Victor, I would like you to be one of them."

A bit of barbeque sauce squirted out the sides of Vic's burger. He grabbed a napkin and wiped some off his shirt-sleeve, then looked back at Baz as if waiting for further explanation. Receiving none, he nodded once, said, "Okay."

"I change names and places, of course," said Baz.

"Okay."

I understood Vic's hesitation. Most people didn't like the thought of their every move being observed, documented, organized, categorized—the idea that their actions and words might be recorded for all to read. I didn't really mind so much, which probably had something to do with my want-ing to leave a mark, something to let the world know I was here long after I wasn't.

"So, I know I don't have to understand *everything*," said Vic, "but I'd really like to understand this."

Baz laughed, nodded. "Fair enough. A while back, some kids from the Chute were vandalizing Babushka's, breaking in after hours, smearing red paint across the windows so it looked like pig's blood. And customers stop coming. Norm, the owner, he comes to me for help. So I helped him."

"How?" asked Vic.

"Ooh, ooh, let me tell it," said Coco, looking up from her

napkin for the first time in ten minutes. "Okay, so get this. Baz takes his baseball bat and a single apple to the Chute. He asks around, ends up finding the kids who kept breaking into Babushka's. It's not hard, you know, they're all bragging about it, the bunch of meatheads. So anyway, he finds them, takes off his shirt—"

"Coke, I didn't take off my shirt."

"Of course you didn't, because that would be ridiculous. I'm saying—for the book—you should write that you took off your shirt. Makes it better. So anyway, Baz *takes off his shirt*, tosses the apple into the air, and hits it with the bat, smashing it to smithereens. Then he looks at the kids and says, 'The next person who vandalizes Babushka's will know what that apple felt.' Ha! Classic, right? Anyway, Norm hasn't had a single break-in since. In exchange, we get five pounds of meat a week, plus access to his back room."

"And his story," said Vic.

Baz shrugged. "We are all part of the same story, each of us different chapters. We may not have the power to choose setting or plot, but we can choose what kind of character we want to be."

"So, where's the book?"

Baz pointed to his head. "I am working on it as we speak. And in the meantime, I'm reading a writing instruction guide by Dr. James L. Conroy. You've heard of him?"

Of course Vic hadn't heard of Dr. James L. Conroy. No one had heard of Dr. James L. Conroy, but that didn't stop Baz from talking about the man like he was the definitive voice in the midlevel writing tutorial handbook industry.

"Is there a title?" asked Vic.

I said, "*The Kabongo Chronicles*."

"*The Book of Baz*," said Coco.

Baz glared at us. "There is no title yet, but I have time. Nzuzi and I are saving for a car and, ultimately, a fleet of cars. Renaissance Cabs will be the premier taxi service in the greater Bergen County area. The way I see it, what better job for a collector of stories than a cabbie? Just imagine the Chapters."

"Just imagine the freak shows, more like," said Coco under her breath.

Vic looked at Coco. "What about you? Are you an early Chapter too?"

"No way, Spoils. What happened to me was my mom left when I was born, see. I never knew her. And her leaving, well, that made my dad really sad. Like sad in his bones, if that makes sense. The kind of sadness that takes time to really sink in, you know? Dad took care of me when I was little. He didn't jump right into being a lazy bum, I mean. He eased into it until eventually he just stopped getting out of bed in the morning. I cleaned the house, got myself ready for school every day, all that stuff. He hit me sometimes, and out of nowhere. He just didn't really wanna be a dad anymore, I don't think. He had this pretty good job at a bank, which he lost. Went from that to working at a convenience store. We were barely getting by, so he started looking for other ways to make money. Found out you got paid if you took in foster kids. Or at least, the government gives your taxes a break, or something. It's crazy, man. Anyway, Dad spent the next few days cleaning the apartment, cleaning himself, and stocking our pantry so full of food, I thought he'd hit the lotto. Then this lady is walking around our house taking notes, asking all kinds of questions, and the next thing I know—*bam*—I've got two brothers. Baz and Zuz. I mean, Baz didn't actually live with us, but he was there so much, it felt like he did."

"I'd aged out of foster care," said Baz. "Tried many times to get custody of my brother, but"—he shrugged, but it felt less like a gesture of nonchalance, more like an imitation of Atlas—"by the time they moved Nzuzi to Queens, he was almost eighteen, so I decided to stick close until he aged out too."

"So yeah, anyway," continued Coco. "They needed a family, they got us, which *I* was thrilled about. I just felt kind of sorry for them, getting paired up with my dad."

"We were paired up with you, too, Coconut," said Baz.

Coco blushed, went on. "So, then one day, Dad's gone. Poof. Left just like Mom. I was really sad at first. We'd just had this huge fight that morning. I don't even remember what I did to make him so mad, but I said something, and he hit me pretty hard, and then I left for school and that was the last I ever saw him. But you know—I figure he just needed to find his own thing. I mean, he wasn't happy with me or with the life he had, that's for sure. So I figure he went looking for a new one. And that was fine by me. I wasn't gonna stand around and cry like a baby. I thought, *Well, if Mom and Dad can go off and start a new life, so can I.* So I asked Baz and Zuz if they wanted to come to Hackensack with me. Baz got a job, we met Mad, and we all lived happily ever after in a motherfrakking greenhouse. The end."

The table was eerily silent for a beat.

Vic cleared his throat. "I'm really sorry, Coco."

Coco polished off her burger, licked her fingers. "About what? Things turned out great. I've never been part of a real family." She motioned around the table. "Not like this, like us. Anyway, I'm no Chapter. If Baz wants to use my story, he's gonna have to get in line and pay for it. Man, that burger was good. Margo may be batshit, but girl can *grill*."

My heart hurt like it got punched. Coco was far too young to have had a front-row seat to the horror show that was her life. I leaned across the table and hugged her neck right there in front of everyone.

"Love you, Coco."

"Love you too, Mad."

She'd told this story before, and while it probably wasn't far from the truth, it didn't take much to spot the holes. Clearly there were things Coco didn't know, things that had been kept from her. I could only guess what they were.

"Wait, why Hackensack?" asked Vic.

I sat back down in my seat. "Remember that commercial the city ran for, like, a decade, trying to promote Hackensack tourism?"

"The one that claimed Hackensack was 'on the verge of a Renaissance,'" said Vic.

I winked. "Bingo."

"Don't tell me . . ." Vic looked at Coco, then the Kabongos. "You guys came to Hackensack because of the ad?"

"It's coming, guys," said Coco. "The Renaissance is just around the corner. I can feel it."

I snorted in my straw, blew soda across the table.

"Keep making fun," said Coco. "We'll see who's laughing when the Renaissance gets here. Baz and Zuz will start Renaissance Cabs, and I'll write a hit song about Renaissance stuff, and then I'll become rich and famous and the only people I'll invite to my Renaissance parties are people who don't laugh at me."

Zuz snapped once.

Coco waved him off. "Yeah, Zuz, you're golden."

"I didn't know you wrote songs," said Vic. "What kind?"

"All kinds," said Coco. "Rap, mostly. I like beats and

rhymes. I've been working on my Renaissance rap for a while now—it's basically awesome."

Margo Bonaparte appeared out of nowhere. "All right, guys. Dessert's almost ready. Follow me."

We slid out of the booth, shooting worried eyes at one another, and followed Margo through the near-empty restaurant all the way to the kitchen. "Come on back," she said. "Sorry about the mess. Haven't quite got the whole clean-as-you-go thing down yet."

Margo stepped up to an industrial-sized stove with four simmering skillets cooking something sweet and caramelly, and my mouth started watering like a faucet. On the floor next to the stove, she bent down, grabbed the corner of a large kitchen floor mat, and pulled. Underneath, in the floor, was the outline of a hatch with a small brass handle.

I looked at Vic, who pointed at Margo and whispered, "*Super Racehorse*."

I made a mental note to tell him about Margo's situation, about her gambling habit and how, when she ran out of her own money, she'd dipped into her father's business account. Atlantic City was only a couple of hours away—it wasn't an uncommon story. Luckily for Margo, her father was a frequent patron of Cinema 5, where he divulged his woes to a very understanding employee. Baz knew that Hubert Bonaparte had soft spots for his daughter, for his restaurant, and for independent film. So he spent the next three weekends at Napoleon's, painting the interior and exterior walls, ceiling, and trim; he also arranged for Hubert to have unlimited access to the back alleyway entrance to the Cinema 5 (an entrance with which I was very familiar). The results of these actions were trifold: first, Margo's

debts to her father were considered paid in full; second, the Bonapartes, while somewhat baffled at the request, agreed to let Baz have their story for his book (which, according to Baz, could use a chapter on family redemption); and third, both Margo and her father turned a blind eye when it came time for us to pay the check.

Oh, and a fourth thing: Margo Bonaparte was relentless in her own pursuit to "repay" Baz Kabongo. Her advances had, as yet, remained unfruitful.

"This used to be the grease trap," said Margo, pulling the handle and swinging the door up and open. "You guys ever clean one of these things? Stinks something awful. Every time we had it cleaned, it scared customers off left and right. So Dad had a new one installed outside—way smaller than this one. This old one's huge. Here, look."

We stepped up to the edge of the trap door. Margo was right. Probably five by seven feet, it was roughly the size of an old hatchback, and had the ambience of a tiny unfinished basement with smooth gray floors and walls.

Margo Bonaparte hopped down through the hatch door. "Stopped using it years ago, but it still smells like sulfuric shit down here." A couple of seconds later her hand appeared, and in it, a full bottle of Bacardi Silver. Coco took the rum, while Baz pulled Margo out of the grease trap. "Never hurts to order an extra bottle or two," said Margo, closing the hatch door and pulling the kitchen mats back into place. "Off the books, of course."

"Is this real rum, like what pirates drink?" asked Coco, every word in her question at a fever pitch.

"You're adorbs," said Margo, taking the bottle from Coco, "and maybe a little nutso. Yeah, it's real rum like what pirates drink." She unscrewed the lid, took a swig while nursing the

skillets with the other hand. "You guys ever had Bananas Foster?"

We all shook our heads, and as much as I hated admitting it, Margo had my full attention.

"Who's Bananas Foster?" asked Coco.

"Not *who*," said Margo. "*What*."

"What's Bananas Foster?" asked Coco, who had officially become a broken record.

"Fried bananas," said Margo, pulling a box of matches off the counter, tipping the rum over the stove, and pouring a healthy dose in each skillet. Then, lighting a long match, she touched the flame to the sizzling bananas, setting them aflame. "On *fire!*"

Zuz snapped once.

We were inclined to agree with him.

VIC

I sat in a high-backed, purple suede Victorian-style chair with brass studs and ornate angels and demons carved into its legs.

The chair was one hell of a Super Racehorse.

The Parlour's waiting room followed suit. Antique furniture, framed posters of old movies (including one of *Casablanca*, my parents' favorite), a crystal chandelier dangling from a high ceiling—the whole place was saturated in patchouli, but other than that, I found it quite surprising. Not at all how I pictured a tattoo parlor. But it didn't end with the décor. Even the architectural design was unique. The entire ground floor was the waiting room. A spiral stair-

case wound up and up to an open loft space above our heads. If the electronic humming was any indication, the actual tattooing took place up there.

We sat in the room and waited.

The waiting room was a very literal place.

Back at Napoleon's Pub, we'd used Margo's phone to find out when the Parlour closed for the evening: eight p.m. It was only a few blocks away, which left us just enough time to walk over and try to figure out where to "hang" Dad's ashes. (I still had no idea what this meant, but I trusted Dad would compass me in the right direction.) On the walk over, Mad cited a few quotes from her favorite book, *The Outsiders*. I'd never read it, but the one I liked best was something about two people admiring the sunset from different places, and how maybe their worlds weren't that different because they saw the same sunset.

I think Mad saw in books what I saw in art: the weightless beauty of the universe.

She sat now with Baz and Coco, the three of them combing through a photo album of the Parlour's prior handiwork; Nzuzi stood by the window, gazing into the nighttime snow, while I sat in my Super Racehorse of a chair and thought about my first real encounter with tattoos.

I was six. Maybe seven. We were in Ocean Grove. Mom sat in a chair, her toes in the sand. She was a beach reader. Dad lay on his back on a towel, his ankles in the sand. He was a beach dreamer. I built a sand castle because I was six. Maybe seven.

I was a beach anythinger.

A piece of my castle crumbled into the moat. Dad sat up, helped me rebuild it. He was leaning across my lap to grab a shovel when I saw the tattoo on his shoulder. *What's that, Dad?* I asked. He said, *A compass. Points due east, see?* I asked

why, as six-maybe-seven-year-olds are wont to do. He looked at Mom. *Let's show him*, he said. At this point I'd forgotten all about my messed-up sand castle. *Show me what?*

Mom set down her beach read.

Dad set down his shovel.

Things were happening. Things I wasn't privy to. This was a real problem for me.

They turned around and stood side by side, close enough for their shoulders to bump together. To my shock, Mom had the same tattoo as Dad, except for one difference: her compass pointed due west.

Their compasses pointed toward each other.

So we never get lost, said Dad.

I emerged from my Land of Nothingness to the sound of two snaps. Still standing by the window, Nzuzi was smiling at me. He nodded very slightly, but it seemed more a question than an answer. I nodded back, and he turned and looked out the window. Earlier, Coco said Nzuzi had plenty to say if you knew how to listen. I hoped I learned to listen like that. I was no stranger to people making the wrong assumptions about me, or to the punch-in-the-gut feeling that immediately followed. The last thing I wanted was to be the one doling out punches.

"Oh God," said Coco. Baz flipped to the next photo in the album.

"God," she said again.

Baz flipped the page.

"Oh my—"

"Coco," said Mad.

Coco's eyes were laughing and a little crazy. "Mad. This guy tattooed his balls. His *balls*. And I don't even know what *that*"—she pointed to the current photo in Baz's lap—"is."

Baz hastily flipped the page.

Before Coco could grill him any further, footsteps clanked down the spiral staircase. A shiny-bald man with a short stick through his nose, gaping holes in both earlobes, and layers upon layers of tattoos joined us in the very literal waiting room.

"Okay, guys, sorry for the delay. Chump upstairs keeps changing his mind, and I've been alone all motherfrakking day, so it's like"—his entire demeanor changed once he saw us—"Baz, you *scoundrel*!"

They hugged so hard, Baz's Thunder cap fell off his head. It was the very opposite of a sideways hug.

Coco hopped off the couch, ran over, and wrapped her arms around the guy's waist. "Hey, Topher!"

"Coco, my darling, how you doing?" The guy—*Topher*, apparently—bent over, pulled her into a tight hug.

"Great! I haven't even cursed today."

Someone in the room, maybe even two someones, cleared their throats.

"Well," she said. "It's been at least an hour."

Topher slow-clapped, nodded in approval. "Frak yeah."

It's him, I thought. *The Battlestar Galactican.*

Topher stood, smiled at Baz. "I miss you, brother. Thought you guys must have moved without telling me, or something."

"It has been way too long," said Baz. "You're clean?"

Topher pulled a necklace out from under his shirt, a long chain with a round chip on the end. "Eight months, six days, and . . . nine hours." Tucking the necklace away, he looked around the room, his eyes landing on me.

It didn't take long, maybe a second or two, for a person to check off the usual suspects—*Burn victim? Stroke? Birth defect?*—before quickly looking away, averting their eyes like

I was the very surface of the sun. I often thought the most unfair thing about having Moebius wasn't Moebius at all, but other people's inability to define me by anything else.

It was a real problem for me.

Topher pointed to Baz's arm. "You need some detailing, brother? Whatever you want is on the house, of course. Not like a few free tattoos squares us. I could never repay you guys for—"

"Yo, Toph!" interrupted a voice from the upstairs loft. "Where'd you go, man?"

Topher raised his head toward the ceiling. "Simmer the frak down, Homer!" He looked back at us, lowered his voice. "Homer's a turd. Been waffling on this butterfly tattoo all evening, like whether he gets it on his forearm or bicep is gonna make or break him in the biker community. It's a motherfrakking purple-winged butterfly."

"I can hear you up here, you know!"

Topher smiled, shrugged. "What can I do for you guys?"

Baz introduced me, gave a quick overview of our situation. I handed him Dad's Terminal Note, hoping he might see the momentousness of the moment.

"Hang me from the Parlour," said Topher, studying the letter. He rubbed his shiny-bald head, and it sounded like this: waxing a brand-new car with olive oil. He looked up at the crystal chandelier. "You got the ashes with you?"

I unzipped my bag and pulled out the urn. "I didn't used to be able to touch it. The urn, I mean. But now I can. I touch it all the time. The urn."

. . .

Smooth, Benucci.

. . .

There were times—socially, or whatever—when I pic-

tured myself crawling into a hole only to have the hole spit me back out.

But hey.

Topher passed the letter back, smiled at me, and this time he didn't look away. And I could tell this shiny-bald man with holes in his ears and a stick through his nose saw the momentousness of the moment. He started up the stairs, pointed to the ceiling. "Only place I can think to hang a person here is the chandelier. Y'all chill for a sec. I'll be right back."

Mad walked to the center of the room, pulled off her knit cap, and looked up at the chandelier. Her long yellow hair tumbled to one side like a dripping wet sun. "This doesn't feel right," she said.

. . .

The thing about uniquely pretty girls is that their prettiness cares nothing for time or place. It cannot be rescheduled or relocated. They are pretty wherever they go, whenever they get there. It can be quite distracting. For example: right now, instead of thinking about the best way to hang my dead father from a chandelier, I was thinking about the best way to keep Mad's hair out of our mouths should we ever kiss. Actually—yeah, never mind. I'd rather her hair get in on the action. Not like it would ever actually happen. Not like someone like her would kiss someone like me. Not like I'd ever know what the skin side of her head felt like, or her legs around my waist, or her tongue on—

"What are you doing?" said Mad.

Shit. I'd stared so hard, she felt it.

"What?" I said.

"You're sort of . . ." Mad looked over at Baz and Coco, who had gone back to the photographs of tattooed body parts.

Before I knew what I was doing, I stepped closer to Mad,

right up in her space. Of all the girls I'd fallen for in the past—and there were many—I'd always fallen from a distance. But that was impossible with Mad. Something about her was inherently up close. And if I couldn't reschedule or relocate her prettiness, it was best to acknowledge it head on. "Finish the sentence," I said, close enough to smell her lips—honey and sweat, and I loved them. "I'm sort of . . . what?"

She looked right back into my face. "You're sort of staring."

. . .

. . .

"So are you," I said.

We both stared into the sun. And we didn't look away.

Maybe the two worlds we lived in weren't so different.

* * *

"This ain't gonna work," said Topher, standing on the top rung of the ladder. After a few seconds of deliberation, he climbed back down. "I thought maybe there'd be a spot up on one of those old candle-holder thingies, you know? But one good draft through the front door and your dad's gonna blow all over the place."

Nzuzi—who had been standing by the window this whole time—walked across the room, picked up my backpack, and started for the door.

"Zuz," said Mad.

But he didn't stop. Cradling my backpack like an infant, he walked out the door and into the snowy night.

I no longer felt distracted. It had taken a very short time for Dad's urn to become part of me, not unlike a limb. Now that it was gone, I felt its physical absence. Without a second thought, I was out the door too.

The Parlour was set back at least three hundred feet off the road; the lawn had become a thick blanket of snow that was only getting thicker. Ahead of me, Nzuzi walked toward the street. I had no idea where he was going, and he gave no indication whether he'd be walking ten feet or ten miles.

I didn't care.

He had my compass.

Suddenly a hand was in mine. Next to me, Mad trudged through the snow, and I turned to dust and feathers and other things that float.

"It's pretty," she said quietly, looking around. "The snow."

I've always found a certain warmth in words when they're spoken in the cold outdoors. I don't know. It's like words take the breath of the person speaking them, and wear that breath like a sweater.

. . .

Up ahead, Nzuzi stopped in the faint glow of a streetlight. We caught up and he snapped once, pointing to the Parlour's wooden sign dangling chest high between two posts in the ground.

The Parlour

Hackensack's Premier Tattoo Shop
since 1972

Ink Up!

I stepped up to it, nudged it with my fist. It swung slightly, toppling the layer of snow. "Hang me from the Parlour," I said.

Nzuzi handed over my backpack, nodded once. Unlike his last nod, this one was an answer. And I knew Coco was right:

Nzuzi had plenty to say if you knew how to listen.

"Thank you," I said.

Again, Nzuzi nodded.

"Colder than tattooed balls out here," said Coco. Behind us, she and Baz and Topher stood shivering in the snow, a look of hesitant anticipation on each of their faces. I felt bad, like I was to blame for more than the cold, but also for not knowing what exactly came next.

"Look," said Coco, walking right up to the sign and pointing near the bottom. Under the words *Ink Up!* was a small inscription carved just deep enough in the wood to last: B. B.→ ←D. J.

"What's it mean?" asked Coco.

"They're my parents' initials," I said, my words hanging like smoke in the air. They were clunky words. Awkward. The cold had a way of doing that, of making each word feel hard and heavy. "They had tattoos on their shoulders. Compasses. Dad's pointed east, Mom's west. So they would never lose each other."

The cold snow fell.

The warm words rose.

My whole life, I'd felt the capacity for bitterness and self-pity. But never more so than on those rare occasions when I wanted to smile *and* frown at the same time, yet was capable of doing neither. I remembered the way my parents were together, like the world was a tree branch, and they shared the same cocoon. Mom should be here now, scattering these ashes with me, not looking for a new cocoon-mate. The letter was written to her, and no matter how much Frank the Boyfriend wanted to be Frank the Husband, he would never be Frank the First Love. Mom was Dad's *due everywhere*. This ought to be her mission.

Suddenly Coco's tiny arms wrapped around my waist in

a tight hug. It lifted the weight a little, made Singapore feel possible, however unlikely.

I turned to Topher. "Could I borrow some tattoo ink? And a pencil?"

Topher nodded, ran back toward the Parlour.

Before I knew what was happening, Mad and Baz and Nzuzi gathered around Coco and me, bracing us against the cold like a waddle of penguins. I wasn't sure how it happened, but I suppose fulfilling the wishes of a romantic dead man speeds up the bonding process a bit. I wasn't complaining.

I'd never been a penguin before.

A minute later Topher returned with more than ink and a pencil. He also handed me a photograph. "We take pictures of most of our work," he said. "This was long before my time, but those tattoos you described—I had a feeling I'd seen them in our photo album."

I stared at the photo.

The tattoos were jet-black, pinkish flesh, fresh. Two shoulders, two compasses. Due east, due west. A perfect match.

"You're an early Chapter, right, Topher?" I asked.

Topher's eyes gleamed. "I was messed up, man. These guys took me into their magical frakking greenhouse, let me sleep on the couch, took turns watching over me during withdrawal. Then Baz got me plugged in with the local AA group. They saved my life, man. I'm proud to be part of the book."

Coco departed our waddle to go hug Topher. I smiled with my heart, held up the old photo of my parents' tattoos. "Can I keep this?"

"All yours, my man."

I slid the photo into my backpack and pulled out the urn. Strange, how long it had taken me to touch this thing, and now here I was about to dip into it.

I popped open the bottle of navy blue ink. Next, I peeled back the tape on the urn and pulled opened the lid. Inside, I pinched a small amount of Dad's ashes, then sprinkled it into the bottle of paint, closed it up, and shook it in.

I dipped the tip of the pencil into the blue, ashy ink, and turned to the sign.

B. B.→ ←D. J.

The paint in my hands reminded me of Matisse and his belief that each face had its own rhythm; ergo, I thought about Dad, who taught me about Matisse; and now here I was using a combination of Matisse's medium and Dad's bones.

"Hang me from the Parlour," I said aloud. Because it felt right. And I painted in the initials using the ashes of the very person who'd carved them in the first place. The very person who taught me to think and smile with my heart.

"Hang me from the Parlour," I said again.

And again.

And again.

MAD

It must've been close to ten o'clock. Snow still fell, but gently, like the flakes were stalling for time, swinging every direction but down. A few steps behind me, Baz presided over what sounded like an epic game of Rock, Paper, Scissors between Coco and Zuz.

Vic led the way back to the greenhouse with utter confidence, verifying his earlier statement that his grandparents used to live in the neighborhood. A minor coincidence, though that wasn't what he called it.

He'd called it a bump.

A couple of blocks away from the orchard, something came over me. I skipped ahead, fell in stride next to Vic.

"Hi," I said.

"Hi."

"How you doing?"

"Fine."

"You need a hat."

"What do you mean?"

"What do you mean *what do I mean*? I mean it's cold and you need a hat."

Behind us, Coco yelled excitedly, having won a round of Rock, Paper, Scissors.

"Yeah, I left the house in sort of a hurry last night."

"I have an extra one at the greenhouse, remind me to give it to you." It was as though my body had had an idea, one it forgot to tell my brain. Ultimately it was the nighttime snow that triggered it—I remembered last night's conversation, also in the snow, the two of us in the shadow of the *Ling*, Vic hunched over his dad's urn while I watched, listened to him whisper what seemed gibberish at the time.

You were the Northern Dancer, sire of the century, the super-est of all racehorses.

There it was.

The idea.

"Vic."

"What?"

"Do horses ever race in the snow?"

He looked at me for the first time since the Parlour. And I couldn't tell for certain, but it sure felt like he was smiling.

And then we raced. And it was super.

* * *

We waited on the old stone wall for the others, the fig tree like an awning over our heads, its branches glistening with ice. Across the street, the orchard awaited our arrival. Weird how just this morning Vic and I sat on the bridge over Channel à la Goldfish and talked while staring at this stone wall—like our current selves were mirroring our former ones.

"Why did you call it a bump?" I asked, still trying to catch my breath in the thin air.

"Why did I call what a what?"

"This afternoon. When you told me how you used to sit here and look at the orchard. You said your grandparents lived around here. You called it a bump."

Vic looked a little left of the orchard, at the neighboring graveyard. "It's a weird word, don't you think?"

"Bump?"

"No. *Lived*. My grandparents *lived* around here. *Lived*—the literal past tense of life. Also known as death."

I understood the urge to brood, maybe better than anyone. And even though another person's brooding is never quite as appealing as your own, I knew better than to respond.

"The word just makes sense, I guess," said Vic.

"Lived?"

"No. *Bump.*"

"In what way?" I asked.

"So like—imagine each person is a unit, and each unit makes so many decisions in a day, and each decision takes each unit in so many directions, it seems kind of silly to think we'd never run into one another, you know? Especially considering units tend to cluster and linger."

"We cluster and linger, do we?"

His eyes turned from the graveyard to me, and there it was again—the suggestion of a smile. "Yes. It's called home." He reached up and brushed my eyelids closed. "Consider this. You're flying in the sky, not in a plane, but with your arms and hands. Like a miraculous bird. You're thousands of feet above the earth, drifting through the night. And far below, you see thousands of tiny red lights on the ground. The red lights are in constant motion, blinking, shuffling between buildings and trees and houses. Old ones disappear, new ones are born. Over time, you notice the lights bump into one another occasionally. Are you surprised?"

I shook my head. "No."

"I call it the inevitability of corresponding units."

I opened my eyes. "So, we're the red lights."

He nodded, turned back to the graveyard. "People talk about coincidence like it's some big thing. But it's not. We bump into one another all the time. Mostly I think people are just too blind to notice."

It was a nice thought—or reminder, really, that whatever shitty situation I'd been dealt wasn't my fault. It was, in fact, nothing more than a sequence of unfortunate bumps.

"Wait here," said Vic. He plopped down off the wall, unzipped his bag, and pulled out his dad's urn.

"Where are you going?"

"I'll be right back."

Funny how many times I'd seen the graveyard, yet had never quite built up the courage to venture over. Vic navigated his way through tombstones and trees, a cautious but easy gait as if he knew exactly where he was going but wasn't quite sure he wanted to go there. The streetlight shone just bright enough for me to see him stoop in front of a large tombstone, set the urn in the grass in front of him, and

begin speaking. I couldn't hear of course, but it suddenly hit me what was happening.

After a few minutes, he made his way back across the street, tucked the urn in his bag, and sat back on the stone wall.

"Your grandparents?" I asked.

He nodded. "They died in the same month, of the same thing. My dad buried his father, then came back two weeks later and buried his mother."

"Shit, Vic."

"I try to think of Dad from far away, as a unit, as a disappearing red light. But it's like you said about the dying stars—sometimes I still see Dad even though he's gone."

"I thought you said that was bullshit."

"Oh, it's bullshit. But I mean—the theory holds up. Anyway, Dad's gone. But I still smell his aftershave. I still hear him clear his throat. Little things that made him my dad, and not just *a* dad, you know?" Vic's eyes had not left the graveyard. "I wonder if that's how he felt about his parents. And I wonder if I'll have kids who'll feel that way about me. I hope so. Our past tenses last way longer than our present ones."

Before I could respond, Baz and Zuz and Coco rounded the corner, effectively dissolving the conversation. Eager to get out of the cold, we all hurried under (or in Baz's case, over) the fence, and were halfway across Channel à la Goldfish when a silhouette froze us in our tracks.

I'd only seen Gunther Maywood once, as he rarely emerged from his house; I'd completely forgotten how tall the old man was. He stood on the opposite end of the bridge, blocking our way across, and in the dark I could barely make him out, so when he spoke, the voice seemed to come from the cold itself.

"What was our deal, Mr. Kabongo?"

I saw Baz's breath, felt him carefully calculating his surroundings, his words. "Groceries in exchange for the greenhouse."

Gunther Maywood raised his right hand. "I found eye drops. In the gift shop bathroom. Was the gift shop bathroom part of our deal?"

"It was not," said Baz.

Gunther tossed the eye drops to Baz. "I'm a patient man, Mr. Kabongo. But if I discover you, or your friends, trespassing again, I will call the police. Do I make myself clear?"

"You do," said Baz.

The silhouette slowly stepped to one side of the bridge. We hustled across, didn't say another word until we were safely inside Greenhouse Eleven. I tried to catch Vic's eye—knowing he must have left his eye drops in the bathroom this afternoon when he changed his pants—but he wouldn't look up.

"Don't sweat it, Vic," said Coco, tucking herself into her sleeping bag. "Heck, lots of people use eye drops. Might not even be yours."

Baz set the Visine on the card table, offered Vic a small smile, and assured us there was no need to worry about Gunther, that we wouldn't have to live in the greenhouse much longer. In the meantime we would just need to be extra careful when using the gift shop bathroom, be sure to take a lookout. Baz often referred to the future in vague and passing expressions, and I could hardly fault him for it. None of us knew what would happen, least of all me. In light of my previous conversation with Vic: it hardly mattered *where* we all clustered and lingered, so long as we clustered and lingered together.

Within minutes we were tucked inside our sleeping bags by the space heater. I lay on my back and stared up at the plastic ceiling and the fuzzy stars on the other side.

"Mad?" said Coco. I only remembered how truly young she was when she spoke in the dark.

"Yes?"

"I need a story."

Zuz snapped once.

I looked over to the couch where Vic lay on his back. He had his earbuds in, his eyes wide open.

"Okay," I said. "Which one?"

"Fro-Yo, please."

I stayed on my side, cleared my throat, and watched Vic as I spoke. "Once upon a time, there was a little girl named Frozen Yogurt. Her friends called her Fro-Yo for short." Coco giggled. She always giggled at this one. "Fro-Yo lived in a magical land called the Eleventh Aisle, where there were no houses or streets, only freezers and shelves and sweet things that melted. But Fro-Yo was lonely. She had no friends, and nobody anywhere—not in the freezers or on the shelves— ever wanted to play with her. Poor Fro-Yo."

"Poor Fro-Yo," said Coco.

Vic pulled out a single earbud.

"One day," I continued, "a little girl named Coconut—who lived in a far-off land called Greenhouse Eleven—happened upon the Eleventh Aisle. Coconut pulled Fro-Yo off the shelf, out of the cold, misty freezer, and said, 'Yo, Fro-Yo! Hello! I will be your friend and love you forever. Would you like that? I'm from Queens, so tell the truth.'"

Coco giggled again.

"Well, poor Fro-Yo, who had been feeling very low-low, said, 'I would like that, and that's the truth, but alas, my

parents—Ben and Jerry—are very strict and will only let me be friends with people who are from the Eleventh Aisle.' This was odd, because Ben and Jerry were pretty progressive parents in some ways, but that's a different story for a different bedtime."

This time Baz chuckled.

I went on. "'Yes, I suppose we are very different, aren't we?' said young Coconut. 'Though doesn't it seem odd?' Poor Fro-Yo tilted her head. 'Doesn't what seem odd?' she responded. 'Well,' said Coconut, pointing her finger to the window, and the world beyond the Eleventh Aisle. 'Do you see that sunset?' Fro-Yo took a look out the window and said, 'Why, yes, I do see that sunset.' Coconut tapped her chin, and said, 'It seems odd that the sunset *you* see from the Eleventh Aisle and the one *I* see from Greenhouse Eleven is the exact same one. Maybe the two worlds we live in aren't so different. We see the same sunset.'"

Vic turned on his side, and we stared at each other in the dark.

"'Why, yes,' said Fro-Yo, 'we do see the same sunset, don't we?' And together, they walked hand in hand out of the Eleventh Aisle."

"Where did they go?" asked Coco. "Here? Did Coconut bring Fro-Yo back here?"

"No," I said. "They walked into that sunset, because it was something no one had ever done or heard about, or seen at all anywhere ever. And they lived drippily ever after. The end."

Coco let out a long, contented sigh. "That was your best yet, Mad."

It was quiet and dark and, before long, Coco snored soundly in her sleeping bag beside me.

Sometimes a thing should be strange, but it's not. I couldn't explain it, but Vic and I stared at each other for a long time that night. We never said anything, never smiled, and he never blinked. I imagined what he might say, what he wanted to say, and I wondered if he was thinking the same thing about me.

What is that story really about? Vic never asked.

You know what it's about, I never answered.

I fell asleep, looking at his eyes. And it should have been strange, but it wasn't.

FOUR

OUTWARD SYMBOLS
(or, Cool in the Traditional Sense)

"'Eye of the Tiger'?" I ask. "Or no, wait, wait . . . 'Don't Stop Believin'.' That was Zuz's favorite. We had it on vinyl, he used to play it over and over again."

Bundle twists in his seat, his back cracking like knuckles. "I told you. I don't have a favorite song."

"What? Come on, man. *Everyone* has a favorite song."

"Well, *I* don't."

I lick the dry part of my lower lip. "I guess we're all part of the bountiful bourgeoisie."

"Madeline, for the most part—and don't take this the wrong way—I never know what the fuck you're talking about."

I shift uncomfortably in my seat. "Smoke break?"

"No."

"No, like, not *now*, or no, like, *never*?"

Bundle stares at me, says nothing.

"It's something Mom used to say"—just saying the word *Mom* is slightly painful, like a pinprick in my palm— "whenever she found something disappointing. She'd remind herself we were all in the same boat, just trying to do the best we could."

For all Mom's bizarre inclinations, she was a great mother. She instilled in me a sense of independence and did her best to cultivate a creative environment. When I said I wanted to be a fashion designer, she bought me a sewing machine. When I showed interest in archeology, she bought me a dig kit. Growing up, I'd have friends whose parents were always flabbergasted when their kids' interests suddenly changed. *What do you mean you don't like mustard? You've always liked mustard. Mustard is your favorite.* Parents forget what it's like to change so quickly, to feel completely yourself one minute, then the next minute it's like a total stranger wrapped themselves in your skin. But not Mom. Mom was like a mood meteorologist, always ahead of the curve, seemingly unfazed by my adolescent whims.

"Okay," says Bundle. "Well. I think it's safe to say we've gotten somewhat off topic."

"You wanna know what my favorite song is?"

"Not really, but I have a feeling you're gonna tell me anyway."

"'Coming Up Roses' by Elliott Smith. It's on his self-titled record. Lo-fi and melodic and perfect-perfect. Pretty much everything Elliott ever recorded had that sort of so-honest-it's-terrifying quality."

"Please oh please, Madeline, tell me more." Bundle rubs his eyes as if we've been at this for days. How long have we been at this? It does feel like a long time, but with no windows and no clock, it's impossible to tell.

"Before Mom died," I say, "she always gave me three bucks a week for allowance. It wasn't much, but we didn't have much. I never complained, just saved. After five or six weeks, I'd have enough to buy a record. That was the first one I bought, Elliott Smith's self-titled. A while back I came home

from school—well, not *home*, I mean Uncle Lester's. I went to my room and pulled my crate of records out from under my bed, but it was empty. He'd sold off the record player already, and all sorts of other shit to buy liquor. I knew I'd have to hide the records to keep them safe, and even if I didn't have anything to play them on, I don't know—I found them comforting."

"Madeline, what does this have to do with anything?"

I twist around in my seat, lift my hair, and pull my shirt collar down a few inches so my left shoulder blade is exposed. "Earlier, you asked about my *abrasions*. Well, here's one for you."

I close my eyes, imagine what Bundle's looking at: a pink mark of perfectly curved grooves, one-quarter of a circle, five or six inches in length. I sit frozen like this as I talk, the most tragic show-and-tell. "Uncle Les sold all my records but one. He needed that one, he said, to teach me a lesson. Said we were a family now, and families had to 'share the wealth.' So he held a lighter under the record and asked where I would like this lesson to be taught."

"Jesus," says Bundle. "He branded you."

"Vinyl warps pretty quickly, but you'd be surprised how hot it can get before it melts." I let my hair drop, my sweatshirt covering the pink grooves, and turn back to face Bundle. And when I speak, I do so fiercely, and I don't even care that it's just Bundle who hears me, because sometimes you say a thing for yourself and not for the person listening. "But the joke's on him because I saw the record he used. Elliott Smith's self-titled. Fitting, don't you think? Saved me a tattoo."

Bundle clears his throat, looks away, then back. "You moved in with your uncle after your parents died?"

I nod.

"You mind my asking how they passed?"

"Drunk driver," I whisper, staring at my wristband. "We were all in the car, Mom and Dad and me. They died instantly. I was thrown from the vehicle. Just got this scar." I point to the shaved side of my head.

Detective Bundle pushes pause on the recorder, and stands. "Okay, let's go."

"Where?" I ask as he slips on his coat.

"Smoke break."

I pull my jacket off the back of my seat before he changes his mind. It feels good to stand, productive even. I'm still sore in places, but getting the blood flowing helps. In the corridor, I spot the outline of Vic through the blurred window across the hall, and I think maybe that was all I really needed—more than a cigarette, just the visual reminder of his company.

Down the hall, cops are everywhere, milling about, drinking coffee, whispering in hushed tones. A few eyes land on me, then dart away quickly.

"This way," says Bundle, leading me in the direction opposite the lobby. "And not a word about this, okay? Lieutenant Bell would have my ass so fast, it'd make your head spin. Against a million regulations, not the least of which is you're too young to smoke."

On our way out a side door, we pass a clock on the wall.

5:13.

Just under three hours to go.

Outside, it's colder than it was this morning, which I didn't think was possible. Even by Jersey standards, it's been a brutal December.

I pull out my pack of cigarettes, light up, and . . .

Drag.
Blow.
Calm.

I hold the pack out toward Bundle. "Want one?"

He shakes his head. "Trying to quit."

The sidewalk is completely frozen over; traffic on State Street idles by, bumper-to-bumper during rush hour. One block over is Main Street, with its delis and cafés and a string of markets. Weird to think it was only eight days ago that I led Vic right by this spot on our way to Babushka's. If that was the Genesis of our story, I couldn't help wondering what the Revelation might be.

Drag.
Blow.
Calm.

"So, what exactly is Moebius syndrome?" asks Bundle. "Is Vic, you know . . . a credible witness?"

I almost drop my cigarette. "Bundle, what the fuck?"

"Oh right. I forgot, the bountiful bourgeoisie couldn't possibly understand. Come on, Mad, you know what I mean. Is he, you know . . . ?"

Drag.
Blow.
Calm.

"You waited till we were outside, didn't you?" I say. "That's why the smoke break. So you could ask that question without sounding like an ignorant asshole on record?"

"Madeline."

"Don't *Madeline* me. You saw Vic's face and assumed there was something wrong with him."

Bundle blows into his cupped hands to warm up. "Well, is there?"

My knee-jerk is to put my cigarette out on his arm. But I don't.

"You ever read *The Outsiders*?" I ask.

"You know, Madeline, you have a serious problem answering questions."

"I'm trying to answer your question. Have you ever read *The Outsiders*?"

"Not much of a reader," says Bundle. "Saw the movie years ago. One too many good-looking guys as I recall."

I bounce up and down on my toes, try to get the blood circulating. "Okay, well, there's this character called Dally, short for Dallas. He's one of the roughest greasers. Lived on the streets in New York for a while and all that. Anyway, the main character, at one point, says, '*Dally was so real he scared me.*'"

I feel Bundle staring, waiting for more. "And?"

Drag.

Blow.

Calm.

Until this moment I'd considered Bundle to be my exact opposite, but it seems we've reached the heart of our Venn diagram, the fractional intersection where Detective Bundle and Madeline Falco cohabitate. I clear my throat and speak quietly, as if diminishing the volume of the statement might also diminish its gravity.

"I thought there was something wrong with Vic too." Nope. Gravity intact. "There's not," I continue. "Moebius syndrome is this really rare neurological disorder that causes facial paralysis. It's different for different people, but in Vic's case he can't blink and he can't smile. Since he doesn't appear to respond during conversations, everyone just assumes he's not picking up their social cues or what-

ever. But he's really smart, maybe the smartest kid I know."

Detective Bundle nods, his bloated face twisting in thought, his red lips puckering in the frigid air. I stare at the many factions of Bundle, and I wonder at the injustice of the world: Vic's outsides can't reflect his insides, as much as I want them to. Bundle's outsides can't help but reflect his insides, as much as I *don't* want them to. But that's not even the worst of it. I have to turn away, because what I hate most about Bundle right now has nothing to do with him, and everything to do with me.

It's a sad thing, recognizing yourself in a sad thing.

Drag.

Blow.

Calm.

"What did that have to do with *The Outsiders*?" asks Bundle.

I shake my head. "Never mind."

"Okay then. Well, the bountiful bourgeoisie is freezing his bountiful nuts off. You about done?"

I drop the butt, stomp it, and follow Bundle inside. Down the hallway, I see Vic's blurry image again and think about that line from *The Outsiders*.

Dally was so real he scared me.

I wonder if anyone will ever scare me as much as Vic.

VIC

"You need a haircut." Mad said it in a yawn the way a person says *I need coffee* when they first wake up.

"Uh, what?"

Coco snapped her fingers. "Vic! Spoils. Dude. A new cut for the new you."

"I like the old me," I said.

False.

However, there was one thing I liked about the old me: his hair. And Old Me's hair was suddenly facing great peril.

"We have time," said Baz. "If we hurry. The bus leaves at ten forty, and we still need to stop at Cinema Five for my check, and Rainbow Café for coffee."

"And a muffin!" said Coco.

The morning sun had just begun to peek in through the plastic ceiling of the greenhouse. Baz didn't have to work until later that evening, so our plan was to spend the morning and early afternoon on Dad's list. We would catch a bus from downtown Hackensack to Englewood, then walk up the Palisades Parkway (where buses were not allowed), and stop at the first scenic overlook we came to. There, I would toss Dad off the cliffs of the Palisades and into the Hudson below. Even though it would mean we'd checked off two locations in two days, I felt an impending sense of dread. Of the five clues, the last three were by far the more obscure.

Mad pulled on her yellow knit cap. "Can't Rachel just pick up your check when she gets hers?"

"Rachel quit," said Baz. "It was only part-time while she

finished nursing school. Now that she has, she got a job at Bergen Regional Medical Center."

"Rachel is your girlfriend?" I asked.

"Quit trying to change the subject, Spoils," said Coco. "Mad. Get your tools. Let's do this."

Mad grabbed some clippers and a pair of scissors off the Shelf of Improbable Things. "Think of it as a symbol, Vic. Your induction as a Chapter. An outward sign of, you know, something greater within."

"Like baptism," said Baz. "An outward sign of inward transformation."

"Inward transformation," said Mad, nodding. "Exactly. So what do you say?"

Honestly, after last night's run-in with Gunther, I was just happy they were still talking to me. The Visine debacle almost cost them their home, which would've made me the sideways hug of the century.

So: I agreed to the haircut.

We put on our coats, exited Greenhouse Eleven, and started toward the woodshed. Mad handed me a hat, identical to hers only blue.

"You know, Mad, between this and the haircut, you're pretty preoccupied with how I style my cranium."

"That's kind of a weird thing to say," said Mad.

"It's kind of a weird thing to be."

Still. I put on the hat. It was incredibly comfy.

Baz explained that the idea to live in a greenhouse had come to him when he was considering new settings for his book. It had to be someplace cheap, of course, but he wanted it to be unique, too, bordering on "something out of a fantasy novel."

I told him he'd pretty much hit the nail on the head.

We arrived at the woodshed, which, according to the kids, was the spot least frequented by Gunther Maywood. And since we couldn't very well have dead hair all over our living quarters, it was to be the site of my haircut. Basically, the woodshed was this: a dilapidated half barn, total Americana chic, like one of my mom's Restoration Hardware catalogs had grown hair on its chest. Inside, there was lots of wood, and lots of things made of wood.

The woodshed was a very literal place.

Mad pulled out a stool, dusted it off, and motioned for me to sit.

"Is this necessary?" I asked, looking for a way out (as sideways hugs are wont to do).

"A good shear is therapeutic," said Mad, running her hand against the shaved side of her head.

Baz and Nzuzi sat in unfinished rocking chairs, while Coco hopped up on a table covered in sawdust, her tiny legs swinging in anticipation. Outmatched, I made my way to the stool and sat. Within seconds my ass was frozen.

"So, what are we doing here?" Mad studied my hair like a block of marble.

Coco clapped her mittens together. "Rattail!"

"What's the funny one called?" asked Baz. "Business in the front, party in the back?"

"Ooooh, a mullet!" said Coco. "Even better."

I tugged my new hat (which in a very brief time had become my fortress of wool, a material not known for its wartime prowess, but hey) down low over my ears. For a moment the only noise was the sound of chairs squeaking as they rocked. And then . . .

"The Cinematic Sodapop," whispered Mad.

"Oh, hell yes," said Coco.

Nzuzi snapped once.

"Wait, the what?" I asked.

Mad unplugged some sort of ancient-looking electric saw, and plugged in the clippers. "It's very cool. Well, not, like, cool in the traditional sense."

"Oh, good," I said, sticking my hands into the pockets of my Metpants. "We wouldn't want anyone thinking I was cool in the traditional sense."

Coco giggled from her belly. "Sodapop is a character in *The Outsiders*. Mad says Rob Lowe is dreamy."

. . .

They had totally lost me.

Mad flipped the clippers on then off then on again, revving them up like the engine of a muscle car. "Sodapop— portrayed in the film by the very fine, very young Rob Lowe—had slightly different hair in the movie than he did the book. So, like, the Literary Sodapop would basically be what you have now, only with a little more shape, and combed straight back. The Cinematic Sodapop is badass in a fifties-slash-eighties sort of way. You basically leave some length on top, and on the sides, then it sort of, you know, tufts out in the back."

"Tufts out?" I asked.

"Yeah, but I'll rein it in a bit from how it is in the movie." She set down the clippers, picked up the scissors, and snipped at the air. "We'll start with these."

As if I cared how she went about tearing down my wall.

"You ready?" she asked.

Before I could say, *No, in fact, I am not*, she pulled off my hat and got to work.

Snip. Snip. Snip.

And the sinking feeling in my gut went away.

Snip. Snip. Snip.
It had been a while since my last haircut.
Snip. Snip. Snip.
I forgot how much leaning and tilting there was.
Snip. Snip. Snip.
I forgot how much touching there was.

MAD

I reread the same paragraph for the fourth time, gave up, and closed the book. It took a lot to break my concentration, to pull me from my world of greasers and Socs, knife fights, and young love. The bus to Englewood did the trick (and then some) by combining the worst parts of Dante's nine circles of Hell in a reeking smorgasbord of stale food and sweat and visceral misery. I couldn't wait for the day Baz and Zuz got Renaissance Cabs up and running, and we could kiss public transportation good-bye.

If I'm even here when it happens.

I sipped the last of my coffee, stuck the empty cup in the pocket of the seat in front of me, and tried to focus on the reason we were here: *Toss me off the Palisades.* Had I not read the Terminal Note myself, I would have assumed Vic's dad had an incredibly morbid sense of humor. But I'd heard the quiet depth and desperation in his written voice, and knew it was far from morbid. Should I ever be so unlucky as to be terminally ill, I could only hope to handle it with as much headstrong candor as Mr. Benucci had. Helping to toss him off the Palisades was the *least* I could do for the guy.

The Palisades were a row of steep cliffs lining a twenty-

mile stretch of the Hudson River. After some discussion, we'd agreed that tossing some ashes off the first convenient overlook would do. Outside, snow-covered trees passed in a silvery blur. Behind me, Zuz snapped in time with the tires of the bus against the reflector lights on the highway. Coco sat next to me, snoring like a bear in hibernation, muffin crumbs all over the front of her jacket.

I shimmied forward in my seat, pressed my face between the two seats in front of me, where Baz and Vic sat.

"Hey," I said.

"Hey, yourself," said Baz.

I couldn't be sure, but over the course of the last few minutes, I thought I'd heard my name uttered a few times. I hopped up on my knees and peered down at the two of them. "You know that makes me crazy."

"What?" said Baz.

"The whispering. About me. You got something you wanna say?"

They gazed up at me, then at each other. "We weren't talking about you," said Baz. "I was just telling Vic that Gunther Maywood is the only Chapter who doesn't know he's a Chapter, and how we just trade groceries and supplies for rent."

"And if your book actually gets published?" asked Vic. "And he reads it? You don't think he'd recognize his own orchard, or name for that matter?"

I'd had this conversation with Baz a few times—it was nice to see it play out with someone else.

"First off," said Baz, "it's not *if* my book gets published. It's when. Secondly, as I told you before, all names will be changed. And lastly, the man is a recluse. He'll never even know the book exists."

"What about the Internet?" asked Vic.

I smiled down at Baz, wrinkled my forehead dramatically. "Yes, Baz, what about the Internet?"

Baz sighed, turned toward the window, and mumbled something under his breath. I looked at Vic, said, "I've been trying to tell him it doesn't matter whether Gunther leaves the grounds. He'll find out—"

"We were talking about you," said Vic, wiping his mouth with his handkerchief.

"What?"

"Earlier. Before we moved on to Gunther, I asked Baz if you ever read anything other than *The Outsiders*. He said I should ask you about your theory."

"Okay, well, the Hinton Vortex is *not* a theory, it's a fact. The last lines of S. E. Hinton's masterpiece are, word for word, the same as the first." I grabbed the book, read the first paragraph, then flipped to the back and read the last. "Brilliant, right?"

"Right," said Vic.

I shut the book, studied its cover. "You know, Hinton started writing this when she was *fifteen*. I'm almost eighteen, look what I've done. Nada." Greatness had never been an aspiration of mine, but even so, who didn't want to leave a mark? Something that said, *I was fucking here. Remember me.* "Anyway, I guess you could say I keep reading because I haven't finished yet."

"The Hinton Vortex," said Vic.

I nodded. "The Hinton Vortex."

"Vortex time!" Coco's voice came out of nowhere. I wasn't even sure when she woke up.

"What?"

She slid up a full foot in her seat, enough for her feet to

touch the floor. "Every time you talk about the vortex, Mad, it makes me think of an amusement park ride or something. *Welcome to the infinitous Vortex!*"

"Infinitous isn't a word, Coco."

"Sure it is. To reflect, you know, the foreverness of a thing. *Infinitous.*"

I slid down in my seat, gazed out the window at the trees. "Coke, I love you, you know I do. But you are insane."

She shrugged dramatically, leaned over my lap, and looked out the window too. "I'm not the one stuck in the infinitous of a story."

VIC

From the Englewood bus stop it was about a two-mile walk to the bottom of the Palisades Parkway, where we ended up hitching a ride with a girl named Jane. We sat in the back of Jane's SUV while she told us all about Stewart, her long-time boyfriend, now fiancé, who was an "aspiring car rental entrepreneur."

This, I thought, sounded fairly wishy-washy.

But hey.

I sat in the far back passenger-side seat, and Mad was in the middle-back driver-side seat. Ergo, I had a direct line of vision to the right side of her face, and since I was slightly behind her, I could stare without getting caught.

I was an absolute ace at caddy-cornered-nonchalant-backseat staring, and these were prime conditions for my particular skill set. And so it was, staring at the right side of Mad's face, I thought about her tone of voice when she spoke

of young S. E. Hinton's accomplishments. I watched her flip her hair to one side, all those waves in a single motion—and I wondered how someone who could flip her hair with such angelic efficiency could sound so sad. Maybe it was some sort of cosmic balance, or secret human equilibrium. *Here, you may take this lovely thing, but not without also taking this awful thing. Knock yourself out.*

Here's what wasn't a maybe: everything Mad said, every delicate movement she made—from her hair, to her hands, to the way she read a book like it was the last thing on Earth worth doing—was pure verve and value.

If a poem could be a person, it would be Madeline Falco.

And hey. Maybe *that* was the secret human equilibrium.

Jane pulled over at the first official overlook: Rockefeller Lookout. There was a parking lot and a couple of high-tech, quarter-for-use binoculars. It was all very official.

"Thank you very much, Jane," said Baz, hopping out of the SUV. "And many congratulations on your engagement."

"Thanks, dude. You guys want me to hang around till you're done seeing the sights? I'm totally fascinated watching people watch things."

. . .

"That's a pretty strange fascination you got there, Jane," said Coco. "Anyway, we're not sightseeing. Vic here is tossing his dad off the cliff."

The look on Jane's face turned rascally. Like, clearly this wasn't her first go at driving a pack of wayward kids up to a cliff so one of them could toss a dead parent into the Hudson.

"Right on, my man," said Jane, winking and shooting gun-fingers at me. *Peugh! Peugh! Peugh!* "Careful you don't toss yourself over with him!"

As Jane drove off, we stood in an uncomfortable silence. Some people, you spend any amount of time with them, and

things make sense. *Of course* Jane was engaged to an aspiring car rental entrepreneur. I could not speak for the others, but after five or so minutes with the girl, I, too, felt like an aspiring car rental entrepreneur.

I put on the blue knit cap; Mad put on her yellow one, then lit a cigarette, and we all stared at the old SUV as it disappeared down the snowy highway.

Coco reached for Baz's hand. "Frakking freak show, that one."

Baz just nodded.

* * *

Rockefeller Lookout was approximately four hundred feet above sea level. According to the sign, you could see the following:

1. The Hudson River (Which, uh, I would hope so. It was right there.)
2. New York City (Ergo, Citi Field, home of the New York Mets.)
3. Henry Hudson Bridge (Great.)
4. Long Island Sound (Terrific.)
5. Westchester County, New York (Why not.)

Posted just below this was another sign urging people to observe park rules. The rules themselves were pretty obvious: do not climb the cliffs, stay on the trails, alcohol is prohibited, and the like. I suppose some kid at some point, after one too many cheap beers, had probably thought rappelling down the cliff would be a rad idea. And I felt sorry for that kid. But I felt sorrier for his parents. Because their house was filled to the brim with green bean casseroles and sideways hugs.

Together we walked toward the precipice of the Palisades. Nothing but a thin metal rail separated us from the edge of the rocky cliffs below. There were no crowds. Probably because it was still snowing. We stepped up to the fence, stared across the Hudson, and saw all five things from the sign. What the sign hadn't prepared us for was the sweeping grandeur of the view. In fact, this should have been included:

> 6. Sweeping grandeur of the view (Super Racehorse.)

It was a shame people didn't come up here during winter; snowy sights were a thousand times better, the giant rocks of the cliff face either wet or white with the stuff. I was just about to pull out the urn when Coco said, "I need to piss like a lover."

"You mean like a *mother*," said Mad.

"Why would I need to piss like a mother?"

"Why would you need to piss like a lover?"

"I don't know, Mad, but I'm about to piss my motherfrakking pants, and we'll find out real quick what it's like."

"Coco, you'll have to hold it," said Baz. "There's nowhere to go."

"I can't hold it," she whimpered, crossing her legs.

Baz sighed, pointed toward a bustle of snow-covered bushes. "Go ahead then. We'll wait."

Coco shuffled from one foot to the other. "I need a guard."

Nzuzi snapped twice, turned, and walked in the opposite direction. Baz rolled his eyes and started toward the bushes with Coco.

I rezipped my backpack. "So Mad and I will just wait here, then?"

But Mad was gone too, smoking next to a nearby park bench. It did not appear as though she was admiring the bench so much as keeping an eye on it. As if it might come to life, shimmy loose its blanket of snow, and trot off down the highway.

I should probably help her keep an eye on that bench, I thought.

Making my way over, I heard her say, "Memories are as infinite as the horizon."

"Poetic mood?"

She pointed to a plaque on the bench:

SYLVIA & MORTIMER ALTNEU

MEMORIES ARE AS INFINITE
AS THE HORIZON

"What do you think it means?" I asked.

"Got me," said Mad. "*Altneu*. Strange last name."

The Land of Nothingness was upon me without warning.

We were in a car. Ages ago. Dad drove; Mom laughed. *Your father is the funniest person I know*. There were mountains. And trees that had just turned colors, so it looked like we were driving into a swirling tsunami of burnt orange and yellow. Mom finally stopped laughing and it was quiet, the peculiar kind of quiet where the leftover energy from the laughter hangs in the air. With some laughter, you just have to let the dust settle. From my seat in the back of the car, I saw my parents' heads. And then Dad's arm reached across the middle console, his hand resting in Mom's lap. *Till we're old-new*, he said. She responded in a whisper: *Old-new*.

Consider this: billions of memories in a brain, each one drowning in a furious river, grasping and gasping for life, a

twine of rope, an olive branch. It's no accident, the memories that last. They are survivors.

"Old-new," I said.

"What?"

I turned from the bench to Mad. "People always talk about growing old together like it's the greatest, most romantic thing ever. But how often does it end up that way? People grow in different ways. More often than not, they just grow bitter."

I imagined my father's hand, resting in Mom's lap. And I knew the older they got, the younger they seemed.

"I took two years of German," I said. "*Alt* means 'old.' And *neu* means 'new.' It's the signature from Dad's Terminal Note. *Till we're old-new*."

. . .

. . .

"So, what do you think it means?" asked Mad.

I looked at my worn-out boots, crusted with dirty salt and snow, and thought about Dad's old New Balance sneakers. "Mom and Dad were here. This is where they found that motto, I bet. Probably stood in this exact spot."

Mad took a final pull from her cigarette before stomping it out on the ground. "The inevitability of corresponding units."

"I mean—it's not the middle of nowhere. It's an official stop, or lookout, or whatever. But still. It feels like quite a bump."

"We can't wait around all day!" yelled Coco behind us, apparently done relieving herself in the bushes. Baz and Nzuzi stood next to her at the cliff's edge, and miracle of miracles, Mad took my hand just as she'd done at the Parlour. As she led the way to the precipice, I felt her up-closeness, thus proving my prior sentiment: some beauties require tragedies.

At the edge, Baz scooped Coco into his arms, and Nzuzi stared across the Hudson. It felt nice not being alone in such heavy things. Nice being with people who knew what mattered: this infinite horizon where time was nothing, where I was at once old and new.

"'The heavens declare the glory of God . . .'" said Baz, "'and the sky above proclaims his handiwork.' This will definitely go in the book."

White snow fell like a polka-dot panorama against the gray sky. We soaked in the silence and beauty of things until, eventually, Mad leaned over and asked if I was ready. And for some reason—I really couldn't say why—I thought of the USS *Ling*. Floating in impotency. And that rock I'd kicked, the one that had hit the deck gun, then plunked into the dark water of the Hackensack River. It was still there. It would always be there.

I thought of all my momentous multitudes. My many *I ams*.

"I am," I said.

I unzipped my bag, pulled out the urn—wind whipped around, tossing tiny snowflakes into a sort of tornado, swirling around us, up and up and up into the ether.

"We're too far away," I said.

The edge of the cliff was at least ten feet away, much too far to chuck a fistful of ashes and expect them to clear the brink. The rocks were roped off with clear signs posted every twenty feet or so: DO NOT GO BEYOND BARRICADE. One of the signs had been vandalized in pastel colors, so it now read: ~~DO NOT~~ GO BEYOND BARRICADE.

"Guess we should go beyond barricade," said Mad with a grin. Whenever I saw her do this, I felt like a pilgrim glimpsing the aurora borealis.

Nzuzi snapped his finger in agreement, the sound echoing off the surrounding cliffs, and Baz rolled his eyes, and all of it made me want to smile. If I'd had a Northern Light, I would have too.

Mad chanted, "Go-be-*yond*. Bar-ri-*cade*. Go-be-*yond*. Bar-ri-*cade*."

"Fine." Baz sighed. "We'll all go."

On the other side, a flat rock, massive and snow-covered, jutted out into emptiness. From there, it was a steep drop to the water, four hundred feet down.

Baz said, "Everyone, be careful."

"Ouch," said Coco. "You're squeezing too hard."

Baz was imagining green bean casseroles too, I think.

I held the heavy urn in both hands, and noticed the flat rock under our feet had been defaced. It must have been recent; the snow had been cleared off. It wasn't usual graffiti fare, like a skull or a slur; it was a rainbow-colored heart to match Mad's coat.

To match Mad's everything, really.

Suddenly my foot slipped on the ice, and I saw my own death in the water below. Mad grabbed my shoulder and helped me regain my balance while I tried to play it cool. I nodded at her, bent down, pulled out a fistful of Dad.

. . .

"Toss me off the Palisades," I said.

"Toss me off the Palisades," said Mad.

"Toss me off the Palisades," said Coco.

"Toss me off the Palisades," said Baz.

Nzuzi snapped once.

I pulled my hand back and tossed the ashes . . . directly into the wind. Fusing with the tiny tornado, the ashes of Bruno Victor Benucci Jr. came flying back into our faces

where three curses, two snaps, and Baz's silence fused into one glorious choir of profanity.

"Did any of him make it?" asked Baz, shifting Coco to his other arm.

We each tried to shake Dad from our coats and faces.

"I don't think so."

Mad picked up a nearby rock the size of a grapefruit, and spit on it so the snow melted a little. "Here," she said. "Put some on this."

"Some what?" I asked.

"Some of your dad."

I sprinkled a pinch of the ashes on the mushy spot, part melty snow, part melty Mad. She scooped up another fistful of snow, and covered the rest of the rock in it, packing it tight.

Hey, Dad. You okay in there?

Yeah, V. Freezing my balls off, but good.

I heaved Dad right off the cliff, down four hundred feet, and into the Hudson, where he would lie forever. Dormant. Like the rock under the *Ling*. Like me. Like all of us, really.

Coco dusted off her mittens. "Who's hungry?"

MAD

By the time we returned to Greenhouse Eleven, it was late afternoon. Baz had the evening shift at Cinema 5, which put him home close to midnight. Having had nothing to eat since our mediocre muffins from Rainbow Café we ravaged the rest of our weekly haul from Babushka's. It was mostly cold cuts and cheeses, which we kept latched in an old file cabinet behind the greenhouse, a sort of makeshift refrigerator during the colder months.

I decided tomorrow would be the day: Operation Check on Jamma. Since Vic's arrival, I'd effectively ignored all the pertinent sections of my Madifesto in this regard, the ones extolling loyalty, family, and remembering one's roots. I would stay tonight while Baz was gone, get a good night's sleep, then disappear tomorrow.

Baz headed off to work, and not for the first time, I was tempted to tell him everything—Jamma, Uncle Les, all of it. But after examining every possible outcome of that conversation, I couldn't think of one that didn't end in confrontation; and if Uncle Les had been drinking (which, these days, was a pretty safe bet), I couldn't think of one that didn't end with Baz getting punched, or worse, Baz doing the punching. I'd yet to see him resort to violence, but everyone had a limit. Leave it to Uncle Les to find Baz's. So I said nothing as he left the greenhouse.

The rest of us ate cold cuts while Zuz spun the same Journey record over and over again, and we all discussed the remaining places on Vic's father's list.

"Okay," said Coco, staring at the Terminal Note, willing it to reveal its innermost secrets. "So, we still have to find the 'smoking bricks of our first kiss,' which, WTF, Bruno? Great

clue, dude." Coco had taken to referring to Vic's father on a first-name basis. "Also, a 'wishing well,' and the top of some stupid rock." She looked at Vic, who was currently on the couch, applying eye drops. "Spoils? Any ideas?"

Vic shook his head, and Coco speculated, and Zuz danced, and on and on it went, like the broken record it was.

Like the broken record *we were*.

Very little was done that evening, and we all ended up going to bed early with that specific feeling of having accomplished next to nothing. In and of itself, it was no big deal. Countless nights our collective head hit the pillow without having done much of anything at all, which was fine because there was nothing to do anyway.

The Madifesto dictates: *when nothing is required, doing nothing is something; when something is required, doing nothing is nothing.*

We lay in the dark, listening to the hum of the space heater, tossing in a rotten sort of laziness. The thing is, something was required of me. And I'd let it go far too long.

"Mad?" said Coco.

"What?"

"Can you tell a story?"

"I'm really not in the mood, Coke."

I focused on the sound of Zuz's snores, closed my own eyes, and tried to channel whatever peace he'd found. From here, I could see Vic, earbuds in, and I wondered if he was listening to that same opera from before, the one he shared with me on Channel à la Goldfish.

Coco cleared her throat.

I opened my eyes. "What, Coco?"

"Nothing. Shit."

I rolled onto my back, pulled my sleeping bag up over my

head, and there in the darkness of my supreme, extreme consciousness, I saw Jamma lying in bed, staring at the ceiling, a Coca-Cola on the nightstand. I really shouldn't have waited this long—

Coco cleared her throat again.

"Oh my God, what, Coco?"

"I can't go to sleep without a story. Or at least . . . a declaration of some kind."

"You want a declaration, huh?"

"If it's not too much trouble."

Vic pulled out one earbud. Zuz snapped once, sat up in his sleeping bag. Guess we were all present and accounted for.

"Fine," I said. "How about this . . . *And Madeline drop-kicked the little girl who kept everyone awake, and there was much rejoicing.* Better?"

Coco didn't say anything at first, but in the veiled moonlight of the greenhouse I thought I could make out a determined frown. "I've been working on one," she said.

"One what?"

"A declaration." Coco cleared her throat again and spoke with the tone of someone who believed the whole world was listening. "And when the kids needed someone most, someone to love and trust, they found one another, and they called themselves the Kids of Appetite, and they lived and they laughed and they saw that it was good."

In the wake of Coco's declaration, there was a long silence, though I had no idea *how* long, because there was just no way to calculate something like that.

"What do you guys think?" asked Coco. "I know Vic is just a Chapter and all, but—I dunno, after today, it feels like we're a real *gang*, you know? Like the greasers, right, Mad? From *The Outsiders*? Figured we should have a name."

Zuz snapped once.

"The Kids of Appetite," continued Coco. "Get it? Cause we're always hungry, and always at Babushka's or Napoleon's or White Manna, and our shenanigans at Foodville with the ice cream. Plus, you know, hunger for life and whatnot. So, double meaning. Kids of Appetite."

I sat up, slid out of my sleeping bag. "We get it, Coco. It's fucking guileless."

Coco's red curls whipped around in the semidarkness. "What the frak does *guileless* mean?"

"Guys," said Vic.

An irrational anger boiled from my stomach to my throat to my face and forehead, and now my hair was on fire. And how strange, to possess all my faculties at such a time, to understand that what I was pissed about, I wasn't really pissed about. I wasn't mad at Coco, not really. So who *was* I mad at? "It means it's not nearly as clever as you think it is."

Coco's tiny figure sat fully upright now, her bottom half still in the sleeping bag like a partially stuffed pepper. "You're just mad you didn't think of it first. For once, *I* made a declaration. A guile*full* declaration."

Zuz snapped twice.

I put on my shoes, stood, and started toward the coat rack by the door. "I am so sick of this place."

"Well, good," said Coco, "because it's sick of you. So sick, it's gonna vomit you right up."

At the other end of the greenhouse, Vic was propped up on one elbow, his earbuds in hand. I slipped on my coat and hat, and only then did I realize that at some point, I'd picked up *The Outsiders*. The book wasn't really a book at all—it was a limb, an appendage. I walked out, slammed the door behind me, and started down the frozen path. My head flooded

with images of Jamma laying like a sloth in her own filth, or worse, bruised, or worse . . .

Approaching Channel à la Goldfish, I heard the shrill voice of Coco. "And we lived and we laughed, Mad!" She must have stuck her head out the door, her voice echoing throughout the orchard; I said a silent prayer that Gunther didn't have a window open. "And we saw that it was good!" she yelled. "We saw that it was really frakking good!"

In the stream, Harry Connick Jr., Jr., swam idly toward me as I crossed the bridge. His bulging eyes seemed to say, *Who are you, Madeline Falco?*

"Give it up, Junior."

But I knew he wouldn't. That fish would not quit.

FIVE

INWARD TRANSFORMATIONS
*(or, The Magnificent Enigma of
Simultaneous Extreme Opposites)*

"Mind if I see your dad's list?" asks Mendes. I slide my backpack out from under my seat, pull out Dad's Terminal Note, and hand it across the table.

There's a knock on the door, and Detective Ron pops his head inside.

"News?" asks Mendes, slipping Dad's note into her file.

"You're not going to like it," says the detective.

"Oh my God, Ron, I swear, one more preface out of you, and—"

"She's not home. She's not at work. Every call goes to voice mail, which, as I mentioned before, is full."

"Shit," spits Mendes.

I stare at the file where Mendes stuck Dad's Terminal Note, suddenly wishing I hadn't given it to her.

"At the very least," says Ron, "we'll talk to her when she checks in tonight."

Mendes nods. "Keep trying. Ask around the neighborhood, coworkers, etcetera."

Detective Ronald nods but lingers.

"Something else I can help you with?" asks Mendes.

"Can I speak with you in the hallway, please?"

Mendes stands, disappears through the door—taking her file with her—and for the first time in a while, I'm alone.

I unzip a side pocket of my bag, pull out my prized possession: a photograph of Mad. The photo has many qualities, but the thing I like most is that there are no distractions, no annoyances, no obstructions between my eyes and Mad. I don't have to pretend to look at anything or anyone else, because there is nothing and no one else to look at.

It is just Mad. Sitting on a street curb somewhere.

"What do you have there?"

Mendes studies me from the doorway. "Nothing," I say, stowing away the photo. "Can I have Dad's note back, please?"

She crosses the room in a few quick strides, places her file on the table, and sits. "Of course you can. Just as soon as I make a few copies."

"What if I don't want you to make copies?"

"And here I thought you wanted to cooperate."

. . .

. . .

I pull out my handkerchief and dab my leaky mug. "What time is it?"

Mendes sighs, looks at her watch. "Five forty. Listen, Vic. You don't know where your mom is, do you?"

I shake my head, fold the light blue cloth, and finish the fold in a tight square.

Mendes watches with vague curiosity. "Because we can't seem to contact her. Not that we haven't *been* in contact with her. Every night for the last four nights she checks in by phone. Always just after midnight. Do you know why she does that?"

I don't answer.

"She's worried sick," says Mendes. "And judging by the

hour of her calls, my guess is she's not sleeping."

"Look, what do you want from me? I don't know where she is."

"Okay."

"I don't."

"Okay." Mendes sips her coffee. "It's just I've heard a lot of frustration from you today—about losing your dad, feeling like you might be losing your mom, too. I know things have been difficult recently, but I think you should know how much your mom cares about you, how worried she's been. That's all I'm saying."

Quiet observers tend to be loud thinkers.

And this particular thought is shot through a bullhorn into the unsuspecting ether: *If Mom is so worried, why are Detective Ronald's calls going to voice mail in the first place?*

(FIVE days ago)

VIC

Elton John's "Rocket Man" spun in the background.

Coco sat directly across the coffee table, cards spread out in a fan in front of her face, eyes leering over the top. Her feet dangled a couple of inches off the ground, legs swinging in time with the song.

"Got any aces?" I asked.

She shook her head.

I drew a new card.

Last night, after Mad left, sleep had been slippery. I kept

my earbuds in for a while, tried to let the soaring sopranos do their work. But it was no use. At some point, Baz came in smelling of stale popcorn. If he noticed Mad's empty bedding, he didn't say anything. And just when I wondered if I would ever find sleep, it found me. When I woke up this morning, Coco was at the table, shuffling a deck of cards.

Baz had left early for a breakfast date with Rachel, which, according to Coco, was most likely a breakup breakfast. "He prefers dumping his girlfriends in the morning," she said, shuffling cards by haphazardly spreading them out all across the table. "Baz says it's impossible to yell over pancakes, says it's scientifically proven. I told him I wasn't so sure about his science, but if he wanted to bring me some pancakes with extra maple syrup, I could get on board with whatever."

Baz had left a note with instructions to meet at Foodville at noon to discuss the third place on Dad's list. When I asked Coco where Nzuzi was, or if she knew where Mad had gone last night, she dealt the cards, said I'd have to earn my answers.

Three games of Go Fish later . . .

"Twos haff you kot to give me?" asked Coco.

"What?"

"Twos. Haff you kot twos?"

"Why are you talking like that?"

Her legs stopped swinging. "Talking like what?"

. . .

"I don't have any twos," I said.

She drew a card from the pile, inserted it into her fan, and went back to staring at me. I was no stranger to the courage of little kids, or to their lack of inner monologue. They usually said out loud what most adults only thought, which

part of me admired. The other part of me dreaded going out in public, knowing at least one kid would most likely act on that courage.

. . .

Coco stared at me over her cards. And even though there could be no doubt she was stuffed full of little kid courage, she had yet to ask about my face.

"Got any sevens?" I asked.

"Ko fishing."

"Okay, what are you doing?"

"What do you mean?"

"With the accent."

Coco set her cards on the table, stood, and grabbed a jar of peanut butter off the Shelf of Improbable Things. "I've been working on accents. This one is my Norm."

"From Babushka's?"

"Yes."

. . .

"Okay," I said. "Why?"

She dug her little fingers into the jar, scooped a healthy portion into her mouth. "What's that old saying about something being a riddle wrapped in a mystery or something?"

In my Land of Nothingness, I saw Frank the Boyfriend's book left open on the living room couch like he owned the place. He had several Churchill biographies, most of which had abandoned bookmarks somewhere in the first third. Frank liked chipping away at things even if they never quite tumbled.

"Winston Churchill was talking about Russia's role in World War Two."

"Russian!" said Coco. "See? Just like Norm."

. . .

"Churchill said Russia was 'a riddle wrapped in a mystery inside an enigma.'"

Coco smacked her lips, her mouth full of peanut butter. "You're kind of a nerd, huh?"

I am an Aspiring Car Rental Entrepreneur.

"Well, anyway," she said, putting the jar away. "I'm the riddle wrapped in the mystery inside the whatchamacallit."

Considering the fact that I was currently playing Go Fish with an eleven-year-old in a greenhouse while waiting for our friend to finish his breakfast breakup over pancakes so we could discuss the third of five prearranged locations at which my deceased father wished his ashes to be scattered, I thought maybe we were all riddles wrapped in mysteries inside whatchamacallits.

Coco sat back down and, within minutes, completed her third annihilating victory over me.

"I'm never going to beat you, you know?"

She smiled, dealt a fourth round. "I know."

"So how about you tell me where Mad went?"

She fanned out her cards again, and even though I never had a sister, this entire interaction was beginning to feel the way I imagined having a sister might be. Slightly annoying behavior combined with slightly hilarious antics.

"Listen, Spoils. I'm from Queens."

"So you've mentioned."

"People in Queens don't bullshit each other, okay?"

"Okay."

"So here's the truth. I have no idea where Mad went. But she'll be back. She always comes back."

"You mean she's done this before?"

Vinyl Elton came to an end. Coco hopped down from her chair, stood on the couch. She took Elton John off the

spindle, replaced it with an old copy of the Sugarhill Gang. "Vic, you need to chill. We all have things, you know? Mad reads *The Outsiders* and tells kick-A stories, and sometimes she leaves. It's one of her things. But she always comes back."

Coco reclaimed her spot at the table, fanned out her cards, and resumed staring. "Got any tens? Tell the truth."

* * *

Bury me in the smoking bricks of our first kiss.

We stood in the eleventh aisle of Foodville for a solid hour, dissecting the third clue. Baz came straight here from his breakfast date, his face stoic, steadfast, covered in emotional camouflage. There was no way to tell how the breakup had gone, or if Coco's assessment as to the calming power of pancakes was remotely accurate. I hadn't participated in many breakups, seeing as how a breakup necessitated an initial get-together.

I had not had much luck at initial get-togethers.

But hey.

I had some kick-ass Metpants and a cool-but-not-in-the-traditional-sense haircut once worn by dreamy young Rob Lowe, so I wasn't sweating it.

Nzuzi showed up too, and neither Coco nor Baz acted like his brief absence this morning was any big deal, but I couldn't help wonder at the timing of his departure, close as it was to Mad's own.

After drawing a complete blank on clue number three, Baz suggested we move on to the fourth one: *drown me in our wishing well.*

"What about the mall?" said Coco.

Nzuzi snapped once.

"What about it?" I asked.

"It has a wishing well, right? In the food court?"

I had no memory of a well in the mall food court, and no earthly idea what significance such a place might have had in my parents' lives. In the end, I had no better alternative than to convince myself that perhaps Mom and Dad had had some special bonding moment (at the freaking mall) of which I was completely unaware. Baffled, I agreed that, yes, I supposed the mall could have been a possibility.

And off we went.

We took a quick detour by White Manna. Since Coco had an indefinite ban, I waited outside with her while Baz and Nzuzi went in to order. They returned a few minutes later with a bag of world-class sliders, which we shared as we began the mile-and-a-half walk to the mall. (Baz removed the buns from his sliders, in keeping with his anti-bread philosophy.)

Before, I'd admired the kids much the way I admired Matisse's *The Dance*: they were fantastical, otherworldly, and even though they were real, it wasn't like I could just jump into their painting. I could stare at them, wonder about them, imagine what they were like. But I could never *experience* them. And now here I was, experiencing the Dance from inside the circle—*in* their painting. But it wasn't complete. Without Mad, it felt like I'd simply taken her spot in the Dance. Which was a real problem for me, considering how badly I wanted to dance with her.

The walk was pretty brutal: even under the blue knit cap, my Cinematic Sodapop had yet to acclimate itself to such temperatures.

Also, I almost got run over by a very large produce truck.

Here's what happened: I saw Roland (the bully with the mismatched shoes) and his little gang across the street.

Before they saw us, I suggested we take a slight detour through a connecting alley. Baz agreed, and just as I started to cross into the alley, he grabbed my backpack and pulled me out of the way of a produce truck lumbering by.

"No worries," said Baz after I thanked him. "Dr. James L. Conroy says one of the most important things in writing a book is raising the stakes."

"This is the guy who wrote a book on how to write a book, yeah?"

"One and the same," said Baz. "And your almost getting squished by a produce truck certainly raises the stakes."

He chuckled about this all the way down the alley. I followed behind, wiped my leaky mug, and wondered if it was possible to feel entirely comfortable around someone who was always looking for the literary angles.

By the time we arrived at the mall, we were all pretty much frozen to the bone. Without removing our coats, we made straight for the center of the food court. One little kid pointed right at me, asked his mom what was wrong with my face. There it was. The little kid courage. My eyes immediately darted to my boots. There were always things I wanted to say, comforts Dad offered after remarks like this, about value not being contingent on sameness, comparisons to Matisse, beauty in asymmetry, and all the rest. I wanted to tell this kid a lot of things.

But I didn't.

And then—something miraculous—the arms of the Dance made themselves known.

1. Baz put an arm around my shoulder.
2. Coco put an arm around my waist.
3. Nzuzi glared at the kid and his mother.

"People are dickwads," Coco whispered in my ear. "And I'm from *Queens*."

Tears threatened, but the good kind. We walked like that, arm in arm, passing no fewer than four vendors offering free samples of curious-smelling meat on a toothpick. No one, not even Coco, accepted.

* * *

Much like the Parlour and the Palisades, a thick anticipation hung in the air. Unlike those places, however, the anticipation felt manufactured. For starters, the wishing well was a momentous eyesore. Parked right in the middle of the food court, it was a measly construction of turquoise tile and rough white grout. The reservoir itself was about ten feet in diameter, and in the middle, a faucet dripped foggy water through the mouth and ears and nostrils and backside of— the heart-thinker in me could scarcely believe mine eyes—a unicorn.

"What the motherfrakking frak . . . ?" said Coco.

"Coco—"

"Baz, seriously though. Come on. I mean it looks like this thing is having, like, universal, like, superhuman diarrhea. Hey, whoa, also—can you believe people throw *real* money in there?"

Nzuzi snapped twice.

The speed with which Coco could change subjects made my head spin. Nzuzi was the only one who seemed able to keep up with her.

"People," whispered Coco, shaking her head. "What a bunch of dickwads."

Nzuzi snapped once.

Baz nodded toward my backpack, and even though it all felt wrong, it was now or never. I removed the urn, opened it, and pulled out a pinch of Dad. Rationally, I understood that even if this wasn't the right place, even if we later discovered that Dad had actually meant a different wishing well, I could always scatter him there, too. It wasn't like I was running out of ashes. There was, literally, plenty of Dad to go around. But the finality of putting him in the *wrong place forever*— specifically *this* wrong place—made me sick to my stomach.

Because Dad would not rest in peace.

He would rest in pieces.

The horn of the unicorn pointed directly at my chest. I tried to imagine my young parents being happy here, laughing at this stupid unicorn. I tried to let the image take root in my soul, a necessity should I ever be able to cross this place off Dad's list, and do so with a guilt-free conscience.

"Drown me in our wishing well," I said.

"Drown me in our wishing well," repeated Coco.

"Drown me in our wishing well," said Baz.

And just as I was about to toss Dad's ashes around the hooves of the unicorn, Nzuzi snapped twice. He stood off to the side of the turquoise monstrosity, pointing at something.

Coco walked over to see what it was. "Uh, Spoils? When did your old man die?"

"December second, 2013. Why?"

"'Welcome to the Barbara Tetterton Memorial Well, erected May 2014.'"

. . .

. . .

Coco cleared her throat, patted Nzuzi on the back. "Well, that was a close frakking call. Good catch, Zuz."

I felt Dad in my hand, thinking how close I'd been to toss-

ing him in this kitschy nightmare of a well forever and ever. We stood silently for a moment, staring at the lavish, phallic unicorn, water flowing from its every orifice, appropriately, the heart of the food court, pumping snacks and bourbon chicken and stale subs through its veins.

This mall was one hell of a sideways hug.

Coco said, "I wonder what a person has to do while they're alive to get the local mall to build them an exploding unicorn statue when they die. Barbara Tetterton, the world's biggest riddle wrapped in the mystery of a whatchamacallit."

Nzuzi snapped once.

And quite suddenly I was exhausted. More than a lack of sleep, the notion of an entire day wasted, with a forecast of nothing but wasted days ahead, ached my bones, my heart, my brain. I dropped Dad back in the urn, placed the urn in my bag, and we all turned to leave. On the way out, Coco accepted no fewer than four free samples of curious-smelling meat on a toothpick.

MAD

Baz slept heavily, steadily, his chest rising and falling in peaceful rhythm. In his arms he cradled a baseball bat like it was an infant. Zuz snored too, though his sounded more like radio static. Coco lay in her signature sleeping position: facedown in the sleeping bag, butt in the air, legs tucked up under her chest.

I crept up to the couch and peered down at Vic. He had his earbuds in, and even though he was clearly asleep, his eyelids were half open like a stalled garage door. The bottoms

of his irises were completely visible, which tempted me to sit here and wait for him to go into REM just to see what that would look like.

But this couldn't wait.

I pulled out one of his earbuds and watched his pupils dilate as the garage doors finished their ascent. "How do you do that?" I whispered.

"Do what?"

Baz's snoring stopped abruptly.

I put a finger over my mouth and froze. Baz turned on his side, pulling the baseball bat with him. He took in a breath, held it for a second, and just when I thought we were in the clear, he started with the mumbling. It was not uncommon, Baz talking in his sleep, and even though it was never in English, I didn't need to understand the words to hear the fear in his voice.

Whatever his dreams were, they terrified him; and this terrified me.

He calmed down eventually, and when the snores revived, I leaned in close to Vic's ear. "Follow me. Bring your bag."

Vic tucked away his iPod, slipped on his coat, and followed me down the walkway and out the door. If I were honest with myself, I would have to admit I'd missed him. Just a little. The Metpants, the eye drops, the way he looked at everyone the exact same way as if all of humanity was on an even playing field—I mean, yeah. I missed him.

Outside, the night was cold and silent. We made our way across Channel à la Goldfish, our shoes clumping softly against the wood, then under the chain-link fence and across the street. We stopped in front of the graveyard, and I thought about bumps and the thousand red lights and the inevitability of corresponding units.

"We're going to your grandparents' old house," I said.

"Okay."

"You said they lived around here." I turned, began walking. "Which gave me an idea."

Vic jogged to catch up. "What was the idea?"

"You'll have to wait and see."

He followed silently, and I don't know what I was expecting—a question or two, I suppose. At the very least, I figured he'd ask how I knew which direction to go in. But he didn't say a word, just kept his head down.

I flipped my hair to one side as we walked. I'd actually spent some time on it tonight, which wasn't something I normally did. The shave, the hat, the length—my hair just didn't require that much maintenance, which was good because I never felt like the upkeep. But yeah, for some reason, tonight . . . I upkeeped.

I glanced sideways at Vic, wondering if he noticed, but more important, wondering why I cared. I pulled out a cigarette, lit up.

"You shouldn't smoke, you know," he said, just like last time by the stream, with Harry Connick Jr., Jr., and the debilitating opera.

Drag.

Blow.

Warm.

"What was that song you had me listen to a couple of days ago?" I asked. "The last time you nagged me about smoking, I mean?"

"'The Flower Duet.' It was Dad's favorite," he said. "Now it is mine."

Now it is mine. More than Vic's favorite song, apparently, he owned it. That fucker belonged to him lock, stock, and barrel.

"My favorite song is called 'Coming Up Roses,'" I said. "By Elliott Smith. You know it?"

"No."

Disappointing but not unexpected. Music was more than subjective; it was erratic. It was the ship on the horizon that one sailor saw, the other sailor didn't.

The Madifesto dictates: *smoking in the cold will bring out your inner existentialist.*

"It is weird, though," said Vic.

"What's that?"

"Both of our songs have a flower in the name."

We walked through the middle-of-the-night streets of New Milford, the soles of our shoes pat-patting against the pavement, and our breath walked with us, this exhale shooting a bit of soul into the air, that inhale sucking a piece of heart into our throats—exhale, inhale, exhale in the cold night.

"What do you think Baz was dreaming about?" asked Vic, his words cutting through the shivery silence.

"No idea. Not sure I wanna know."

To our left, the Hackensack River wasn't visible, but that didn't mean we couldn't feel it. Like a distant fire, the river made itself known in the smells, the sounds, the way the air felt like a cloud. And then Vic stopped walking and I stopped walking and we stared at each other and this new quiet joined the old cold, and I had no idea what was going on.

"We're here," he whispered.

I dropped my cigarette butt on the pavement, stomped it, looked around. "Oh. Right."

In front of us was a modest two-story with brown siding and brick trim. The only signs of life were a single lit window and a steady stream of smoke from the chimney. Even in the dark it was obvious the house had been neglected through the

years: at each corner the gutters dangled like limp arms, and everything from the giant rotting tree in the front lawn to the crooked porch light confirmed total architectural atrophy.

"You're probably wondering why I brought you here," I said.

I waited a beat, but Vic gave no indication that this was true. As far as he let on, I may as well have presented him with nothing more than an old toothbrush, or one of those fake certificates of authenticity guaranteeing the validity of some celebrity's autograph.

"So, I got to thinking about that third clue," I said. "*Bury me in the smoking bricks of our first kiss.* When we were all at Napoleon's, you said your parents got together when they were young, right? 'Silly young,' you said. Well, if they had their first kiss in high school, it's not like they would have had their own place or anything, which means there's a decent chance it went down at a parents' house. And what kind of bricks smoke?"

I pointed to the roof, at the crumbling chimney with the tiny billows of smoke.

"It could have happened at school," said Vic. "Or at . . . camp, or something."

"Maybe. Or maybe it happened here. Maybe it happened up there, on that roof."

I had a plan, see, wherein I would explain the details of my rationale to Vic, and those bright eyes of his would grow brighter still, and he would thank me profusely for my brilliant deduction, and I would graciously bow my head and tip my knit cap.

"How did you know where they lived?" asked Vic.

I saw another question behind his eyes: *Where have you been?*

"I did some research," I said.

"So, like, Google, or what?"

I didn't answer.

Vic turned toward the house. "Who lives here now?"

"Some old lady. She can't hear a thing."

"Did Google tell you that?"

I sighed, wishing we could go back in time a few minutes so I could start this whole explanation over. "I pretended to sell magazines."

"You what?"

"I knocked on her door, pretended I was selling magazines. I rang the bell a dozen times, she never heard. Practically knocked the door down before she answered. I'm not worried so much about getting caught. The real question is how we get up th—"

Vic stepped onto the lawn.

"Vic, wait a sec."

But he didn't. Instead he marched lightly through the snow toward the enormous tree, its rotted branches drooping under the weight of a pitiless winter; he tightened the straps of his backpack as if approaching the face of an enormous cliff, with every intention of climbing it, mastering it, owning it. In a surprisingly agile move, I watched Vic hop in the air, do a chin-up on the lowest branch, and swing himself onto the limb like a skinny-nimble superhero. I stared at the lit window—willing the old lady to be as deaf as she was earlier today—then ran through the snow to the base of the tree trunk. Already four or five branches up, Vic climbed and climbed, and all I could think was, *Don't let him fall, don't let him fall, don't let him fall.*

"Vic!" I shout-whispered. "Be *really* careful, okay?"

I took one more glance at the lit window, pulled my coat tight around my waist, and swung myself up each branch

with relative ease. Above me, Vic had reached the topmost limb, and was now eagerly eyeing the edge of the roof a good three feet away.

And then—like *that*—he jumped, clearing the gap fairly easily, landing on the roof with a dull thud. I breathed into my hands to warm them, pulled myself up and up until it was my turn to jump. As it turned out, watching someone leap a three-foot gap at that height was far easier than leaping it yourself. From here, three feet felt a lot more like thirty.

"You don't have to do it," whispered Vic from the other side. "Actually. Please don't."

I breathed in quickly, held a soulful breath—and jumped.

VIC

In no time at all, we found a loose brick in the chimney. Then another. And another. Mad pulled them out, and with each one my breath caught a little in my chest. Behind the bricks was a solid square foot of space, like a miniature cave.

And in the cave was a box.

The box sat there like it belonged, like it had been among bricks for so long that it thought it was a brick. I pulled it from the chimney, tried not to think about whatever dreams my parents had had the last time they'd touched it.

Bury me in the smoking bricks of our first kiss.

Suddenly the box looked a lot more like a coffin.

I took off my backpack and sat on the roof, carefully placing the tin box next to me. Mad sat on the other side.

It was a very small box. Ergo, she sat like this:

1. With extreme up-closeness.
2. Knees tucked under her chin.
3. Punk cut tilted toward me. (I wanted to put my hand on the shaved side of her head and rub her scalp. Big-time. I do not know why.)
4. On the other side of her head, her yellow hair tumbled in waves. It looked different—not better or worse, necessarily. But a little more . . . aware of itself or something. It crashed like a waterfall down her shins, splashing a foot shy of her painted Nikes. I wanted to wash myself in that hair. That hair could make me clean.
5. Eyes literally sparkling in the moonlight, eyes so gray, they redefined the word.

"I'm not going to make out with you or anything," said Mad.

I am an Aspiring Car Rental Entrepreneur.

"What?" I said.

"You're looking at me like you think I might make out with you. I'm not going to."

I swallowed hard, focused on my bisyllable answer. "Okay."

"I mean . . . I didn't know if maybe that's what you were waiting for."

"It wasn't."

Mad nodded. "Some guys think I'm like that."

"I didn't think you were like that."

"Well, you don't really know me."

Even though the phrase cut like a knife, I found myself entirely content. Mad's speech was so intentional, I could al-

most hear the functionality of it, her lips and tongue and teeth operating as one. She spoke so quietly, all these little sentences just for me. The eyes, the sentences, the hair—these pieces that composed the single unit called Mad were astounding. They walked inside my brain, pulled up comfy chairs, and made themselves at home.

"Mad, I know you well enough to know you wouldn't make out with anyone on impulse."

She smiled, and I felt warm all over.

I looked down at the box and felt cold all over.

The human body is a mysterious machine, capable of feeling an extraordinary amount of emotions—often opposing—at the same time. Like coincidences, it's not as improbable as it seems. As complex beings, it stands to reason that the mathematical probability of a single unit experiencing multiple stuffs would be quite high.

Dad used to talk this shit all the time.

He called it simultaneous extreme opposites.

. . .

. . .

Mad glanced at the tin box between us, did this sort of tossy-twirl thing with her hair where it shot around to one side and landed on her back, then sang, *"I'm a junkyard full of false starts; and I don't need your permission to bury my love under this bare lightbulb."*

"What's that from?" I asked.

. . .

"My favorite song. 'Coming Up Roses,'" said Mad. She sang a few more lines, which only increased my general non-brain, non-heart-thinking way of thinking.

I was such a mess.

"I like it," I said.

She looked up at the moon and sang in a small melty voice. And as she did, I was transported to another world where kids were nice and no one ever pointed and we all just danced and stayed up late telling stories and drank hot chocolate with marshmallows and lived in greenhouses with unique friends.

"*While the moon does its division*," sang Mad, "*you're buried below. And you're coming up roses everywhere you go.*"

She lowered her hand, rested it on top of the tin box between us.

"Who sings that again?" I asked, staring at her hand, trying to build up the courage to reach out and grab it.

"Elliott Smith," she said.

Do it, Benucci. Be the racehorse. In a rare wave of courage, I reached out toward the box—just as Mad moved her hand.

Such was the way of the world.

She shifted, her shoes scraping the shingles of the roof as she slid toward the chimney, then turned and leaned her back up against it and tucked her knees under her chin again. I watched all her pieces move as one, thinking some machines were just more mysterious than others.

"So," said the most mysterious machine. "How do you sleep with your eyes open?"

I looked at the box. It sort of tipped the timing of everything, like a third party was up on this roof with us. Our conversation was sporadic, even for me. Talking, then thinking, then no talking, then singing.

I met Mad's eye. "Are we asking all the questions now?"

"What do you mean?"

"I mean, we've been doing that thing where we say we won't ask this and we won't ask that, but . . ."

"Right."

"Right. So. Are we asking all those questions now?"

"Sure. Let's."

I nodded. "Fine. I'll trade you."

"You'll what?"

"I'll trade you. Questions. But we each have to agree on them before giving our answers."

"Okay," she said. "What's your question for me?"

Mad's eyes were a strange sort of smile. She knew what I wanted to ask, that I wanted to know where she'd been, why she'd left. And I think she would have told me too. But I had this feeling like even though she *would* have told me where she'd been, she really didn't want to. And I never wanted to be that to Mad. I never wanted to be the one to make her go against her wants.

I wanted her wants intact.

"Other than the Hinton Vortex," I said, "why do you like *The Outsiders* so much?"

Her eyes changed into a different smile. They said thank you.

"Do you agree to your question?"

She nodded. "I do. And you'll tell me how you sleep with your eyes open?"

"I will," I said. "But you first."

Mad spent the next ten minutes talking about *The Outsiders*. No theories or analytics. Just pure, unadulterated fangirling. In the moonlight, I stared at her lips as they moved in succinct elegance, praising story and character and setting. Apparently, the best characters in *The Outsiders* valued loyalty above all. And I remembered what Coco said, that if Mad's "thing" was leaving, her other thing was coming back. I thought maybe loyalty, for Mad, was in the coming back. She recited her favorite quotes,

and one of them was something about being so real that you scared people. Mad said she wanted to be *that* kind of real. I thought I understood. In our many conversations about art, Dad always challenged me to look past "the pretty," as he called it. He taught me that what really mattered wasn't beauty, but what drove that beauty, the stuff that bubbled just below the surface. *Don't look at the colors that are there, V,* he used to say, pointing to various prints in my Matisse book. *Look at the colors that aren't.* Dad called this "the simmering underneath," said you could find it in books and music and art and just about everything. Listening to Mad describe the scary realness of the characters in her book, I thought she probably understood the simmering underneath.

As she continued, hair splashing, lips crashing, heart singing, she spoke of the joys of fiction, and about sinking *into* fiction, and I imagined sinking with her. I wanted to be part of all things if they were her things.

I wanted to go to Singapore and take her with me.

. . .

And I wanted her lips.

. . .

Just to taste them. To put my own lips on top of them, all around them. I wanted to put my tongue in there too. I wanted to feel her wet mouth and the sharp edges of her teeth. I'd never kissed anyone before. Kissing was hard for leaky-mug-dry-eye type reasons. And sympathy-smile type reasons. Also, kids-on-the-bridge type reasons. But man. I wanted to. With Mad, I really did.

"Okay, your turn," she said. "How do you sleep with your eyes open?"

I pulled out my handkerchief and wiped my leaky mug.

Across the street, an old pickup was parked in someone's driveway. The streetlight next to it shone down on the truck. It looked isolated, like it was alone on a stage. Barely within the circle of light, a garden gnome stood in the grass. Alone in the dark.

"'Expression, for me, does not reside in passions glowing in a human face or manifested by violent movement.'"

. . .

"That's a quote?" asked Mad.

"Henri Matisse."

Mad nodded, like this was perfectly reasonable, like of course this Matisse quote explained how I slept with my eyes open. It didn't, but for some reason, whenever I thought of my having Moebius, I thought of this quote. It just made me love Matisse all the more. Really what it did was solidify my belief that we—you know, me and Matisse—would have been close friends.

"I have Moebius syndrome."

And I plunged into these words I'd read, words I'd heard, words I'd thought . . . but words I'd never spoken. Mad sat, her chin on her knees, her back to the bricks, listening intently.

"It's a neurological disorder that causes facial paralysis," I said. "Something like two to twenty per one million are born with it, so . . . lucky me. But lots of people with Moebius have it way worse. Some can't move their mouths at all. Some have other problems with their hands or arms or feet. I am lucky. In some ways." I held up Dad's monogrammed handkerchief. "Swallowing is difficult. I can't smile. I can't move my eyes sideways. I only cry on rare occasions. I can't blink, which causes severe dry eye, hence the Visine. I had speech therapy when I was younger, which helped a lot. Before that,

people had a hard time understanding me. I can't curl my lips around the rim of a cup, so I had to train myself to drink without spilling. And to answer your question, I can't close my eyes when I sleep. Not all the way, anyway. There are different surgeries I could have, but . . . I don't know. I've never known any different."

Sometimes you tell the truth, and things are better for it. Other times truth hangs in the air like a fog, clouding the pretty lies. I hoped Mad could see me through the fog. I hoped she heard this truth and saw that I was trying to be real with her—as real as the realest character in *The Outsiders*. And just as I was hoping this, Mad pushed herself away from the chimney, her knees landing on the shingles in front of her. She had this look on her face, like . . . I don't know . . . she was hungry for more. But also satisfied. Eager. Reckless. Wild. Content. Happy. Sad.

The look was a simultaneous extreme opposite. I wanted to live inside this look. It was a look that would eat me alive if I let it.

"You going to open this thing, or what?" she said, picking up the box.

"Is that your next question?" I asked.

"Sure."

I smiled with my eyes, hoping she noticed. "I accept your question."

She handed the box to me. "So what's your next question for me?"

"I want a picture of you," I said without hesitation. "With no one else in it."

Mad squinted. "That's not a question."

"May I have a picture of you? With no one else in it?"

"That's two questions. And the second part is kind of . . ."

She stopped, sighed, stared. Still staring. Still staring. Still staring.

"What?" I asked.

"Nothing."

"What?"

Even though there was no smile on her face, I saw one written there. And for this reason, I was glad I hadn't opened up the box yet.

"Ask me again," she said, moving in closer. So close, I felt her breath on my nose. So close, I felt certain impulses in my nether regions, a bulge in the deck gun of my USS *Ling*.

"May I have a picture of you with no one else in it?"

. . .

. . .

"I agree to answer your question. But you go first." She tapped the tin box in my lap. "Open Sesame."

Heart beating like a drum, I clicked the latch and opened the box. Inside was a pack of cigarettes. They were old; it didn't take a seasoned smoker to see that.

"Clever," said Mad, pulling the pack out.

"What's clever about it?"

"Bury me in the *smoking* bricks of our first kiss." She pointed to the chimney, pulled a thin cigarette from the pack. "Double meaning. You mind?"

I took the pack into my own hands. "I didn't know my parents smoked."

Mad lit the ancient cigarette, took a puff, and choked. "God, these are terrible."

I set down the tin box, pulled the urn from my bag, and grabbed a pinch of Dad, stuffing the ashes into the almost-empty pack of cigarettes. As an afterthought, I took a second pinch of ashes and dropped them down into the chimney.

"Covering my bases," I said, sitting in the exact spot I was in before. I wanted to sit closer, but as a sideways hug, it was my unfortunate lot in life to be spineless.

. . .

. . .

"Memories are as infinite as the horizon," said Mad.

I raised an invisible chalice. "To Sylvia and Mortimer."

Mad lifted her cigarette. "May their memories be eternally horizontal." We laughed, and something about the moon—or maybe Mad—made me want to say things. So I did. I conjured brand-new words, simple words, threw them out into the thin cold ether. "I miss my parents."

"Me too."

"Dad could make Mom laugh like nobody. And now she laughs like everybody. Frank isn't hers. They weren't made for each other. Mom says you can't base a relationship on literary preferences, but she and Dad totally liked the same books, so you tell me. Frank wouldn't know old-new if it hit him in his stupid face. He loves canned green beans. Can you believe that? What kind of grown-ass man loves canned green beans? Would it kill him to eat a fresh green bean once in a while? And God, his kids are the worst. They have this band called the Orchestra of Lost Soulz—Soulz-with-a-Z, mind you. And they're sneaky mean."

"In what way?" she asked.

"In every way. In all the ways. They're sneaky in too many ways to explain, okay?"

"Okay."

. . .

We stared at the moon, and at the dormant truck across the street, and at the garden gnome.

. . .

Mad stomped out the rest of the cigarette. "What do you think it means?"

"What do I think what means?"

"Being old-new. Clearly it's a sweet thing to say, some sort of subtle, indefinable quality."

"Clearly."

"So let's define it."

I loved that after I had spilled my guts, this was what Mad wanted to discuss. She offered no solutions, no apologies, no pity. It wasn't because she wasn't listening, rather—because she was.

"You first."

Mad cleared her throat. "Okay, well. Maybe it means feeling old, but remembering what it feels like to be young."

"Or being young, but understanding what it feels like to be old. Like an old soul."

"Or some utopian mindset that long after you've seen everything and heard everything and done everything, there's still some newness out there somewhere."

"Or maybe it's just a name," I said. "Sylvia and Mortimer Altneu."

"Sylvia and Mortimer. Old-new."

"Simultaneous extreme opposites."

Mad raised her eyebrows. "Simultaneous whats?"

This time, I thought about what to say before saying it. I wanted to get it right. "Lots of things are two things at once." I pointed to one side of her head, where her waves fell down past her knees. "Mad has long hair." Then, I pointed to the other side of her head, the shaved punk cut. "Mad has short hair. See? Equally true. Extremely opposite. Happening simultaneously."

"Simultaneous extreme opposites," she said, then sort of

laughed, which made me feel like this: my work on Earth was done. "Quite the enigma."

"A riddle wrapped in a mystery inside an enigma."

"The most magnificent enigma," she said.

Mad leaned sideways, closer, until her face was inches from my own. She stared right into my eyes, and my insides turned to molten lava. She made me forget the unforgettable things.

I don't know.

I wanted her. But not like that. Or not *just* like that.

I wanted Mad in *every* like that.

And I tried to imagine what she saw when she looked at me this up close.

"*While the moon does its division,*" she sang, "*you're buried below. And you're coming up roses everywhere you go.*"

The song did it—what all good songs try to do. It made me feel like it was about *me*. And suddenly Mad grabbed my right wrist. Tight. But careful, too. And I let her.

She turned it over in her hands so the inside was faceup.

And I let her.

She raised my sleeve so my skin was bare and cold.

And I let her.

She looked from my face to my wrist, and she studied my scabs, and in the light of the sickle moon they looked more sad than usual. Ragged and haphazard were my tiny paths going nowhere. My pain threshold had been pushed many times. Fingernails, mostly. Construction paper, credit cards, cardboard—never a blade.

I'd thought about it though. What it would look like, what it would feel like.

But I always stopped at thinking.

"Does your mom know?" asked Mad.

What a thing to ask. Just get right in there, right up in my head, right in all the important places.

"Yes," I said. "We used to talk about things. She asked if I hurt myself on purpose. I told her yes, but never too bad."

Mad, still holding my right wrist, pulled the sleeve of her own jacket up.

She did not have tiny paths. But she did have bruises. Dark ones. Going nowhere.

"These are recent," I whispered. I don't know why I whispered it. It just needed whispering. And while mine clearly were self-inflicted, hers clearly were not. "Who did this to you?"

She didn't answer, just shrugged. And as much as I wanted to hug her, to pull her to me, I didn't. We just held each other's wrists, inches apart, under a lit sky, letting the moon do its division, all our shit getting buried below, submerged in the bricks of my parents' first kiss, on the roof of my once-handsy, now-deceased grandparents' house, having completed the third task on my dad's wish list, soaking in the scary-realness of the moment.

"You may," whispered Mad.

"I may what?"

"You may have a picture of me with no one else in it."

I am a Super Racehorse.

SIX

THE BUS, THE BELL, & THE TWO RED ROOMS
(or, It Was Not His Fucking Orange Juice)

"Madeline Falco," I say out loud. "Madeline. Madeline. Madeline. It's weird, saying your name out loud. I mean, you hear it so often in other people's voices, but how often do you hear your own name in your own voice?"

Bundle scrunches his face up like a pug. "Madeline—"

"See?" I interrupt, pointing at him. "Right there. I hear that shit *all* the time. But your name sounds different in your own voice, I'm telling you. Madeline . . . Madeline . . . God, that's weird."

"It's weird, all right."

"What's your first name, Bundle?"

He sighs, and I can almost hear the *whatever* behind it. "Herman," he says. "Herman Bundle."

I smile a little, nod slowly. "See? How'd that feel?"

"How did *what* feel?"

"Saying your name out loud. Felt good, right?"

"This is ridiculous."

"Herman Bundle," I say dreamily. "Any idea what it means?"

He shakes his head. "You know what yours means?"

"I don't know what Madeline means, but Falco is the root

of *falcon*, Italian for 'hawk.' Which makes me a mad hawk. I'm basically a superhero."

A man in a wrinkled suit and a shock of red hair walks in holding a cup of coffee and a newspaper.

"Hey, Ron," says Bundle, pushing pause on the recorder.

The fact that this man's name is Ron, that he has bright-red hair, and that his suit looks like it hasn't been washed in weeks, is simply too much for my Hogwarts-loving brain to handle.

"Let me guess," I say to Ron. "Your father is obsessed with plugs." He stares at me with a tired perplexity, then scratches his head so his hair kind of frizzes all over the place. God, this man is more Weasley than Bill. Or was it Charlie? Whichever one went to Romania to study dragons.

Ron calmly turns to Bundle. "*Any-who*. Thought maybe I'd see if you wanted a coffee or something."

Detective Bundle rolls his eyes back in his head and grunts.

Ron chuckles. "Yeah, I thought so. I'll be back." Just before stepping into the hallway, he turns and looks at me. "You stink, you know that? You and your boyfriend over there. Like someone shat sour eggs."

After Ron leaves, Bundle smirks at me.

"What?"

"Told you."

"And here I thought we were getting to be friends."

"Friends tell each other when they smell like shit. Also, *why* they smell like shit."

"Now, now." I take a sip of water. "Let's not spoil the ending."

I set the glass down and press record.

MAD

"You're lying," said Coco, staring at the ice cream. She turned to Baz, her bottom lip quivering. "He's lying, right? Tell the truth."

Baz couldn't stop laughing long enough to talk, truth or otherwise.

"I'm not lying," said Vic. "I saw it on *60 Minutes*. Or . . . *20/20* or CNN or something. In a list of ingredients, 'natural flavors' isn't necessarily a good thing. Take castoreum, for example, the anal secretion of beavers. They use it in the wild to mark territory, but apparently it smells like vanilla and raspberry, so we use it—"

"Don't say it," I said.

"—as a food additive."

Zuz snapped twice.

Very slowly, as if the freezer handle were wired with explosives, Coco pulled open the door, flooding us in a cloud of cold fog. She pulled out a pint of mint chocolate chip, scanned through the ingredients on the back. ". . . *natural flavors.*" She grabbed another one, then another and another, each time reading the ingredients, and each time letting out a sort of low-pitched whine.

"Um, Vic?" I said. "I think you broke Coco."

"It just can't be," muttered Coco, staring blankly at the back of a tub of cherry cordial.

"Sorry," said Vic, staring at his boots.

Coco slammed the freezer door and looked on the verge of tears. "That is all frakked up." She crossed her arms. "Well, I don't even care. I love ice cream more than I hate a beaver's anal secrets."

"Secretion," said Vic.

We all pretty much lost it. I mostly gagged; Baz only stopped laughing long enough to declare that this scene was *definitely* going in his book.

I raised my hand. "Okay, okay. Everyone, quiet down. I have declarations."

The Madifesto dictates: *the longer you hold on to an apology, the harder it is to give it away.*

Coco, who'd been giving me the cold shoulder all morning, glared at me.

"I declare that I was, in fact, a Grade A assclown the other night," I said. "I declare that, heretofore, we shall be known as the Kids of Appetite, as it is officially, irrevocably, and otherwise authoritatively one kick-ass gang name, and that I was supremely jealous of the fact that Coco thought it up first."

"The kids of what?" asked Baz.

"Oh right," I said. "You weren't there. Coco named us the Kids of Appetite."

"You can't just—Mad, you skipped the declaration." Coco cleared her throat. "And they called themselves the Kids of Appetite, and they lived and they laughed and they saw that it was good."

Baz looked like he was holding back a smile. "You stole that from the Bible."

"Did not."

"Sure you did. *And God saw that it was good.* It's all over the creation story."

"Oh, so okay, no one but God can see that things are good? I see that things are good all the frakking time, for your information. Sometimes I see that things are *very* good, in fact."

"*Anyway,*" I said, "it would seem we've derailed." From my jacket pocket, I pulled out the finishing touches of my declaration, the pièce de résistance of my apology. "I declare that we, the Kids of Appetite, wear these wristbands proudly, loudly, and in perpetuity, as they are an outward sign of our inward transformation."

I handed a wristband to Baz, then Zuz, then Coco, saving Vic for last.

Two nights ago I'd stayed up all night making these, sewing the cotton together, then stitching on the three white letters, bold and simple: KOA. They were wider than most wristbands, five inches at least, long enough to cover the entire wrist and then some. This was a crucial detail. The idea came to me when I thought back to that day I'd first seen Vic's scabs on Channel à la Goldfish.

I handed the wristband to Vic, tried to speak with my eyes. *Here, this should cover those up.* If I couldn't heal his wounds, I could at least hide them. He stared back at me, and I felt waves of the same flutterings I'd felt last night on the roof. I smiled at him, pulled my hair to one side, then looked around at everyone.

"I declare that we, the Kids of Appetite, are a family."

Coco's arms came flying. I felt a whiff of air and hair, and before I could stop her, she'd wrapped herself around me in a forceful hug. It was hard to tell over the sobbing, but I'm fairly certain she was thanking me.

We all slipped them on, and Baz held up his wrist. "It is so declared."

Coco clapped her hands, chanted low and rhythmically, "*Kids . . . of . . . App-e-tite. Kids . . . of . . . App-e-tite.*"

Vic and I caught everyone up on last night's occurrences: the completion of the third place on the list and the true

meaning of *smoking bricks*. We discussed number four on the list—*drown me in our wishing well*—and they told me about their fruitless excursion to the mall, and Barbara Tetterton's diarrhea unicorn statue.

"The Parlour was where they made a permanent commitment to one another," said Baz. "The rooftop was where they first kissed. The common thread is that they are personal places."

"What was so personal about the Palisades?" asked Coco.

"Sylvia and Mortimer Altneu," whispered Vic. He then explained the plaque on the bench at the Palisades, how it was dedicated to the Altneus, and how Altneu translates to *old-new*. "My parents used to say they'd love each other until they were 'old-new.' And look"—he pulled his father's Terminal Note out of his backpack and pointed to the bottom—"the signature."

There was a certain palpable energy in the air—we all felt it. As if the Terminal Note were a treasure map and we'd just pinpointed *X*.

I said, "Okay, let's come at this the other way."

"What do you mean?" asked Baz.

"Well, instead of trying to figure out the wishing well, Vic, can you think of any other locations that meant something special to your parents? Their first date, maybe, or high school, or—"

"How about where they got married?" said Coco.

VIC

Coco informed us she would need eleven-ish additional minutes to decide which ice cream to choose (*natural flavors* be damned). This would, according to her, "square us up," considering she'd been the one to figure out the clue.

Ergo, Mad went outside for a cigarette.

Ergo, I followed.

We sat on the curb and she lit up and I wished she wouldn't. I just wanted the earth to have Mad for as long as it could. And her smoking habit was historically and scientifically proven to foil these plans.

"We're not going to find the wishing well, you know," I said.

"That's the spirit, Spoils."

"Not at the church where my parents got married, I mean."

"How do you know?" asked Mad.

I told Mad it was just a feeling I had, but the truth was, since Dad died, I'd spent hours going through old family photos. I was probably the only teenager who could tell you exactly what his mom's wedding dress looked like. And the cake, and the flowers, and the groomsmen and bridesmaids, and yes, even the church. (St. Bart's on Bridge Street.) I'd memorized it all. The thing was, had Dad *not* died, I probably never would have studied those photos for hours on end, which means I wouldn't know that St. Bart's is constructed of old stone and has a giant red door with a crack running straight down the middle like it was the only church ever to get struck by lightning.

But he did die and I did know those things.

I also knew there was no wishing well. I hadn't been there, but the photos were thorough and comprehensive. That said, I had no better suggestions. And part of me wanted to see

the church in person anyway. If Dad's list was a blueprint, St. Bart's was like ground zero or something.

"Uh-oh," said Mad.

Behind us, a group of kids walked our way, their footsteps heavy and hard. One of them wore Asics: one purple, one black. Roland and company, the kids from the bridge. There was no way to avoid them this time. As they neared, I kept my head down, tried my best to ignore the barrage of oh-my-Gods, and what-the-fucks, and get-a-load-of-thats.

So many feet, so many words.

The mocking continued as they passed us, headed into the grocery. And just when I thought it might be safe to look up again, Mad yelled, "Hey!"

"Wait. Mad. What are you doing?"

She stood from the curb, dusted off her jeans. "Come here a sec!"

"Mad, don't."

But it was too late. Led by Roland and his mismatched Asics, the group slowly spilled back out of Foodville, practically landing in our laps. And like that, Mad completely transformed. She smiled like a siren and tossed her hair around in that way guys like. In that way *I* like.

I don't know. I guess the old deck gun had pretty shit timing.

"Whaddup, girl?" said Roland.

I still couldn't remember his nickname. It had something to do with cereal. Or a rapper, or something.

"Yeah-hey," said Mad, siren-smile intact. "What's your name again?"

I barely recognized her voice, all high-pitched and flirty.

"Name's Roland, but my boys call me the Pops."

There it was. *The Pops*. Classic.

One of his sidekicks crossed his arms. "Mad props to the Pops!"

"Mad props to the Pops!" they chimed.

This is the language of boys.

It is why I'm an alien.

Mad pointed at me while I kept my head down; I wondered if it were possible to shrink my entire body into my boots. "You see him?" she asked. "That's Bruno Victor Benucci III."

"So?" said the Pops.

"*So*," said Mad, "Bruno Victor Benucci III is son of Dame Doris Benucci, and the late Bruno Victor Benucci the Second. Ring a bell?"

The Pops consulted his minions, returned with a staunch "Um, no."

"Well," said Mad, "Bruno Victor Benucci the Second was a big-time earner for the Northern Dancers."

"The whatsits?"

"Northern Dancers, aka our friends up north, bada bing, bada boom . . ." She snapped her fingers, and did a few non-sensical hand-to-elbow gestures.

One of the minions said, "Dude," to which the Pops nodded in agreement. "Th'fuck you talking about?"

"What I'm talking about," said Mad, "is the *mafia*."

The effect was immediate. The Pops gazed up and down the street as if Al Capone himself might round the bend with a tommy gun pointed at his head. "*Shit*, yo," he whispered.

"Shit, yo is right, Mr. Pops," said Mad. "Now, what you guys do is none of my business. I just wanted to make sure you knew who you were laughing at, is all."

I watched the mismatched Asics slowly make their way toward me. Roland "the Pops" kneeled so we were eye level.

"Sorry, yo. Had no idea you were connected." He cleared his throat, looked around nervously. "Say, uh. Could you put in a good word for me with the Northern whatsits—?"

"Dancers," said Mad.

God, I could marry her right now.

The Pops nodded enthusiastically. "Dancers, right. If you could do that, yo, it sure would mean a lot, Mr. Benucci. And of course, you don't gotta worry about anybody at school making fun of you anymore."

I looked him dead in the eye, daring him to look away. "Why would anyone make fun of me?"

His Adam's apple bobbed. "Right. Nah, I mean, of course, no reason. I just meant—I'll look out for you. That's all." He wiped sweat off his forehead. "So. Will you? Put in a word?"

Dad was an absolute ace at finding the advantages of his disadvantages. And he'd done his best to teach me the same. Right now I was grateful for my killer poker face and for once took comfort in my inability to smile.

"I'll take it under advisement," I said, shrugging. "That's the best I can do."

The Pops broke into a huge smile, shook my hand, and led his army of cretins inside Foodville. As soon as they were out of sight, we burst out laughing.

"Guess you don't have to worry about those guys anymore," said Mad.

"Thanks to the Northern Whatsits."

"Thanks to the Northern Whatsits."

. . .

. . .

"How do you do it?" asked Mad.

"Do what?"

"How do you stand guys like that?"

If I thought hard enough, I could recall my earliest memory of getting picked on. First grade. Mark Something, with the big ears. There have been many Marks through the years—kids who made fun of others before someone could make fun of them. I guess I just never understood why anyone had to make fun of anyone.

"I'm used to bullies," I said. "But bullies never seem to get used to me."

She lit another cigarette, blew smoke into the frosty ether, and again I wished like hell she'd quit.

Across the street, an attractive couple holding hands quickly turned their heads away from me.

. . .

. . .

"Sometimes I think it's better than pity," I said.

Mad picked a piece of filter off her tongue. "What?"

. . .

I often argued with myself. Usually in the shower, but it could happen anywhere. I wasn't sure if this was normal, probably not. But hey. I'd pick a side and argue myself silly. And in the ongoing debate between ridicule and pity and which was the greater offense, here were the sides in short summation: ridicule was generally thoughtless, but intentional; pity was generally thought through, but unintentional.

I still heard the laughter, felt the undiluted revulsion from the Pops and his absurd gang.

Ridicule cut deep.

I watched the attractive couple across the street, their eyes pointed dead ahead, careful not to look back in my direction.

Pity cut deep.

So which cut deeper? Okay, definitely ridicule, but the

better question was, *who the fuck cares?* It was like asking if you'd rather get hit in the head with a wooden bat or a metal one. You're on the ground either way, and I guarantee the last thing you care about is the physical properties of the tool that put you there.

"Vic?"

"What?"

"You zoned, man."

I cleared my throat. "You should really quit smoking, you know."

Mad stomped out her cigarette, looking at me through firework eyes with the opposite of pity and ridicule, whatever that was. And I was absolutely blown away by her morning-type beauty. It was altogether different from her evening-type beauty. I don't know. Mad had many beauties, and some of them were time sensitive. And all of them made me want to do things I'd never done before.

There were lots of things I'd never done before.

MAD

From Foodville, it was about a fifteen-minute walk to St. Bart's. For much of that time, I watched Coco eat ice cream straight from the carton, and more than once I caught her admiring her KOA wristband out of the corner of her eye, or holding her wrist in an unnatural position so people passing might see it. Baz always cautioned against drawing too much attention to ourselves, so rather than announce our newly minted gang status to the general public, Coco quietly informed Vic that people around us "best recognize"

the Kids of Appetite as more than just a rough-and-tumble type gang, but the kind of gang that "was not lacking in scruples."

I honestly couldn't say where the girl got her material, but it sure was a sight to see.

The church sat back off the road, surrounded by dead bushes and trees, things winter had wrapped its cold dead hands around, yet to release. The grounds felt hallowed, but also empty, as if the church were the limb of a thriving organism, now amputated. An old stone structure, St. Bart's was essentially a giant triangle, starting wide at the bottom then rising from the ground like a child's drawing of a Christmas tree. The roof was severely slanted except at one end where a bell tower rose straight into the sky. The closer we got, the more enchanting it became, beautiful and picturesque in the looming winter.

We trudged across a parking lot, where someone had scattered rock salt; the only vehicle in sight was an old blue bus with the words GOD'S GEESE painted in red across the side. Underneath the letters, running the entire length of the bus, someone had painted what was probably supposed to be a goose, but had ended up looking more like a furry airplane.

I reached out a hand, brushed the long neck of the goose as we passed. "I declare this to be the ugliest bus on Earth."

Zuz snapped once.

We crossed the snowy lawn, reached the front door of the church, and just before opening it, Coco let out a low moan and leaned over, hands on knees.

"Coke, you okay?" I asked.

"I don't feel so good."

Baz rolled his eyes. "I warned you not to eat the whole pint."

Coco shook her head. "It's the natural flavors."

I tried not to smile but couldn't help it. Vic cracked open the heavy red door, poked his head inside. "There are pews in there. She could lie down."

"*Oooooooh*," moaned Coco. "I think the anal secrets gave me hemorrhoids."

I chuckled. "Strangely enough, that's probably not the first time that sentence has been uttered."

"Coco," said Baz, shaking his head, "we've talked about this. It's your own fault."

They had, in fact, talked about Coco's inordinate lack of self-control when it came to the consumption of ice cream. This was not the first time she'd made herself sick, which sucked for all parties involved because absolutely no one could wallow in misery like Coco.

"Hey," I said, thinking maybe if I could make her laugh, it might defuse the situation. "You guys ever think about how hemorrhoids plus ass equals asteroids?" I raised both arms in the air, shook my hands around. "Hemorrhoids from spaaaaaaace!"

Coco placed the back of her hand on her forehead, threw her hair back in dramatic fashion. "You guys, go on without me," she said. "I'm done for."

Baz rolled his eyes and scooped her up in his arms while Vic and I held the front door open.

The inner workings of St. Bart's were cold and old: in the one giant room, high ceilings came together at the point of the triangle; dark wooden pews, stained-glass windows, and paintings of men in robes filled every nook and cranny; and dust was everywhere. The whole place seemed untouched by

time, unsoiled by man, the same yesterday, today, and forever, amen. Incredibly old-new.

"Simultaneous extreme opposites," I said.

Vic took off his hat, tilted his head back until the bottom of his Cinematic Sodapop touched his backpack. I looked up too, saw a mural of Heaven and Hell with angels on one side of the wall, demons on the other.

"Simultaneous extreme opposites," he agreed.

Baz helped Coco lie down on a pew, then made his way to the front of the church, where he knelt in the shadow of a large, hanging crucifix. Zuz wandered up to a ten-foot-tall painting of some plump pale-faced saint, while Vic and I walked down the side of the pews, passing a closed door labeled CHURCH OFFICE, which seemed funny somehow, this touch of modern in a world of ancient. We approached a pulpit at the front of the church. Baz's eyes were closed, his hands folded, his lips moving quickly in fervent prayer; on the other side of the room, an opening led up a darkened staircase.

"Maybe we'll see the wishing well from higher ground," I said, starting toward the door. Vic gave me a look like he wasn't convinced, but he followed anyway. As if the church were lacking in mystical portentousness, each wooden step creaked under our feet, and the whole thing suddenly felt like we'd stepped into an episode of *Scooby-Doo*. We took the rest of the steps two at a time until we reached the top of the stairs.

"Hey," I whispered, my voice cutting through the inky blackness.

"Hey," said Vic.

"There's a door here."

"Okay."

"Why are we whispering?" I asked.

"I am because you are."

"Right. Okay, I'm gonna open the door now."

"Wait," whispered Vic.

"What?"

"I don't know, just—hang on."

"Okay."

Neither of us spoke for a second; somehow the silence seeped into the air like steam, making the pitch-blackness of the stairwell all the darker.

"You okay?" I asked.

"Yeah. It's just weird being here. You can open the door now."

"You sure?"

"Yes."

We stepped through the door and onto the weathered floor of the bell tower, and I instinctively raised both hands to shield my eyes from the sun. Vic kept his head down, eyes shielded, and I tried to imagine how painful it would be not being able to blink right now. Once my eyes acclimated, I took in our surroundings: stone walls rose in a circle around us, arching above our heads, coming together in a dome-shaped ceiling. Wide openings were spaced out every five feet or so, and in the middle of it all hung a giant, rusty bell. It reminded me of pictures I'd seen of the Liberty Bell, like an ancient relic, like decades had passed since it was last rung. We stepped up to one of the open-air windows, and I felt like a sentry standing guard on top of some medieval castle, awaiting news of battles from afar.

"So beautiful," said Vic. I turned to find him looking out at the view, still shielding his eyes, but with less urgency than before.

The view, I thought to myself. *He's talking about the view.* I was surprised how disappointed this made me. I'd hoped he was talking about me.

For a minute nothing else was said. The view spoke for itself. It spoke of fields and trees, lovely in their winter-deaths. It spoke of rabbits and birds, what few stuck around during the elderly months of the year. It spoke in bright blankets of snow, miles and miles of it spread out like a down comforter or marshmallow cream. I wanted to crawl under those covers, and I wanted to eat my weight in cream. I wanted to be part of this winter conversation.

I would say, *I'm afraid.*

Of what? the winter would ask.

I'm afraid for Jamma, and for myself. I'm afraid for our future, afraid we won't have one. I'm afraid of being so many selves, I'll never be myself. *Is that enough, Winter? Are you happy now, you inquisitive son of a bitch?*

I looked out over the panorama, at this winter conversation I would never be part of, and it occurred to me how much I wanted to interrupt things.

As if reading my mind, Vic said, "Here."

I turned to find him standing by the giant bell, gripping its frayed rope in both hands. And just then as he held out that rope, there was something in his eyes . . . I couldn't explain it. It was like Vic was a blank sheet of paper, and I was a pen, and at any moment I might write my entire history all over his face. And where there was no smile, I would see one. And in my heart, where there was fear, I might feel a shudder-shock of courage. And in the fields, where the rabbits and birds and pillowy lands carried on their elusive conversation, I knew exactly how to interrupt things.

I took the rope in my hands and smiled at Vic.

I smiled *for* Vic.

The Madifesto dictates: *bells are loud.*

VIC

Some time ago I did some computing. (This was before I found comfort in numbers; I was not very good at computing yet. But I was very good at using a calculator to do my computing for me. At this, I was an absolute ace.) Assuming the average person sleeps 8 hours a day, they are left with 960 waking minutes, or 57,600 waking seconds per day; assuming the average person blinks every 5 seconds, that's 11,520 blinks per day; assuming each blink lasts the average .1 second, that is 1,152 seconds per day spent blinking, or 19.2 minutes. Multiply this by 7 days a week, times 52 weeks a year, times the average male life expectancy of 78 years, and you are left with a grand total of 9,085.44 hours which the average male spends blinking.

Further computing verified this as 378.56 days.

54.08 weeks.

1.04 *years* spent blinking.

The average male spends just over one year of his waking life with his eyes closed.

I spent years being upset, bitter about my differences. When I looked in the mirror, I saw only the abstract. There was no splendor to be found. I did not understand how to find the advantages of my disadvantages. I did not see the beauty simmering underneath.

Not yet.

But Dad did.

Which is why he gave me the calculator in the first place.

* * *

Mad dropped the rope, covered her ears with both hands. I covered mine, too, wishing I hadn't left my sunglasses at home. The bell rang loud from its origins in this little stone tower and out across the snowy fields and all through Hackensack. I pictured this: a flock of birds multiplying, swarming the streets of the city, singing the same two notes over and over as they flew.

Chirm-chong! Chirm-chong! Chirm-chong!

Mad took a step closer.

Inches away now, those gray eyes blinked. And blinked again. And again. And I watched her, uninterrupted by annoyances such as the closing of eyelids. Just like Dad taught me, I found the advantage in my disadvantage.

And the bell tolled.

And the birds sang.

And still, Mad inched closer.

. . .

. . .

Long ago I had resigned myself to the possibility that I might go my entire life without ever being kissed. Ergo, all the nodding and one-word answers. Especially around the unique ones, the smart ones, the ones I found pretty. (If magazines and movies were any indication, there was quite a discrepancy between the ones *I* found pretty, and the ones everyone else found pretty. But hey.) And here was Mad: unique, smart, my kind of pretty.

Yes, a kissless reality had not been outside the realm of possibility for me.

But my realm, it seemed, was ever-expanding.

Time slowed, and I cashed in on a few of those nonblinking milliseconds. Mad's hands were pale white and pink from the cold, and they looked like freshly blown glass. The yellow hair, the yellow hat, the gray eyes, the rainbow jacket: Mad was an easel. Mad was fireworks. Mad was an exploding star in space, exploding in my face, a simultaneous extreme opposite of the highest order.

Her lips moved. There were words, but they were impossible to hear over the bell.

"What?" I said.

She spoke again, slowly this time, emphasizing each word so I could read her lips.

"I'm going to kiss you now," the lips said.

My realm of possibility exploded. Or imploded. Or some other word that hadn't been invented yet but meant: to shatter or blast on a cosmic, interstellar, and multigalactic level.

My lips replied, "Okay," and like a mirror, the two of us moved toward each other.

Toward.

What a word.

Wet, cold lips outside. Molten lava in my blood. Paralyzed, incapable, shy, impotent in my brain. Don Juan, loverboy extraordinaire in my heart. Every smile I'd ever coveted poured out of me and into Mad. And I felt her teeth, and I felt her tongue, and I felt her lips on mine. And I reached up and ran my hand along the shaved side of her head, felt the countless tiny hairs, and the skin of her scalp, and her scar, and *fuck you, Ling, we are not so alike.* And I never felt more like my dad, who I missed, and who taught me to think with my heart.

One hundred things my heart thought while I kissed Mad in the bell tower:

1. I am a Super Racehorse.
2. I am a Super Racehorse.
3. I am a Super Racehorse.
4. I am a Super Racehorse.
5. I am a Super Racehorse.
6. I am a Super Racehorse.
7. I am a Super Racehorse.
8. I am a Super Racehorse.
9. I am a Super Racehorse.
10. I am a Super Racehorse.
11. I am a Super Racehorse.
12. I am a Super Racehorse.
13. I am a Super Racehorse.
14. I am a Super Racehorse.
15. I am a Super Racehorse.
16. I am a Super Racehorse.
17. I am a Super Racehorse.
18. I am a Super Racehorse.
19. I am a Super Racehorse.
20. I am a Super Racehorse.
21. I am a Super Racehorse.
22. I am a Super Racehorse.
23. I am a Super Racehorse.
24. I am a Super Racehorse.
25. I am a Super Racehorse.
26. I am a Super Racehorse.
27. I am a Super Racehorse.
28. I am a Super Racehorse.
29. I am a Super Racehorse.
30. I am a Super Racehorse.
31. I am a Super Racehorse.
32. I am a Super Racehorse.

33. I am a Super Racehorse.
34. I am a Super Racehorse.
35. I am a Super Racehorse.
36. I am a Super Racehorse.
37. I am a Super Racehorse.
38. I am a Super Racehorse.
39. I am a Super Racehorse.
40. I am a Super Racehorse.
41. I am a Super Racehorse.
42. I am a Super Racehorse.
43. I am a Super Racehorse.
44. I am a Super Racehorse.
45. I am a Super Racehorse.
46. I am a Super Racehorse.
47. I am a Super Racehorse.
48. I am a Super Racehorse.
49. I am a Super Racehorse.
50. I am a Super Racehorse.
51. I am a Super Racehorse.
52. I am a Super Racehorse.
53. I am a Super Racehorse.
54. I am a Super Racehorse.
55. I am a Super Racehorse.
56. I am a Super Racehorse.
57. I am a Super Racehorse.
58. I am a Super Racehorse.
59. I am a Super Racehorse.
60. I am a Super Racehorse.
61. I am a Super Racehorse.
62. I am a Super Racehorse.
63. I am a Super Racehorse.
64. I am a Super Racehorse.

65. I am a Super Racehorse.
66. I am a Super Racehorse.
67. I am a Super Racehorse.
68. I am a Super Racehorse.
69. I am a Super Racehorse.
70. I am a Super Racehorse.
71. I am a Super Racehorse.
72. I am a Super Racehorse.
73. I am a Super Racehorse.
74. I am a Super Racehorse.
75. I am a Super Racehorse.
76. I am a Super Racehorse.
77. I am a Super Racehorse.
78. I am a Super Racehorse.
79. I am a Super Racehorse.
80. I am a Super Racehorse.
81. I am a Super Racehorse.
82. I am a Super Racehorse.
83. I am a Super Racehorse.
84. I am a Super Racehorse.
85. I am a Super Racehorse.
86. I am a Super Racehorse.
87. I am a Super Racehorse.
88. I am a Super Racehorse.
89. I am a Super Racehorse.
90. I am a Super Racehorse.
91. I am a Super Racehorse.
92. I am a Super Racehorse.
93. I am a Super Racehorse.
94. I am a Super Racehorse.
95. I am a Super Racehorse.
96. I am a Super Racehorse.

97. I am a Super Racehorse.

98. I am a Super Racehorse.

99. I am a Super Racehorse.

100. I am a motherfucking Super Racehorse.

* * *

We walked back downstairs in the semidarkness, my brain on overload, swinging from one thought to the next like an overzealous chimp between branches.

Here is what I knew: we kissed.

Here is what else I knew: I wished we were still kissing.

Did Mad wish the same thing? Did she like it at all? Would she ever kiss me again? Probably not. Probably I sucked at kissing. Probably I kissed like an aspiring car rental entrepreneur who wore fancy suits and loved Winston Churchill biographies. But maybe not. Maybe I felt like a Super Racehorse because I *was* a Super Racehorse. Maybe this, maybe that, probably yes, probably no, back and forth between branches, e'er the overzealous chimp.

I am the monkeyman.

Back in the sanctuary, Baz sat in a pew, holding Coco's head in his lap, while Nzuzi sat behind them, staring straight ahead like he was watching a movie.

"What's so funny?" asked Baz.

I looked at Mad. She was smiling.

She liked it.

My heart was so full, I thought it might explode into the ether, creating some bizarre new solar system whose inhabitants ate only love, drank only hope, and breathed only joy.

What a substantial galaxy that would be.

Baz gestured to the back of the church. "Madeline. Vic. This is Father Raines."

Only now did I see him—the man standing in the corner. Even in the dim church, I quietly observed the man's blue eyes, his wispy-white hair, his black robe/white collar combo. He looked quite natural, actually. As if he'd been planted and grown, cultivated from the unforgiving stone floor.

I imagined my second favorite Matisse: *The Dessert: Harmony in Red*. But it was also known as *The Red Room*, and I liked that better. In the painting, the table is red, the walls are red, the chairs are red. A woman sits at the red table and all around her, stems and branches and vines grow, seeping from the red redness, and even though it's strange and a little unnerving, it seems natural, because of course life in the painting had grown from the red. Where else would it grow?

Of course Father Raines had grown from the church. Where else would someone like him grow?

He cleared his throat, looked from Mad to myself. "I see you two have met the Iron Maiden?" He pointed a single finger up, and for a moment I thought perhaps the Iron Maiden was some strange epithet for God. "The bell," he said. "I named it after my favorite band. Though I must say, it's a pity she was cast from iron, rather than bronze. She's quite rusty."

"Your favorite band is Iron Maiden?" I asked.

"Well, their earlier work," said the father, pulling up his cloak like roots, stepping lazily toward the pews. "The later albums are rubbish, don't you think?"

We stared at the old man as if he were an attraction in a museum. Actually. No. We stared at him as if he were a vicar with a distinguished palate for Iron Maiden discography. And as impossible as it seemed, there was something

about him that was entirely familiar. I couldn't place it, but I'd seen him somewhere.

"That your bus out front?" asked Mad. "God's Ducks?"

Father Raines's eyes lit up. "God's *Geese* is a mission. Every December, we drive a small population of the Hackensack homeless south for the winter."

"You migrate," said Mad.

"The northern winter is a cruel animal for the homeless, *especially* the elderly population. To that end, the National Coalition for the Homeless has connected us with a program in Tampa that sets up subsidized housing and Medicare. I may not be able to put their lives back together, but I can see that they don't freeze to death in the meantime. I've posted flyers at the local shelters, inviting the homeless to attend my homily this Sunday afternoon, after which we host a charity potluck for gas and travel expenses. We'll hit the road precisely at four. Precision in time is a lost art, don't you think?"

"Must be a long drive," said Mad.

"I take a parishioner with me, and the two of us take turns driving through the night. It's actually quite a treat. Anyway"—he tossed his hands in the air, as if giving up on the thought—"Mr. Kabongo informed me you're looking for a wishing well."

"Yeah," I said, shaking my head. "Sorry. Didn't mean to waste your time."

"Oh, you're not wasting my time at all. It's right out back."

. . .

. . .

"What is?" I asked.

"The wishing well. Though I daresay it's frozen over."

. . .

We all looked at one another for a second, until Baz stood,

picked up Coco, and started down the aisle. "Thank you, Father. We will not stay long."

Father Raines nodded and lumbered around the side of the pews, brushing his hand along the walls as he walked toward the door marked CHURCH OFFICE. And suddenly I knew where I'd seen him before.

"I've seen you in photographs," I said, following him around the pews. Father Raines stopped just short of the door, only a few feet away now, his long robes swinging slightly from the sudden shift of momentum. "My parents got married here. Bruno and Doris Benucci. It was a long time ago. You probably don't remember."

The priest studied me differently from before, as if trying to place my parents' features in my own face. (I'd spent hours trying to do the same thing to no avail. My features were islands unto themselves.)

. . .

"Doris wanted a destination wedding," he said.

My mother's name sounded so natural rolling off his tongue, a familiarity that comes from experience.

"What?" I asked.

"People remember lots of things for lots of reasons. I happen to remember every wedding I've ever officiated. Your mother said she'd always wanted to get married by the water, even if it was dinky little Ocean Grove. But her mother—your grandmother—wouldn't hear of it. Now how did she put it? Oh yes. 'A real church for a real wedding.'"

As I listened to his story, I felt like this: a small boy carrying a suitcase, walking on the distant horizon, the line between my Lands of Somethingness and Nothingness growing thinner by the moment.

"Your mother looked radiant," said Father Raines. "I've al-

ways felt that a bride's happiness is contagious, you know, and as happy as your mother looked, I'm quite certain the guests were downright giddy. I know I was. Just before I began the service, your father turned to the whole church, and said, 'Everyone, follow us!' He grabbed your mother's hand, and they walked out that door." He pointed to the door behind Baz. "The guests were baffled, but more than that, I think they were curious. Their two reasons for attending the wedding had just walked out the back door. What could they do but follow? Your grandmother and I led them outside, and there we saw your parents standing by the wishing well, holding hands. That day, your father managed quite the feat. He found a way to please both his mother-in-law and his soon-to-be wife. They were married on church grounds, and they were married by the water."

"It wasn't in the pictures. The wishing well, I mean."

Father Raines smiled from the roots of his feet to the topmost branches of his wispy hair. He bent down on one knee and whispered the rest of the story. "You won't believe this, but the minute I pronounced them husband and wife, it began to rain. As if God Almighty wanted to do his part in contributing water to your mother's wish. All photographs were taken inside." He tilted his head to one side, a wide smile growing on his face.

"What?"

Father Raines unearthed his root-feet, said, "You look just like them," and shut himself in his office.

I turned and saw my young parents kissing, laughing, loving, living. And there was something to be said for the fact that I'd just had my first kiss in the same church where they were wed. And there was something to be said for the fact that we'd found four of the five places on Dad's list. And there

was something to be said for the fact that, for the first time since he died, I felt like part of a real family. There were lots of things to be said, and if not for the knot in my throat, I would have said them. But the weight in my backpack felt like a thousand bricks, and the pounding in my head was incessant, and I could not hear the miracles of then for the realities of now.

The Realities of Now:

1. There were probably hundreds of little wishing wells scattered here and there, things I didn't know, could never know about my parents.
2. Because no matter how well I thought I knew them, they had had a life before me.
3. And it sure seemed like most of the good stuff happened before I came along.

MAD

I followed Vic out the back door, trudging through and across and between the snow falling and the fallen snow. An absolute blizzard of prepositions. We passed spindly trees and tall thorny shrubs and, pushing through a patch of overgrown vines, finally arrived at the long-forgotten wishing well—frozen over, just as Father Raines had predicted. The well looked like a fire pit—small, circular, stone, and, under the top layer of ice, coins remained sheltered until March or April or whenever the cold decided to thaw this year.

Baz set Coco down, and we all held hands in a circle around the frozen well. Before accepting my hand, Vic

kneeled down, unzipped his backpack, and pulled out his father's urn. He leaned over the well and, with the full force of his weight, dropped an elbow through the sheet of ice.

I suddenly remembered a picture of my own parents' wedding, where Mom and Dad stood in front of a church, and he dipped her and they kissed deeply, and Mom's veil blew in the wind like a white flag. I tried to put myself there now, next to them in that picture. Where would I be standing? What would I be doing? I tried to put myself beyond the church, and into the inner sanctum of time itself. But I couldn't imagine it. I'd seen the photos, but I couldn't quite put myself *in* them.

That's what Vic was doing right now. Reconciling the past with the present. Taking manufactured memories and inserting himself into them, seeing clearly what could have been.

Vic wasn't staring at the well. He was staring at the happy beginning in full knowledge of the unhappy end.

"You mad, Spoils?" asked Coco, who had apparently recovered from her bout with the *natural flavors*. "Wishing ill by the wishing well is bad luck, you know."

"Coco," I said, giving her a telepathic *shut up*.

"What?"

"It's okay," said Vic. "I'm not mad. It's just weird."

Quite unceremoniously, he tossed the ashes through the small hole in the ice, and it was done. And even though he said nothing, he accepted my hand on one side of him, Zuz's hand on the other, and, interlocked around the well, we stood in the cold until someone found the right words to say.

"And they called themselves the Kids of Appetite," said Coco. "And they lived and they laughed and they saw that it was good."

Together Baz and I repeated, "And they saw that it was good."

If Vic said the words, I didn't hear him.

VIC

It wasn't just that I woke up in silence; it was silence that did the waking. For two years I'd fallen asleep with my iPod plugged in beside me, my operatic lullaby on repeat, and for two years I'd woken up to the soaring sopranos. But not this time.

I shifted sideways on the couch, pulled my earbuds out, and tapped the back of the iPod. It was an older model—battery life wasn't what it used to be. Shit luck for me, seeing as I left my charger at home along with my phone and toothbrush and sunglasses. Lying there in the dark, I went through the checklist of things I would have brought had I not left the house in a state of panic, when, across the room, I heard a soft *click*.

The door to the greenhouse. Someone had either just entered or just left. I looked at the sleeping bags: Baz, Nzuzi, Coco . . .

Mad was gone.

I swung my feet to the floor. For the second night in a row, I was grateful for my new sleeping attire: hoodie, Metpants, boots. I stepped over and around the sleeping bags and tip-toed down the center walkway, carefully avoiding the loose stones, then pulled on my coat, and stepped outside.

I am swift and soft.

I am a stealth fighter.

I am a spook, a spy, an agent of speed and silence.

I made my way down greenhouse row, over Channel à la Goldfish, where Harry Connick Jr., Jr., swam aimlessly, not a care in the world. And on the other side of the bridge, I saw the bottom of Mad's Nikes scrape their way under the fence. I needed to give her enough time to get across the street at least, so as not to be detected. I counted to ten in my head, then ran to the same spot, got down on my stomach, prayed she wouldn't hear the rattling of the chain links, and shimmied under the fence to the other side.

Swift. Soft. Stealth. Spook.

Ahead, Mad rounded a bend onto an adjacent street. Even a sideways hug such as myself knew to follow at a distance. (Granted, now that I had kissed Mad, my hugs leaned a little more to the front than they once did.)

At first Mad started down the same street we'd walked last night, in the direction of my grandparents' old house. But after a block or so, she veered. I followed quietly, covertly, passing a slew of houses, some of which were familiar from days past when I took walks to avoid incessant games of billiards, cuckoo clocks, and heightened geriatric sexual impulses.

Swift. Soft. Stealth. Spook. Spy. Speed. Silence.

I had this feeling that the streets of New Milford were wholly unconcerned with the goings-on of its nighttime inhabitants. Like the houses and streets and sidewalks slept as well, not just those living in and around them. The weather seemed to understand this: the wind blew harder, the air bit colder, the night fell darker. I pulled my jacket collar up around my face.

Prime conditions for a covert op.

There was no hurry in Mad's step. It was a mosey, a lei-

surely stroll. A few blocks in, she stopped on a dime and turned in a full circle. At the last second, I dove behind a nearby snowman, knocking off its icicle nose. I waited there, in some stranger's front yard, my back pressed right up against where the snowman's crotch would be if snowmen had crotches. I counted to twenty just to make sure I didn't step out too soon and blow my cover. Thank God for this snowman. This man made of snow.

A snowman is a very literal thing.

. . .

. . .

I poked my head around the side of the top hat just in time to see Mad, now less than a block away, walking through a yard toward the front porch of a house. I watched in amazement as she climbed the steps of the porch, opened the front door, and disappeared inside.

The house Mad had just entered was entirely out of place, set at least twenty yards off the road, with about ten or fifteen yards of space on either side. It looked like it belonged in the country, not the suburbs. A light in one of the front rooms flickered on, and a shadow, possibly Mad's, crossed in front of a large bay window.

Now or never.

I bid adieu to the literal man made of snow and followed the imprints of Mad's feet; at the front porch, I cut sideways through the yard toward the front bay window. Once there, my right foot sank into a storm drain that had been hidden under the snow. I shook my foot dry, shifted to the side of the drain, and put my face right up to the window, where a curtain hung a few inches shy of covering the entire pane. At the very edge, I peered into the house.

Swift. Soft. Stealth. Spook. Spy. Speed. Silence.

It was a living room, or had once been. Magazines and soda cans were strewn across the floor, TV trays stacked with paper plate upon paper plate upon paper plate. The walls were no different: dirty mirrors, crooked frames, pictures so dusty, I couldn't see who was in them. Only one article in the entire room appeared to have been taken care of: a gun rack.

I knew nothing of guns. But these looked very serious. These were not rifles of a sideways-hug nature. Two of them had scopes and seemed pretty modern; the other two looked like antiques. But all of them sparkled, which made me think . . . it took a lot of effort for someone to clean just the one thing in a room this filthy.

Next to the gun rack was a set of mounted antlers, which I would guess once framed the head of a deer. But what did I know. (About this, not much.) The antlers were long and sharp, weaving this way and that with the coordinated chaos of a thick spiderweb.

Antlers and guns.

This was not my kind of house.

Mad entered the dark living room, took off her jacket, hung it on the mounted antlers, then disappeared into an adjacent room. Seconds later she reemerged with a can of soda and a bag of chips. I watched her step through the room, strategically plotting each move, avoiding pizza boxes and used tissues like land mines.

She plopped down in a recliner in the corner, aimed a remote at the TV, and flooded the room in blue light. An old woman walked into the living room next, a can of Coca-Cola in each hand, scooting trash across the floor with her slippers as she walked.

"Hey, Jamma," came Mad's voice through the window.

The panes must have been paper-thin—her voice was a little muffled, but I could hear clearly enough.

The old woman sat on the couch but did not answer. She popped open both cans of soda with ease, took turns sipping from each one. Left, right, left, right, a double-fisted Coca-Cola extravaganza. I stood frozen to the ground, watching them watch TV and drink Cokes, like this was all just a regular night in.

A third person entered the room now, a man as disheveled as the house. I caught my breath because he looked shockingly similar to my favorite Matisse, *Self-Portrait in a Striped T-shirt* (which I suppose meant this man looked like Matisse himself). His hair was thinning on top, receded a few inches off his forehead. He had a bushy beard, angular eyebrows, big ears, and a big nose, like all the pieces of his face just didn't know when to stop growing. But more than anything I noticed his great empty eyes. Just like the painting, there was something entirely terrifying about them.

"Sick of this fucking shit," said the man, crossing the room like a drunken bear. I watched along with Mad and Jamma as he calmly removed a rifle from the gun rack on the wall and slammed the butt end of it right through the television screen, shattering it in a blaze of dancing lights and wires and glass. The man turned, his rifle dangling from his left hand. "You," he said, pointing a single finger down at Mad. "I fucking *told* you, did I not? I have an early hunt tomorrow, and the last thing I need is the goddamn TV blaring through the house all night."

My entire body was numb, and not from the cold. I went to my Land of Nothingness and imagined the painting of this scene. It would be called *Self-Portrait Man Terminates Television*.

Not even Matisse could make that beautiful.

"Well?" said the Self-Portrait Man.

Mad cleared her throat. "You're right. Sorry, Uncle Les."

I emerged from my body, floated up and up into the sky where I looked down at Vic, saw him turn, trip, run back in the direction of the greenhouse. On his way, he picked up the icicle nose from the base of the snowman, pulled back his KOA wristband, and extended his tiny paths going nowhere. "Not too deep," said Vic as he ran. For it had been a long time. And when he arrived back at the greenhouse, he caught his breath just outside the door, opened it slowly, careful not to wake anyone. Inside, he sneaked over to the Shelf of Improbable Things, where he pulled out his old jeans and, avoiding the dried pig's blood, held the jeans tightly over his new cut until the bleeding stopped. It took some time, but when it was done, he lay down on the couch. That night his sleep was fitful, his dreams full of winding, painful paths, and empty-eyed uncles with antlers growing from their heads, and bubbly floods of Coca-Cola.

He barely slept at all.

MAD

My uncle had the uncanny ability to leave his shadow behind. He'd staggered from the room minutes ago, but the damn thing lingered still, a blanket of shade in an already dark room. I stared into the old TV, now nothing more than a pathetic, wood-paneled box, and wondered, not for the first time, what I was going to do.

"Come on, Jamma," I said, heaving myself off the couch. "Let's get to bed."

Good start. Get the grandmother to bed. A micro-solution to a micro-problem. The decisiveness felt good.

Jamma took a swig of Coke from one hand, then the other. "But I'm thirsty."

"You're always thirsty," I said, bending down to grab her under the elbow.

"I don't need help," she said. "I'm old, but strong as—"

"Strong as an ox, I know." I crossed my arms, smiled as she stood without help. It was true: for a woman her age, she was surprisingly strong. We made a pit stop in the kitchen to set one can of Coke in the fridge, then a pit stop in the bathroom where I helped her sit on the toilet (again, with more than a little admonition).

Jamma had been living with us when my parents were killed; Uncle Les wasn't her son, so by all accounts she wouldn't even be here if it weren't for me. But there was no money for a decent nursing home, and we were her next of kin. Uncle Les could have put her in a state or county-run facility, which cost next to nothing, but he didn't. And I knew why.

Jamma could cope by herself if it came to it, but when I was home, the guilt of being away took over, and I found myself mothering her more than was probably necessary. It was her mind that needed the most assistance, and in that respect I was of little value.

We walked to Jamma's room, where I helped her into bed; she set the second Coke on the nightstand, picked up a pair of mittens she'd been knitting since the dawn of time. "I'm almost done with them."

She was always almost done with them, but I nodded and

smiled anyway. "They're going to be quite comfy, Jamma."

"My hands are always so cold, you know. And I'm very thirsty."

It was a constant push and pull: when I was here, I wanted to be anywhere else; when I was anywhere else, I wanted to be here. Wherever I was, I felt guilty for not being in the other place.

I sat on the edge of her bed, took the unfinished mittens, and placed them back on the nightstand. She liked her pillow fluffed; I fluffed it. She liked to lay her head so it fell right in the middle of the pillow; I helped her lay her head so it was exactly in the middle.

"How is school, Madeline?" On her sweet face, I saw a little of her old self where usually there was only vague emptiness. "What's the name of that college again?"

It was her most lucid moment in months. Not only did she remember the fact that I was (supposed to be) in college, she also remembered my name. A home run on a good day was Jamma recognizing my face when I walked in a room, but this . . . this was rare rationality.

"Bergen Community," I said softly.

"Bergen Community. Sounds lovely, dear."

I nodded, swallowed down the lump in my throat, then leaned over and kissed her on the forehead. It was strange, but I'd grown used to being forgotten, which made moments like this—moments of remembering—all the more difficult.

On my way out, I left the door open a crack just in case she needed anything. My room was across the hall, and even though she'd never once called out, I felt better knowing there were no barriers between us. If she needed me, I would know. I crawled under my covers and switched on the light

by my bedside; it had a bright-red lampshade that splashed its color across the room like a painting. I tried reading, but my mind wandered to thoughts of my mother, how she used to sing when she cooked, holding the spatula as a microphone, or how we had to put the Christmas ornaments on the tree in the exact same order every year. I thought of Dad, and how he loved me in his own quiet way. I felt it in his hugs, far louder than his voice. I thought of Jamma before the dementia set in—she was my mother's mother, and the two of them were thick as thieves, always playing pranks or whispering in the other room.

We were a family who knew one another.

And now I had Uncle Les. Dad's brother, though they couldn't be more different from each other. In a Venn diagram where set A = {Designated Guardians of Mad}, and set B = {People Who Don't Give a Shit About Mad}, the intersection = {Uncle Les}.

Uncle Les hadn't always been like this. I had memories of him from years ago, pictures in my head to prove his decentness. But that hardly mattered now. I was here now. Jamma was here now. And here, and now, there could be no future.

Macro-problems.

I switched off the red light. In the new darkness, I rolled over and closed my eyes. And I listened. Across the hall I heard the gentle, rhythmic *click-click* of Jamma's knitting needles, working on mittens she'd probably never finish. And on the other side of my wall—in my uncle's room—there were sounds too. Muffled curses, foul voices, the occasional low and deep moan. And always he sobbed in drunken lethargy before inevitably passing out on the floor.

This was the end of his daily routine.

Behind the relative safety of my closed eyelids, I re-

membered a day long before the accident, back when Mom and Dad were alive and things were still things. That day, we were let out of school early for teachers' Professional Development day. It was around noon, which meant Mom and Dad were both at work—so I walked home. Nearing our house, I heard music coming from an open window, and saw Uncle Les's car in the driveway, which was odd, as he rarely came over. I walked up the porch, recognizing the voice of my mother's favorite artist, Joan Baez. It was turned up pretty good, too. I opened the front door, walked inside, and received an education: about the largeness of the world, and my own smallness in it; about the speed with which truth could change; about how little I knew of the people I loved.

Uncle Les stood in our kitchen, wearing a beige pair of briefs and nothing more. He had his back to me: a mole on his left shoulder blade, a gleam of sweat across his skin. He drank orange juice straight from the container, holding it over the faucet as little trickles poured down the sides of his face and into the sink. Joan Baez was loud enough he hadn't heard me come in. And just when I was about to ask what the hell he thought he was doing, I heard her—Mom's voice from the bedroom down the hall. All she said was "*Lester*," but it was more than enough. I turned around, walked out of our house, and did not come back until dinner, when I was long expected and Joan Baez had been silenced, and no one was standing in our kitchen in their underwear, drinking orange juice straight from the carton like it was *his* fucking orange juice in the first place.

It was not his fucking orange juice.

On the other side of the wall, I heard my uncle collapse onto the floor, thus completing his daily routine. He never

knew I knew. Mom never knew either. I was glad about that. At least she died not knowing I knew the worst thing about her. And at least Uncle Les felt too guilty to put Jamma in a shitty home. But I was still left with the same question.

I opened my eyes in the darkness. "What am I going to do?" The darkness answered, as always, with complete silence.

seven

THE MANY CHUMPS OF SUBURBAN JERSEY
(or, Be the Racehorse)

Matisse's *Woman on a High Stool*.

That's what this room reminds me of.

. . .

"Do you like art, Sergeant Mendes?"

She sips her coffee, leans back in her chair. "Sure."

"Did you know Matisse and Picasso were friends? Or—not friends, exactly, but . . . they pushed each other to greatness."

"I didn't know that."

"Earlier, when you read my file, you mentioned I was obsessed with abstract art. Do you know why?"

She shakes her head.

"I love it because it's the only place where ugly and beautiful can mean the same thing. And if it's something shocking, something totally different, something people have never seen before"—I pull out my handkerchief, wipe my leaky mug—"all the better."

Sometimes you don't know why you feel something until you're talking about it. I've always known I loved Matisse. And since art does not require a why, I'd never quite nailed it down. Until now.

"Dad took me to the Museum of Modern Art," I say. "I saw

my first Matisse. It was called *Woman on a High Stool.* I sat in that room in that museum and stared at it for over two hours."

"What's it look like?"

"Just a woman sitting on a stool in a gray room. With a table. Matisse started the painting with a bunch of blues and greens but ended up covering most everything in gray. Except her knees. Her knees, he left blue and green. Dad always said, *Don't look at the colors that are there, V. Look at the colors that aren't.* He called it the *simmering underneath.* Said if you looked close enough, you could see colors in real life that no one else saw, colors that were there but covered up. Which is really something when you consider Matisse was a Fauve."

"A Fauve," says Mendes, though I can't tell if she's asking what it is or correcting my pronunciation. I choose to believe it's the former.

"Fauvism is a style of painting that finds inherent value in color itself," I say. "The Fauves believed colors were themselves symbols, rather than just physical descriptors. And see, that's what makes *Woman on a High Stool* so great."

"How so?"

"If Matisse believed color was the most important thing in a painting, why cover it all up? I think it means he understood the simmering underneath, probably better than anyone. Matisse knew *exactly* what he was doing."

. . .

"Vic, it seems we've veered somewhat from—"

"Have you ever been to MoMA?"

Mendes sighs, checks her watch. "Actually, no. But I've been to the Frick a couple of times. And the Met."

"So you ever notice how some people can look at a really

good painting or sculpture and they stand there with their hands folded across their waist, or one hand under their chin, their eyes all squinty, and then they nod their heads and say, *Hmm*, like they really get it, like the painting really means something on a deep level, and then—*poof*—they've seen enough? Time to move on to the next piece. They acknowledge the technique, the skill, the creativity, but they miss what's underneath. I don't know how people do that. I don't know how people just nod, and say, *Hmm*, and move on."

"Did your dad sit with you?"

"What?"

"You said your dad took you to the museum. Did he look at the painting for two hours too?"

"He sat for a while. I don't know. There was a multimedia piece in another room. A cellist or something played in front of a giant photograph. It was nice, but . . ."

"No Matisse," finishes Mendes.

I nod. "No Matisse."

. . .

. . .

"Dad likes—*liked* art. But he liked music more. You ever heard 'The Flower Duet'?"

Mendes shakes her head.

"It's part of an opera."

"I didn't know you liked opera," she says.

"I don't—not really. I just sort of . . ."

"Nod, and say, *Hmm*, and move on?"

I smile on the inside. "The only time I ever saw Dad cry had nothing to do with cancer. It was years ago, long before he got sick. I was in the backseat of the car, just tall enough to see his face in the rearview mirror while he drove. He had 'The Flower Duet' on repeat. And he didn't know I could see

him, but I could. And he was crying. I really hated that." I dig my fingernails into my wrist. I want this to hurt. Dad's memory has always been close, but there are times I feel it slipping.

"Victor." Mendes puts both elbows on the table, folds her hands in front of her face. "When this is over, I'd be happy to refer you to someone. It might . . . help, you know? To talk about these things with a professional."

At that moment there's a knock on the door.

Mendes sighs, lowers her hands. "Come in!"

Detective Ronald pokes his head inside the room, motions for Mendes to join him in the doorway. She does, and for a second they whisper. I can't make out much, but I definitely hear the words *still trying*. Mendes steps back a little, stares at Ronald like she only now recognizes his presence in the room. "So you basically called me over here to tell me you have nothing. God, Ron—okay. Where's Lieutenant Bell?"

"In his office, I think."

Mendes instructs Ron to wait in the room with me while she goes to chat with the lieutenant. Alone with Detective Ron, I put my forehead on the table, partly out of exhaustion, but mainly so I don't have to talk to him. He paces the room for a minute, then stops at the desk and flips through my file.

"What'd you think of Rockefeller Center?"

I raise my head from the table. "What?"

He leans over the open file on the table, picks up Dad's list. I'd almost forgotten Mendes still had it. "'Drop me from the top of our rock,'" he reads. "The observation deck on top of Rockefeller Center, right? I took"—his eyes dart to the open door, then back to me—"I went to Top of the Rock last year. Best skyline view in the city, hands down. Especially this time of year."

. . .

Son of a bitch.

. . .

Sergeant Mendes reappears, ushers Ron into the hallway, closes the door, and sits. "Okay, sorry about that." She says something else, but I don't hear her. I go to my Land of Nothingness, where I'm joined by my young parents, fresh-faced, smitten, standing on the rooftop of a skyscraper, the New York City skyline behind them.

Rockefeller Center. The Top of the Rock.

Maybe Detective Ron isn't a purebred poodle. Maybe he has a little racehorse in him after all.

(TWO days ago)

VIC

"Two days," I said.

"Technically, she's only been gone two *nights*," said Coco, scanning the menu as if we wouldn't just eat whatever Margo brought us. "It's only been one and half days, which is nothing. Hey, Zuz. D'you think those pepper jack fries contain any beaver's anal secrets? Tell the truth."

Nzuzi snapped once.

Coco sighed, closed the Napoleon's menu. "Mad was right, Vic. You broke me."

I stared across the table at the Kabongo brothers. Yesterday morning—the morning after I witnessed *Self-Portrait Man Terminates Television*—Nzuzi had disappeared. He was gone until lunchtime.

But hey.

It was no business of mine where Nzuzi went.

"What the frak is tricalcium phosphate?" said Coco, reading the back of a small bottle. She twisted it around to read the front. "'Organic Table Seasoning.' *Tricalcium phosphate* doesn't sound very 'organic' to me." Coco moved on to inspect a bottle of ketchup, while we waited patiently in our booth for whatever culinary scheme Margo had for us today.

All day yesterday, I'd wavered between telling Baz what I'd seen and not telling him. The brain-thinking part of my brain voted yea for the following reasons:

1. It could not erase the image of Mad's uncle, a fierce rendering of Matisse's *Self-Portrait*. (Actually this image made me want to tell Baz to bring his baseball bat.)

2. Those bruises on Mad's wrist—the ones she'd shown me on the roof of my grandparents' old house—now made a lot more sense. I knew the *origins* of those bruises. And that knowledge was now my responsibility. Because a person just can't let shit like that go on.

3. While it was true that I harbored meteoric repugnance for Frank the Boyfriend and his bury-your-head-in-the-sand-wear-a-suit-to-bed type mentality (not to mention the spoiled fruits of his loin, Klint and Kory), I never worried that Frank the Boyfriend might hurt Mom or me. But if that *had* been a concern, and someone else knew about it, I could only hope they would speak up.

The heart-thinking part of my brain voted nay for a single reason:

1. Apparently Mad had not told Baz. Ergo, she
   wanted it to be a secret. And I wanted her
   wants intact.

But: it wasn't enough.

So: I would tell him.

And: if Mad got pissed at me for giving up her secret, I could live with that. Honestly, if her being pissed was the downside to my saying something, I would take it over the downside to my not.

"*Bonjour, mes petits gourmands.*" In the time it took Margo to finish her absurd sentence, she had both hands on Baz's shoulders and a particularly intense gleam in her eye. "I'll get your sodas out pronto—and your water, Mbemba. And hey, I think you guys are gonna be pleased today."

"Why, you got more of those blazing alcoholic bananas?" asked Coco.

"Afraid the old grease trap is fresh outta rum. Have to wait till the next shipment for more Bananas Foster. No, this time I've got something a little healthier. My world-famous lettuce wraps!"

Margo was greeted with a leafy silence.

"Sorry," she said under her breath. "Still have that influx of lettuce."

"We will eat and be grateful," said Baz.

Margo Bonaparte stared at him for a second and then out of nowhere said, "How's Rachel?" She must have immediately regretted it—her eyes darted to the floor; she mumbled something about needing to check on the food and disap-

peared. Coco pulled out a pencil, began scribbling something on a napkin.

"So she's an early Chapter, then?" I asked.

Baz removed his Trenton Thunder baseball cap, set it on the table. "Who?"

"Margo."

"What makes you think that?"

"It was something Mad said just after I met you guys. I asked about money, and she said you guys had early Chapters around town who helped you out. Topher offered free tattoos, Norm seems ready to hand over his entire shop. It seems like each Chapter wants to give you more than a story. Anyway. You never pay Margo. And she never asks for payment. So I just figured—"

"The produce truck."

. . .

"The what?"

"A couple of days ago that produce truck almost squished you like a bug. Do you know why I pulled you back?"

I hadn't considered that Baz might need a specific reason other than saving my life.

"It's because you were not paying attention," he said. "You did not see what was coming down the road, but I did. I saw the produce truck. So I pulled you back."

"Okay."

He sipped his water.

"Baz, I don't understand."

"You do not have to understand."

Shit. Walked into that one.

"Look," he said. "It's simple. There are many people in this world—in this town—who are not paying attention. They do not see the oncoming produce truck."

"But you do?"

He nodded. "Usually. So why *not* do something? People usually sit back, shrug, and watch things happen. Awful things. I know this from experience. But I'm done shrugging. I'm done doing nothing. Anyway, I could use the stories."

I couldn't help hearing my father's voice in Baz's words. *Do something, V.*

. . .

Just as I opened my mouth to tell him what was going on with Mad, Coco said, "That's *perfect*, Zuz. Good call."

Next to me, her pencil flew furiously while Nzuzi leaned across the table, nodding in approval. I watched the little girl as she wrote, her face pulled tight in concentration. The poor girl had witnessed more than her share of tragedies. No reason to pile this on top. I sipped my Sprite, decided it could wait until Coco wasn't in earshot.

Margo returned, carrying a tray full of iceberg lettuce, individual bowls of steak, rice, fresh green beans, cauliflower, sprouts, and some sort of savory peanut sauce.

"Frakking A," said Coco. "I'm gonna have to revise a few of these lyrics."

All four of us ate hungrily, and in no time the table was a mess of napkins and wiped-clean plates. Coco went back to her scribbling, pointing to her napkin occasionally and asking Nzuzi questions about which lines he preferred. Whatever she was working on, he took very seriously, always taking time to consider before his nonverbal answer.

"This is a good one, Baz," said Coco, head down in concentration. "Might even be a hit."

"Oh yeah?" said Baz, winking at me, then looking at Coco very seriously. "What's it about?"

"Uh-uh. Not until it's ready. But I'll tell you what. You give

me a thousand bucks, you can put it in your book."

"A thousand bucks, huh?"

Coco nodded. "And that's a motherfrakking *steal*."

"How about seven dollars?"

"Split the difference—let's say four hundred."

Baz laughed, said he'd have to think about it.

"Where did you get the idea to write a book?" I asked him.

"My mother."

"Was she a writer too?"

Baz tossed his napkin onto his empty plate, crossed his arms, and smiled a little. "Maybe someday I will tell you about her. For now, let's just say that my book is sort of her legacy. Like your father's urn."

I'd been so preoccupied with Mad's situation, for the first time since finding Dad's note, I hadn't given a single thought to the list.

"Maybe it's time you left," he said.

I was right in the middle of prying a sprout from my teeth when he said it. I looked at Coco, then Nzuzi, before I realized he was talking to me.

"What?" I said, leaving the sprout to fend for itself.

"Maybe you should leave."

It felt like this: Father Raines suggesting I fornicate.

"'Drop me from the top of our rock,'" said Baz. "I assume you still don't know what this means, and that's fine. What I want to know is, when was the last time you even thought about it?"

. . .

No one cut to the chase like Baz Kabongo. Occasionally this bluntness was refreshing, but it also kept me perpetually on edge, knowing he might ask anything at any given time.

"I think about it a lot," I said. It was a lie, and we both knew it. Recently my brain had thought nothing but *Madmadmadmadmadmadmadmadmadmad*. "When was the last time you thought about it?"

I regretted the question as soon as I asked it, knowing exactly how he would answer. How anyone other than me *should* answer.

"He was not my father," said Baz. "I like you, Vic. You are welcome to stay with us for as long as you like. I'm not telling you to leave, I'm not even saying I want you to leave. But I made a deal to *help* you do this thing, not to do it for you. And so I will say it again. Maybe you should leave."

"And go where?"

"Home, Vic."

* * *

Before leaving Napoleon's, Margo passed her number to Baz for the hundredth time, reminded him to call. He stuck the paper in his pocket and said he would try.

Outside, we started the walk back to New Milford, passing Foodville along the way. Coco emerged from whatever she'd been working on long enough to beg for ice cream. Baz said there wasn't enough in the budget, to which Coco responded by accusing him of sounding like a soccer mom.

"Still don't know why you won't just let me take it," she said.

"You know my rule," said Baz.

"What rule?" I asked.

Coco's sigh was bigger than Coco's self. "Baz has a rule about stealing. Don't steal if *you* can afford it, *only* steal if *they* can afford it, and what-the-frak else. I can't remember."

Baz said, "Don't steal if *you* can afford it, *only* steal if *they* can afford it, and never steal what you don't need."

We walked in silence for a few seconds, Foodville passing like a tortoise on our right.

"I'm sorry," said Coco, "but it sounds like you want us to steal."

Nzuzi snapped once.

"See?" said Coco. "Your own brother agrees. Why not just say, *Only steal what you need*?"

Nzuzi snapped once.

"Same thing," said Baz.

"Well, one of them is confusing as balls, and one of them isn't. It's like saying, *Don't* not *punch Spoils in the nutsack*, which, I'm sorry, sounds like you want me to punch Spoils in the nutsack."

Everyone else laughed, but I only halfway registered the conversation. I fell into step beside Baz, while behind us Coco went back to her scribbling.

"Baz, I'd like to address what you said—"

"Are you in love with Mad?"

The question should have taken me off guard. Instead I felt relief that someone else had noticed. The snow crunched beneath our feet. I said, "Maybe."

"You've never been in love before?" asked Baz.

"I thought so. Lots of times. But Mad is . . . different."

An image: two compasses, one pointing east, one pointing west. Mom and Dad's love was global. It made no difference which way they went. As long as they lived, they always ended up in the same place. For a heart-thinker such as myself, this was a momentous notion. And I realized that even though it felt like I was spinning in different directions, my entire compass pointed toward Mad.

"She's in trouble," I said. Coco was far enough behind us and totally enthralled in whatever she was writing. "Mad is in trouble, Baz. She needs help."

Baz's face changed, but I couldn't read him. He stared ahead, straight down the road as he walked. "What do you mean?"

"I woke up two nights ago, just as she was leaving. I followed her. She has an uncle. And a grandmother. She lives in a house not too far from the orchard."

. . .

"I know."

I almost tripped over my own feet. "You know?"

"Yes."

. . .

. . .

"Um. Okay."

"Nzuzi checked on her yesterday morning."

"I don't understand. So Mad told you?"

Baz shook his head. "Months ago Nzuzi followed her just like you. He woke me that night, led me to the house, showed me."

"What did you see?"

"She was watching television. With an old woman. It was dirty, but they seemed okay."

"What about the uncle? Did you see the uncle?"

Now that the conversation was out there, it felt urgent that he understood. I needed Baz to see the same painting I saw: *Self-Portrait Man Terminates Television*. The problem was you couldn't force someone to stand in front of a painting.

Baz shook his head. "There was no uncle."

"There *is* an uncle, Baz." I wanted to rip this painting off

the wall and stick it in his face. "And he's awful. I'm afraid he might hurt her."

Baz didn't speak for a few moments, but when he did, I heard the very same conflict I'd felt for two days.

"Okay," he said. "We'll go tonight. After Coco is asleep."

I nodded, felt a small sense of relief.

Coco and Nzuzi ran up behind us. "Finished!"

We were still a solid mile and a half away from the warmth of the greenhouse; it was downright frigid.

"Finished what?"

Coco nodded at Nzuzi, who, astonishingly, began beatboxing.

"Yo, yo. Uh," said Coco in low, rhythmic intervals. "Let us wrap . . . the Lettuce Wrap. Let us rap . . . the Lettuce Rap." Nzuzi's beatboxing remained steady, though somehow increased in complexity as Coco broke into limerick:

We're the real Kids of Appetite here to say
Been wrapping our lettuce since way back in the day
It's crunchy, it's healthy, it's sort of sweet
Gimme those veggies, don't gimme your meat
Lettuce ain't no filler, son, why you playin'?
It's legit delicious, yo, I'm just sayin'
Who are we to boss you around?
I'll tell you in a sec, gotta drag this chorus down

Let us wrap . . . the Lettuce Wrap
Let us rap . . . the Lettuce Rap

Not cola, not classic, I'm Coke, that's enough
Made by Queens machines, so you know that I'm tough
Over here is Baz, he old, but he cool

Right there, that's Spoils, ain't nobody's fool
My boy Zuz dropping truths like a motherfrakking boss
He speaks in other ways—don't hear him? Your loss
Mad ain't here, so you know what to do
Leave a message once it beeps—here, I'll do it too

(Beep!)
Let us wrap . . . the Lettuce Wrap
Let us rap . . . the Lettuce Rap

Suffice it to say, we just took you to school
Played you like a fiddle, done soaked up your cool
Listen up now, chump (and you a chump unanimous)
Said it once, twice, thrice, now infinitous
I'll keep preaching my sermon, keep gettin' knocked down
I know a good thing when a good thing's around
And here's that good thing, imma say it again
It's simple, it's truth, here it is now, lean in
If you wanna hella good thing to munch
The KOA endorse lettuce for lunch

Let us wrap . . . the Lettuce Wrap
Let us rap . . . the Lettuce Rap

The streets of New Milford did not know what hit them. And as we rapped Coco's song once, twice, infinitous times, I went to my Land of Nothingness, and there I saw the many chumps of suburban Jersey, hiding in their basements, waiting for the anthem to end.

They would be waiting a long time.

* * *

After returning to the greenhouse, it took Coco pretty much forever to fall asleep. Juiced as she was from the success of her latest rap hit, she lay in her sleeping bag and beseeched Baz to tell a story. Ergo, he caved, and told a story from the Bible about Moses leading the Israelites out of Egypt. Coco interrupted a couple of times with title ideas for Baz's book (*Pillar of Fire* and *Bible II: The Reckoning*). We were trekking down Mt. Sinai before she started snoring, at which point Baz told Nzuzi to stay with Coco, that we were going to check on Mad, but would return soon.

Baz and I left the orchard together, stepping out into the momentously cold night to *do* something.

My inner sideways hug shuddered mightily.

Baz said, "The Mets suck, you know."

I'd just finished crawling under the fence, where my Metpants had gotten snagged on a link. Baz had hopped over effortlessly and was waiting on the other side, with his cutting remark.

Like I hadn't heard it before.

"Yeah, I know. They've had some decent years recently, though."

As we walked toward Mad's house, Baz held out his Thunder baseball cap, explained how exciting it was to watch the young Yankees up-and-comers. I thought of the spring Dad and I decided to be Trenton Thunder fans. As the minor league affiliate of the New York Yankees, the team played games that provided us with early intel on the enemy. Double-A ball meant fewer suicide squeezes, more raffle tickets and wrinkled hot dogs. But Dad used to say, *Baseball's baseball, V. Beats the hell outta sitting at home, twiddlin' your thumbs.*

I used to hate it when he said *twiddle*. Now? Shit. Missed it.

For a couple of blocks, Baz talked Thunder and Yankees baseball with the enthusiasm of a true baseball fan. Even so, I had little tolerance for a team that prioritized purchasing players over developing them (Jeter notwithstanding).

Twenty-seven championships? Sweet. I'll take my two and go home.

But hey.

It probably made sense, like, on a personal level. The Yankees were *win at all cost*. The Mets were *good game, good game*. The Yankees were Ruth, Gehrig, Mantle. The Mets were Seaver and Piazza. (Gooden and Strawberry both ended up in Yankees uniforms, so Dad said they didn't count.) Much as I hated admitting it, the Mets aspired to certain levels of automobile rental entrepreneurship. But they had heart. And this was the number-one selling point for a couple of tried and true heart-thinkers like my dad and me.

"You should consider switching sides," said Baz.

The suggestion made me unexpectedly happy.

Dad's friends used to say the same thing.

We arrived at Mad's house, where I led the way up to the same front bay window, warning Baz not to step in the storm drain, as I had last time. Baz took off his hat, pressed his face right up against the glass to get a full view of the room. It was still a mess, though less than before. The TV was gone, which shouldn't have been surprising, considering it had been obliterated. Still. I'd been primed to show it to Baz, counting on it as evidence that things were not okay, that her uncle not only existed, but was flat-out dangerous.

After a few minutes of nothing, we walked around the sides and back of the house, looking for other windows or visual points of access. I appreciated that Baz wasn't just here

to appease me. Or at least, I didn't think he was. He seemed genuinely concerned. Likewise, I understood his hesitations. Our being here, however right it might be, was a definite breach of Mad's trust.

We checked the front window one more time, got a brief glimpse of Mad. She was wearing tall rubber gloves and appeared to be cleaning the house, which my current spy-brain found suspiciously domestic.

There was no sign of her grandmother. There was no sign of her uncle.

Everything seemed to be well and in order.

Eventually Baz insisted we go.

"Baz, wait," I whispered.

"What?"

. . .

"Where's your hat?"

He reached up out of instinct. But yeah. It was gone. We searched high and low, did two circles around the house, but found no sign of the hat. Baz kept saying it was no big deal, but the thing was: it was. That hat was a direct link to him, and if Mad found it, she'd know he had been there. We did more circles around the house, but after turning up nothing, we eventually called it quits.

The walk back to the orchard was a quiet one. We didn't talk about baseball. We didn't talk about much of anything.

* * *

I lay in the darkness, wide-awake, waiting on verbal confirmation that Baz and Nzuzi were asleep, kicking myself again for leaving my iPod charger at home. Mostly I could have used the soaring sopranos. Those two ladies were ab-

solute aces at instilling courage, and right now courage was in short supply.

When we left Mad's house, part of me knew I wasn't done for the night. Part of me knew I would go back.

So many parts.

As if pieces of a puzzle had come to me intermittently throughout the day. One piece: the bruises on Mad's arms and wrists. One piece: the growling of Mad's uncle. One piece: a rifle through a TV. At first I'd been confused about why Mad would even go back. Apparently her uncle had been too drunk or apathetic (or both) to notice his niece's absence. There was no talk of school or friends or even, *Mad, my God, where have you been*? She certainly didn't return for him.

It had to be the old lady. Jamma, Mad called her. I'd bet anything it was her grandmother, and I'd bet even more she was the reason Mad continued returning to the house.

. . .

Baz's breath had settled into an even rhythm, his chest rising and falling in time. Nzuzi's, too. I swiveled on the couch, noiselessly lowering my feet to the ground. From here I could see their eyes closed—good enough for me.

I sneaked down the center walkway, grabbed my coat off the rack, and exited the greenhouse. Outside, the night wind turned my leaky mug into a Popsicle. I ran across the orchard, the bridge, all the way to the fence, and was just about to scurry underneath when I heard the sound of a single cough.

I froze.

. . .

. . .

The nearest bush or tree was at least ten yards away. Nothing to hide behind.

"Mr. Maywood?" I said, my voice thinner than string.

No answer.

"Who's there?"

. . .

. . .

. . .

Nothing.

Just a snowy, nighttime quiet.

I tried to convince myself that the cough had been nothing more than a figment of my imagination.

Be the Racehorse, Benucci. Be the motherfrakking Racehorse.

Under the fence I went, and for the second time that night I caught my Metpants on the chain link. Prying myself loose, I retraced our steps from before, only this time I ran. Very suddenly I felt I'd waited too long. Horrible imaginings took root in my brain, but the worst: Mad's face as a TV.

Her beautiful, simultaneously extreme opposite punk cut.

Her smile and her singing.

Her self.

I ran faster.

So fast.

Until I was there. In the same spot.

Under the front bay window.

My right foot fell out from under me. I cursed, pulled it out of the same snow-covered storm drain I'd fallen in last time, when I saw it—a Thunder cap. Relieved, I picked it up and slipped it onto my head. This provided me with an extra measure of incognito recon garb (though seeing as how I had no incognito recon garb to speak of, the hat wasn't so much an *extra* measure, as it was *a* measure).

I stepped around the storm drain and looked through the window.

Mad had been cleaning, all right. And she'd gotten plenty done in the hour or so it took the Kabongos to fall asleep. The magazines and pizza boxes, soda cans and bottles, the greasy paper plates and dust and dirt—all of it was gone. In fact, were it not for the gun rack on the wall, and the mounted antlers next to that, I might have thought I'd had the wrong house. I waited a few minutes, just to see if Mad would enter with a Coca-Cola, plop down in the recliner like last time.

Still nothing. No sign of Mad, Jamma, or the Self-Portrait Man.

I bent low, ran around the side of the house.

Swift. Soft. Stealth. Spook. Spy. Speed. Silence.

At the far right corner of the house, a single light shone through a window. It was dim, slightly reddish, like a lighthouse through a squall. A curtain was drawn, thin enough to let the light through, thick enough that I couldn't see inside.

Behind the house, I stepped onto a patio with stained-brown furniture, a grill, a stone ottoman, and a table that looked like it hadn't been used in decades. A set of sliding glass doors led out to the patio. No curtains this time, just long, vertical blinds.

They were not drawn.

I pressed my face against the glass and quietly observed the makings and colors of a very average American kitchen: beige refrigerator, silver toaster, black microwave, brown stove. I quietly observed something else, though, just below the surface.

Don't look at the colors that are there, V. Look at the colors that aren't.

I'd always suspected Matisse's paintings were alive, that

they studied me as much as I studied them. I wondered if they could feel their own colors, especially the ones that had been covered up. And I wondered about Matisse himself, what it must have taken for a Fauve to cover up all those brilliant colors, inch by inch, with muted tones. Such restraint. But well worth it. The figures in the paintings felt their colors whether we saw them or not.

I went to my Land of Nothingness and felt a pulsing vibrancy, a burst of color underneath this kitchen: red.

So much red.

I reached for the handle and found that it was unlocked.

* * *

The air in the beige-red kitchen was only slightly warmer than the air outside.

This is how I knew I was indoors.

The carpets smelled like cats and cold pizza and Lysol.

This is how I knew I was in the living room.

Blank walls stared at me, whispered of distant memories.

This is how I knew I was in the hallway.

"What do you think of them?" she asked in a whisper, on her bed, in the dark, in a nightgown and slippers, two cans of Coca-Cola on the nightstand beside her. "I finally finished my mittens." She held out both hands to me, admiring the fluffy pink mitten on each one. "I'm warm. Finally warm."

This is how I knew I just met Jamma.

The silence was broken by a whine, something like an animal, only meeker, more desperate and muted.

This is how I knew Mad was here.

Across the hallway, the door was cracked. I put my eye up to the opening. Inside, the red, the dim, the room with the drawn curtain.

This is how I knew Mad was in trouble.

The Self-Portrait Man sat on the floor, his back to me. His words weren't just slurred, they were intrinsically venomous, as if he hated himself for whatever it was he was saying. Through the crack, I watched him raise a large open hand and bring it down with force.

A shriek. And crying.

"No one gave you permission to touch that picture," said the Self-Portrait Man, raising a bottle to his lips, downing what was left in a few large swigs.

My legs were the calmest part of my body: they turned, walked by Jamma's room, made their way to the living room, past the mounted antlers where Mad's jacket hung, and stopped in front of the gun rack. I reached up, pulled the heaviest-looking rifle from its place of prominence, turned, walked calmly back to the red room.

I could never shoot anyone. Even if the heart-thinker in me managed to pull the trigger, I'm not sure the brain-thinker would know how. But here was the conclusion at which my factual heart arrived: a large, heavy rifle was as good as a baseball bat.

I pulled Baz's Thunder cap low over my eyes and pushed open the door. My feet continued walking until I stood right behind the Self-Portrait Man. He sat on top of Mad, pinning down the arms and legs of my Stoic Beauty, my first kiss, my first love, my first everything. I thought of Mad's up-closeness, and the word *together*, the Hinton Vortex, and feeling like an *I am*, and her quiet-lovely voice singing of junkyards and false starts, and the momentousness of

Altneu, and simultaneous extreme opposites, and the comparison of wrists on the rooftop of my dead grandparents' house, all those bruises and the Self-Portrait Man was to blame, to blame, to blame . . .

. . .

It was quick.

Like someone hit the fast-forward button in my body. I hoisted the rifle high above my head, slammed it down with every ounce of myself, and watched my two favorite Matisse paintings become one as the Self-Portrait Man collapsed into *The Red Room*.

I dropped the rifle to the floor.

"I am a Super Racehorse," I said.

And that was how I knew.

EIGHT

COMING UP ROSES
(or, As I Opened the Door)

I see the blood even now. All of it, gushing like water from a hose. And his eyes, turned off. And the other eyes too, lit up like fire.

"Madeline," says Bundle, draining the vestiges of his coffee.

I shift my weight to the other hip. "I once had this cat named Justin."

"What?"

"For my twelfth birthday, Dad brought home a kitten. It was female, but when Mom asked what we should name her, I was all, *Let's call her Justin!* I was twelve, what can I say? Justin it was. When Mom and Dad died, the cat came with me to Uncle Les's house."

"Madel—"

"My uncle had one of those animatronic singing fish. You remember those? The kind that turned its head and sang right at you?"

Even Bundle knows better than to interrupt now; he hums under his breath, low and out of tune.

"'Take Me to the River,'" he says. "Al Green, right?"

"That's the song. I don't know who sings it. Other than the fish."

For a moment the faint hum of the digital recorder is a cricket during silence. And all I can see are the eyes: one pair turned off, one pair on fire.

My God . . .

"Justin the Cat hated that stupid fish. She didn't trust it, but she was too curious to leave it alone. She used to climb up on the back of the sofa so she could reach it up on the wall. She'd sniff at it, claw at it—I think she wasn't sure whether to pounce on the fish, run from it, or take a bite out of it. The whole thing just drove Uncle Les nuts. Said if I couldn't control my own pet, he'd control her for me. What you have to understand—I mean, it's not like Uncle Les was rotten from the beginning. When Jamma and I first moved in, he was nice, even. Sad but not mean. He was trying, you know. But . . ."

"Madeline, what are we talking about here?"

I take another sip of water, the last gulp in the glass. The cut on my lower lip still stings, not to mention the throbbing pain in my back and hips. "One day I came home from school, and Justin was missing. I scoured the house, turned the whole place upside down. I walked out onto the back deck, past the patio furniture and grill, all the way to the edge of the property, where a shallow creek ran behind our house. I found her like that—sopping wet, moving with the motion of the weak current, no telling how long she'd been there. Her eyes were like a doll's or . . . a puppet's. They didn't look dead. They looked like they'd never been alive in the first place. And then, behind me, from an open window of the house, I heard singing."

I wipe my eyes, look straight ahead at Bundle, and quietly hum.

MAD

Vic dropped the rifle to the floor.

"I am a Super Racehorse," he said.

I barely recognized him in Baz's baseball cap, but then it was hard to see much of anything at the moment. My eye was swollen almost completely shut; it hurt like fire and shards of glass. I sat up in a daze, leaned over, and checked Uncle Les's pulse.

"He's alive."

Vic's hand was on my shoulder. "You okay?"

Everything was blurred, fuzzy, like I was peering through a moldy shower liner. Behind me, Vic said something about calling the police, and I vaguely registered him leaving the room. I felt the rest of my life would be this way, one nebulous happenstance after another where I would never quite grasp what anyone ever said or did. I watched Uncle Les breathe, up and down, in and out—life required every direction. It needed the push and the pull, the simultaneous extreme opposites. An empty bottle lay at his feet, and just as suddenly as the vagueness was on me, I pulled back the liner and everything came into focus.

I turned, ran stiffly from the room. My left hip, the one that had taken the brunt of Uncle Les's weight, throbbed from the inside out. I shut the door, looked around for something to barricade it with. An old armoire stood at the end of the hallway. Moving to one side of the armoire, I put my shoulders and back into the pushing, but it barely budged.

Vic came running back. "I called the cops."

"Help me with this."

Vic hesitated. "I think we should go."

"What? No."

"Mad, I hit him. What if he's . . . I don't know. And the cops are gonna ask all sorts of questions."

I pointed to Jamma's room, where my grandmother was in bed, admiring her mittens like the whole world wasn't spinning off its axis. "I'm not leaving her. Now help me."

Vic took off Baz's Thunder cap, set it on top of the armoire, and helped me push the thing so it sat squarely in front of my bedroom door. And I don't know if it was the sight of Jamma right now, or the idea that we'd just called the police on my own uncle, or the fact that things had been so bad for so long, I'd forgotten it was something to call the police about, but at that moment I felt what little food I'd had to eat that day boiling in my stomach.

"I'm gonna be sick."

I ran into the bathroom, slammed the door behind me, staggered to the toilet, and threw up. After, I stuck my face under the faucet to let the cool water run over my swollen eye. On the corner of the bathroom counter sat a framed photograph, the catalyst of the evening. I turned off the water, picked up the photo, and stared at a shadow.

There were no pictures of my parents in this house. Uncle Les had seen to that. I kept my own box of them hidden in my closet. We'd been a family once, with homemade Halloween costumes and broken vases and pulled teeth and cookies for Santa and time-out corners and movie nights— and now, nothing. Whenever I could, I spent some time with what I had left: photographs. And today, I found this photo. I don't remember it being taken, which is just the way families operate. You live with these people; they are in your space and you are in theirs, and even if what you're

doing doesn't require documentation, sometimes documentation happens. And there we were in the photo, all three of us happy together, pleased as pie, just sitting, doing something or nothing, it really didn't matter.

And I liked it. So I put it in this frame and set it on the bathroom counter. I don't know what I thought. Maybe that Uncle Les wouldn't mind. But I knew better. I thought about that day when I came home early and found him drinking orange juice that did not belong to him. I thought about the flirty lilt of my mother's voice from the bedroom, and I knew—they loved each other. My uncle fell in love with his brother's wife, and while her death may have been enough to make Uncle Les drink himself into oblivion, to hit this girl in his house who was nothing but a reminder of a love that was not his to claim, to remove all photographic evidence, effectively wiping Mom from his memory—I would not let him wipe her from mine.

I placed the framed photo back on the counter, carefully standing it upright.

In the mirror, I tried to straighten my hair a little. Bruises and scars, and a swollen eye . . .

"*I'm a junkyard full of false starts.*" I sang the words in a whisper, the way Elliott Smith did, the way a favorite song should be sung. "*And I don't need your permission to bury my love—*"

From the other side of the door: a loud crash.

"Vic?" I said loudly.

Nothing.

Breathe. In and out. *Breathe.*

In my head, I heard Vic's song, the opera of debilitating beauty, and I heard my song, "Coming Up Roses," both of them mashed together in the most glorious medley of all

time. As I opened the door, time slowed, and I saw everything in vivid detail.

As I opened the door, I regretted not finishing what Vic had started, picking up the rifle and ending my uncle's life while I still had the chance.

As I opened the door, I saw the old armoire in my head, and I knew where the crashing sound had come from.

As I opened the door, I saw my uncle holding Vic from behind, his muscular arms wrapped around Vic's neck like a python, choking off any chance of air or escape. They stood in the middle of the newly cleaned living room, and Vic's face was purple, and on his neck I saw a tiny spot of bright red where the jagged-sharp edges of Uncle Les's broken bottle met Vic's skin.

As I opened the door, I heard nothing but our two songs floating around the house like flung roses in slow motion.

I heard nothing. . . .

NINE

COCA-COLA
(or, This Is How It Ends)

Mendes holds her pen between her thumb and forefinger, her hand resting on the file in front of her. "This afternoon you opened our conversation by discussing all the girls you'd fallen in love with. We've talked about art and family, and your own personal struggles."

. . .

"So?"

"So, what am I missing?"

"What do you mean?"

"Vic, you've been telling this story, and I'm happy to listen, but you're stalling. I wanna know why."

. . .

"What time is it?" I ask.

"That's the second time you've asked. What difference does it make?"

Before I can come up with anything, Mendes stands, walks around behind me, leans down into my ear, and whispers, "Victor, I wanna know what you know. Why keep protecting Kabongo? You say you were in the house when it happened—okay, fine, I believe you. No more bullshit. Tell me what you saw."

. . .

"Do you know what the literal translation of *Fauve* is, Miss Mendes?"

"Wild beast."

She says it like it's nothing, like she was just waiting for me to ask.

"I get it," she says, her voice urgent, her whispers tickling my ear. "The simmering underneath. I do. But, Vic—you're not Matisse. This isn't abstract art, and you're not a Fauve. You can't make this pretty, no matter how much gray you throw on it. You know what I think? I think you're a kid who saw something that scared the shit out of you."

I go to my Land of Nothingness. There, few words are spoken, and all beauty is abstract. There, questions are traded and wounds healed. There, moms don't change and dads don't die.

"Victor. Why did Baz Kabongo kill Mad's uncle?"

I go to my Land of Nothingness, where sopranos fly.

"He didn't, Miss Mendes."

(TWO days ago)

VIC

This is how it ends. There is nothing left to consider. My red light is fading, almost gone. I am separated by oceans, far removed from the magic of the bell tower, where I defied mathematics and everything by kissing the loveliest girl I'd known. I am alone inside a reverse cocoon. So many

deaths eluded by inches: that slip on the snowy rock up on Rockefeller Lookout, a mighty plummet off the Palisades; the near miss with the produce truck; my many multitudes boiled down to one, as I become the rock soaring through the air, clanking off the deck gun, plopping into the dark water of the Hackensack River. I will sink to the bottom and exist forever without anyone knowing about me.

. . .

Mad stood frozen in the bathroom doorway. She stared at me. Time was no longer a thing, nor sound, nor slow, nor fast—only separation. The Self-Portrait Man held me from behind, digging the tool of separation into the skin of my throat, slowly carving a new tiny path, a path going somewhere dark, pulling me down . . .

And like *that* . . . sound returned.

Two snaps.

MAD

Zuz came out of nowhere.

The first punch landed squarely on Uncle Lester's left cheek, knocking him back a couple of feet. The shard of bottle fell from his hands; Vic, now released from my uncle's grip, fell to one side. Palm open, Zuz whipped Uncle Lester across the face once, twice, three times. Uncle Les hit back, landed a blow on Zuz's mouth, but it didn't seem to faze him.

I found feeling in my feet again, ran over to Vic, and helped him up. What was left of the bottle I kicked across the room, where it landed next to my jacket on the floor,

and even in the madness of everything, I found this incredibly odd.

Why is my jacket on the floor?

Above it, on the wall, there was the gun rack: three rifles, the fourth still on the floor of my room. Next to it, where Uncle Lester's prized antlers had been mounted on a plaque, there was now only its empty outline on the wall, a light spot where years of sun and dust and grime had been unable to penetrate.

The ivory antlers were gone.

I turned back to the fight, saw Uncle Lester take one last drunken swing, missing by a wide margin. Zuz did not punch back. He'd won and they both knew it. In one last forceful motion, he pushed Uncle Lester into the shadow of the hallway, and I waited for the sound of my uncle's body hitting the ground, but it never came. Instead a different sound—crushing and crackling and ill. And out of the shadows, Uncle Les stumbled forward, his eyes turned off, not the eyes of a dying or dead thing, but the eyes of a thing that had never been alive to begin with, the eyes of a puppet, a doll. I'd seen the look before, though I couldn't say where.

And I saw those ivory antlers emerge from his mouth as if he were throwing them up, their sharp ends impaling his skull from back to front like a toothpick through a ripe grape. The toothpick moved now, ever so gently, as blood gushed like a broken fire hydrant; and, sliding backward by inches, the antlers exited the way they came, the sickest of ingestions.

I saw Uncle Les fall to the ground. Those antlers he so loved, and the hours spent admiring them on the wall, never once suspecting they would be his final undoing.

I saw my grandmother standing in her slippers, blood

spatter across her face and nightgown, and her eyes connected with mine, and I'd never seen that kind of fire. They were ancient and primal, those of a den mother protecting her young. They were lucid. For a moment her entire body shook from top to bottom, the way an animal dries itself off when it's wet. And then her eyes glazed, and she looked down at the mittens on her hands as if they'd acted of their own accord. "I'm still thirsty, though," said Jamma quietly, continuing some imaginary conversation. She turned and walked into the kitchen.

"So very thirsty."

Ten

AND DONE SO MIGHTILY
(or, Those Tenacious Molecules of Chance)

When the dust from the atomic cloud clears, the room is eerily silent.

"I don't believe you," says Bundle.

"Believe what you want."

"Mad, come on. You're telling me—you're saying it was your grandmother. Your eighty-something-year-old grandmother."

"She's strong as an ox, dude."

The door flies open, and a woman walks right up to me, completely ignoring Bundle. "Madeline, I'm Sergeant Mendes. I need you to tell me your grandmother's name."

Vic stands behind her; I smile at him and he inside-smiles back, and I'm breathing steadily for the first time in hours, and God, I've missed him.

"Her name, please," says Sergeant Mendes.

"You took her to the hospital and you don't know her name?"

"I didn't take her personally. What's her name?"

"Olivia."

"Olivia what?"

"Chambers."

Bundle sighs, puts his hands behind his head. "Sarah, please. This is asinine."

Mendes leans over the digital recorder, says, "Interview between Madeline Falco and Detective Bundle terminated at"—she checks her watch—"eight thirteen p.m." She pushes stop, looks at Bundle. "I don't think it is, Herman."

Vic and I sit silently in the room while Sergeant Mendes and Detective Bundle step into the hallway. Bundle doesn't pull the door closed on his way out, so we hear pretty much everything. Mendes sends Ron (a detective, apparently) to call Lieutenant Bell first, then Bergen Regional Medical Center, and inform them the police are on their way to pick up Olivia Chambers. She then mobilizes a slew of Hackensack's finest to check the back room at Babushka's, Napoleon's Pub—any place Nzuzi Kabongo might be hiding—sending extra officers to the orchard, last greenhouse on the right, with instructions to get whatever DNA and prints they can off any and all vinyl records, specifically by the band Journey.

"I knew we moved too quickly with this," she says. "I told Lieutenant Bell, but—*shit*. I should have pushed harder."

"Sarah, DNA does not lie. Now this story they're telling, it's not—"

Mendes reappears in the room, apparently uninterested in Bundle's opinion; Bundle follows closely behind, and there's something in the contrasting looks on their faces, their differences in body language—hers with a sense of urgency; his with a sense of, well, dinner—that is the perfect illustration of the two. Mendes is in charge, and everyone in the room knows it.

"I need to speak to Nzuzi pronto," she says. "Do you know where he is?"

The Madifesto dictates: *when parsing words, avoid the spirit of the question, and answer only what is asked.*

"No," I say.

Vic looks at me, says nothing.

"Sarah, let's talk facts," says Bundle, raising his right thumb. "The baseball cap. Kabongo's DNA was in the cap, the cap was found at the scene."

"Oh," says Vic.

The word sort of seeps out of him, but I hear the revelation behind it. I feel the same revelation, having wondered what caused the police to land on Baz in the first place. Surely it's not just the hat.

"What, *oh*?" asks Bundle.

Vic says, "I wore his hat that night."

Bundle crosses his arms. "Let's say that's true. The DNA on the antlers is rock solid. Kabongo held that thing *in his hands*. We know this. It is a scientific fact."

Utterly confused, I say the first thing that comes to mind. "Zuz tried to pull it out." The room turns to me while I recount the rest of the evening: how Zuz rushed over to Uncle Les, tried to pry the antlers out of my uncle, thinking maybe it wasn't too late; how we cleaned Jamma's face, changed her clothes, put her to bed, and rushed out the back door just as the police arrived; how we burned her bloody nightgown in a trash can back at the orchard; how we told Baz what had happened and stayed up all night, trying to figure out what to do.

Bundle shakes his head. "It was *Baz's* DNA on the murder weapon, not his brother's."

"Was it an exact match?" asks Vic. No one says anything at first; I think we're all surprised at the question. "Brothers have similar DNA profiles, don't they?"

Mendes puts both hands to her temples, rubs in tiny circles. Bundle, sensing his case crumbling, is all kinds of flustered now. "Fine," he says. "The Blythe case, then."

"He's in a coma," says Mendes.

"We have evidence."

"Circumstantial at best," says Mendes. "No weapon, no prints, no eyewitnesses. None who aren't in a coma, anyway."

Bundle stares at Sergeant Mendes for a second, his face red and puffy. He tilts his head a little, turns, and storms out of the room.

"Why do you need Zuz's DNA?" I ask.

"What?"

"In the hallway, you sent officers to get Nzuzi Kabongo's DNA."

"We'll need it to run against what we found at the crime scene. If you're telling the truth, it should be a closer match, which would more or less negate our evidence against Baz." Mendes sighs, picks up the digital recorder. "Do me a favor, you two. Don't leave town for a while, okay? I'm sure we'll have some follow-up questions."

I look at Vic and can tell he's thinking the same thing. "We're not going anywhere without Baz."

She stands there, staring at the recorder in her hands, opens her mouth like she's about to say something, then stops herself.

"You knew he was innocent, didn't you?" says Vic. "Earlier, when you mentioned Nzuzi's twin sister, Nsimba—that would've taken some digging. I've been trying to figure out why a sergeant with an airtight case would go to the trouble. It's because you knew he didn't do it."

"I had suspicions," she says. "Our department has been under a lot of pressure lately—there was a lot riding on

closing this quickly. The DNA from the antlers matched that in the CODIS database, which seemed pretty solid. Throw in the hat—all evidence pointed to Baz Kabongo."

"But you said so yourself." Vic points to the hallway. "Just now. You said you should have pushed *harder*. Which insinuates you pushed at all."

Mendes smiles a little, and I wondered if she didn't see in Vic what I saw: a scary realness. "I was right about you, Vic," she says. "You're smart. And kind of a nerd."

She starts for the door when Vic says, "Can you keep pushing, Miss Mendes?"

She turns and sighs, and I wonder when she last had a full night's sleep. "There are plenty of people who still need to talk to Baz, not to mention a mountain of paperwork to get through. This kind of thing takes time and you should be prepared for that. But yeah, I'm gonna push. Listen, you guys got anyone you want us to call? Someone who can come get you? Vic, we've had zero luck getting ahold of your mom but—"

"Sarah." Detective Ron is in the doorway; I can almost see the tail between his legs.

"Ron," says Mendes. "What have I told you about sidling up like that?"

"Sorry, it's just—I called the hospital." His face is a portrait of perpetual frustration, and in that frustration I find exactly what I'm looking for: our plan worked. "Olivia Chambers disappeared this afternoon. No one knows where she is."

VIC

Winter could not find us down here.

Nothing could. But then, that was the point.

As it turned out, the ex–grease trap in the kitchen floor of Napoleon's was just large enough for five people. We sat facing one another, on either side of the compartment, our backs against the walls, our legs across the floor, interlocked like shark's teeth or a backgammon board. We sat watching one another in the flickering light of a candle, bags in our laps and heaviness in our hearts, wondering if this was the last time we would all be together. And how strange: I'd only been with the group one week. But one week was all it took. I was no longer the straggler with the broken wing.

I was part of the miraculous gaggle.

The grease trap had two vents on opposite walls. *One of them used to lead to floor drains around the kitchen,* Margo had said before shutting us in. She went on to explain that when the new grease trap had been installed outside, they'd closed up that particular vent in order to reroute the drains to the new trap. The other vent led to an old dishwasher, one they never used anymore but had yet to get rid of. It was this second vent that provided just enough air for us to breathe. We'd removed our coats, hats, and gloves long ago, and took turns sitting in front of the vent.

Oxygen: the superest of all racehorses.

"I hate it down here," said Mad.

I held her hand, but not too tight. Mad's bruises were still fresh, a rainbow of pinks and blues.

"I don't know," I said. "We're in cramped, dark quarters

with limited oxygen and minuscule hopes of survival. Throw in Tom Hanks, and this is basically a space shuttle."

Mad smiled and I died, per usual.

"I still can't believe it," she said, her smile already gone. "I can't believe we left her there."

. . .

"We had no choice," I said.

She looks right at my face as if seeing me for the first time. "What if they arrest her?"

"They won't arrest her, she's an old lady. They'll assume what anyone else would—that she *couldn't* have done it. I mean, I *saw* her do it, and I barely believe she did it."

Mad shook her head. "Old age, dementia, none of it gets her off the hook. Jamma can't go to prison, Vic. She'd never last."

"We cleaned her up. Plus, she was wearing those mittens, so they won't find anything on the antlers. They're not going to arrest her, Mad. Baz is right. The plan is going to work."

Mad nods in a daze, reaches down, pulls something from her pocket, and hands it to me. "Here. I almost forgot."

It was a photo of her sitting on a street curb, looking sideways like she didn't even know she was being photographed. It must have been a windy day. Her hair was all over the place.

"A picture of you with no one else in it," I said.

"Hardly seems important now."

"It is. Even more so. Thank you."

She smiled at me, put her head back against the vent, and I'm not entirely sure she didn't fall asleep on the spot.

Consider this: a billion tiny happenings, the tenacious molecules of chance—a gust of wind here, a trip on the sidewalk there—pushing our plot, constructing our setting,

building our character, until we are who we are, where we are, how we are.

Who and *where* were easy:

1. Kids of Appetite.
2. Grease trap.

How was far more complicated:

1. This morning, the *Record*—and presumably the radio, Internet, and television—reported the crime, announcing the police had fast-tracked a warrant for the arrest of Baz Kabongo based on DNA found at the scene.
2. We were all worked up over this, Mad especially. "DNA found at the scene?" she kept saying. "Baz wasn't even *at* the scene." Baz only responded with a small sad smile. It was the same smile he used when he told the story about the broken air conditioner at the Cinema 5, and the severely uninformed employee who wrongly assumed Baz was from the jungle. That story made me shake my head, but this—this made my head spin, slowly at first, gaining momentum like helicopter rotors until my head popped right off my shoulders and into the unjust ether.
3. Within hours the police swarmed the streets of New Milford like locusts, carrying photos of Baz around, knocking on doors—*Have you seen this man?* We did not wait around for

what would surely be a triumphant response from Gunther Maywood.

4. The first place we went was Babushka's. Norm offered to hide us in his back room for a while but was hesitant to let us stay too long. He said police had been roaming the Chute, asking if anyone had seen Baz, offering immunity to nonviolent criminals should their efforts aid the police in the manhunt. Given his store's dangerously close proximity to the Chute, we couldn't blame him for not wanting us around. There, in the dangling shadows of slaughtered swine, we spent the day discussing our options. "We could just leave," Coco had said. "Skip town, and never look back." Mad shot down the idea, saying she wouldn't leave Jamma. I didn't say anything, but I didn't have to. I think Baz saw it in my eyes. Mom was still Mom, even if I barely recognized her anymore. There was no way I could leave, not permanently. After hours of talking in circles, Baz suddenly looked very pleased, smiling around at all of us. "There have been times—so many times I've lost faith. But I am sure of it now, friends. We are blessed by the Living God." Without another word, he walked over to Norm's desk, picked up the phone, and dialed a number by memory.

Baz: *"Christopher."*

. . .

Baz: *"Yes, we are fine. Sorry, I can't talk. We need your help. Can you get away from the Parlour for a while?"*

. . .

Baz: *"I don't know. Days, weeks, maybe more."*

. . .

Baz: *"Thank you. Pack a bag. Tomorrow, be at St. Bart's on Bridge Street at four p.m."*

. . .

Baz: *"You are welcome."*

And he hung up.

It was the "you are welcome" that struck me as odd. Such an outlandish request on Baz's part should surely necessitate a reversal of niceties. But that was not the case. From our brief time together at the Parlour, I'd gathered how much the kids meant to Topher—but this was an altogether different level of loyalty. Baz asked Topher to put his life on hold indefinitely, to which Topher not only agreed but did so thankfully.

Baz stood there, his hand resting on the phone. After a beat he picked it up, dialed another number by heart.

Baz: *"Rachel Grimes, please. Yes, I can wait."*

. . .

. . .

. . .

. . .

Baz: *"Hi, Rachel. Yes, I am fine. Listen, I don't have time to explain much, but . . . we need your help. You should have a new patient by the name of Olivia Chambers, probably arrived late last night, maybe early this morning. . . ."*

He proceeded to hand out complex instructions in a calm and commanding tone. What he asked of Rachel, should she get caught, would surely cost her her new job. But like the

conversation before, the call was concise and successful.

Rachel agreed to the plan.

Baz placed one more call, this time to Margo Bonaparte, whose phone number lived in his pocket in perpetuity. The conversation was also brief, and when he hung up, Mad asked how he knew Jamma would be at Bergen Regional.

"I didn't know for sure. But after such trauma, I thought maybe the police would take her to a hospital," said Baz. "Bergen Regional is closest to your house."

It occurred to me that Baz's belief in God's providence was not unlike my own belief in bumps—that someone might just as easily attribute coincidence to the Almighty as they would mathematics. Mad's grandmother happened to be taken to the very hospital at which Baz's ex-girlfriend had recently acquired a job. Whether we were all tiny red lights bumping into one another, or simply playing out the design of Baz's Living God Himself, I had to admit I was impressed.

We waited for the cover of dark and crept six or so blocks, where we met Margo behind Napoleon's. Per usual, she had her run of the place near closing. She led us inside the pub, instructed us to "take a good long piss," then directed us into the back kitchen, where she doled out six candles, matches, various breads, cheeses, and bottled waters from the pantry (with a warning not to drink too much, as we'd have to hold it for quite some time), and with a *bon appetit!*, she shut us in the grease trap.

I suspected a large part of Margo Bonaparte's eager-to-help attitude was motivated by her desire to have sex with, and produce babies for, Baz Kabongo.

But hey.

I wasn't about to complain. When called upon, each Chapter had come to our aid, and done so mightily.

We spent much of the night drifting in and out of sleep, in and out of conversation; time passed until we lost track of it. As promised, Margo returned before opening the following morning to let us out for a bathroom break. Afterward, we took five minutes or so, stretched our legs and backs, then descended into the grease trap once more. An overwhelming sense of doom set in, like reaching the finish line of a marathon only to hear the starting gun. Margo double-checked our stock of goods, assured us she would return at the agreed-upon time, and shut us in.

"Smells like a beaver's anal secrets down here," said Coco.

Nzuzi snapped once.

I didn't point out the fact that technically, castoreum smelled like musky vanilla, hence its use in perfumes and foods. Even so, I had to agree with the spirit of Coco's comment. The grease trap may have been inactive for some time, but it still smelled like the sweat mark in the armpit of a sideways hug.

We would definitely stink for some time.

Before long, Mad was asleep, slumped on my shoulder. Nzuzi sat by the vent, also asleep, his head against the wall. Across the cramped quarters, Coco lay sideways, fast asleep in Baz's lap.

Baz was asleep too. But not peacefully. Sweat poured from his forehead and face, and he mumbled in the same language from the last time I'd heard him talking in his sleep. This went on for a few minutes, and then, just like that . . . he woke up. There was no scream or jolt; he simply opened his eyes and began talking.

The candle burned low, and as he talked, I went to my Land of Nothingness. There, I saw a different burning: the hell Baz and Nzuzi had lived through.

"One evening a neighbor comes to our house, says armed civilians, rebels, are going door to door with a list of political enemies. Many people are on this list, my family among them. Soon, we hear bombs and gunfire, explosions closer and more frequent. What could we do? We ran. We left our home with the bare minimum, eventually joined by thousands of others, a sea of people afraid for our lives.

"When I asked my mother who was leading us, where we were going, she quoted Exodus 13:21: 'And the Lord went before them by day in a pillar of cloud to lead the way, and by night in a pillar of fire to give them light. . . .' She said it so many times, it came to sound like a poem.

"We followed the road to the Deep South, stopped in many villages, slept in abandoned homes when we could, or else on the road. At some point, it was decided we would head for Kinshasa, in the DRC. There were skirmishes among us—I was too young to know what they were about, but old enough to be afraid. It went on like this for three months. Three months of eating mostly cassava leaves, of watching the sick being pushed in wheelbarrows, of stepping over bodies—*people* who had dropped dead of exhaustion, malnutrition, dehydration. My mother insisted our conditions have no bearing on how we treat others. She recited Luke 21:3–4: *'Truly I say to you that this poor widow has put in more than all; for all these out of their abundance have put in offerings for God, but she out of her poverty put in all the livelihood that she had.'*

"Mother loved the Bible, but other books too. She loved introducing her students to new characters and ideas. She used to say, *We are all part of the same story, Baz, each of us different chapters. We may not have the power to choose setting*

or plot, but we can choose what kind of character we want to be.
Once a day, while we walked, she picked someone out of the
crowd, pointed to them, and said, *Baz, you see? There. That
child with the dirty face. In this chapter, you shall be her brother.*
Or, *There, the woman with the sad eyes. This is not a sad-eye
chapter. Let's make her smile.* We made many smiles, and I had
many brothers and sisters, and the Chapters multiplied."

. . .

Baz stopped talking for a moment; just when I thought he
was done, he continued.

"We crossed the Congo River early in the morning, our
canoes bumping into bloated corpses along the way. It could
be us soon, we knew. Some time later, we reached Mbanza-
Ngungu, where we stayed in a refugee camp. Death was
everywhere. It likes to make itself known, and soon enough
it made itself known to my father. He died in a clinic in
Mbanza-Ngungu. Later we learned he had been secretly di-
viding his meals among us, eating hardly anything at all.
And still, even after Father's death, my mother repeated,
'*Lean not on your own understanding. . . .*'

"A week later we boarded a truck to Kinshasa. I was eleven,
Nzuzi and Nsimba were four. We stayed on a compound with
an old friend of my mother's—I never knew the woman's
name, we only called her *Mama*. Here we dreamed our lives
were not over. We registered with the United Nations High
Commissioner for Refugees. It was a start, but Mother had
her heart set on paying rent, which meant finding income.
She suggested selling cassava leaves to local fishermen.
Kinshasa is an urban city, but there are fishing villages on
the outskirts. During our months of walking, she had de-
veloped unique ways of preparing cassava leaves and asked
what I thought of her idea, if I thought the fishermen would

pay. I said I didn't think it was a good idea. *Maybe it is our turn to be someone else's Chapter*, I said. Mother nodded, said, *Maybe, Baz. Maybe. Our Chapters were beyond helping themselves. For them the end of their story was so near, they could not see any other way. Tell me, Mbemba Bahizire—have we reached the end of our story?* I thought about this a moment, then stood and ran to the door. *I'll fetch the leaves, Mother!* It was the last time we laughed together."

. . .

. . .

"My mother and Nzuzi looked like Tutsis. Everyone said so, even from the beginning. It was not a problem—they simply had Tutsi features. But now, in Kinshasa, it was a problem. The Rwandan conflict had outgrown Rwanda, and many native Congolese were hunting Tutsi, burning them alive. I am speaking of the general population, you understand, not army rebels. Kids in the street threw rocks at my mother as she passed, simply because she appeared to be a Tutsi. Nzuzi was only four at the time, but they were ruthless to him as well.

"The International Red Cross had a camp in Kinshasa for Tutsis, a place to keep them safe. It was decided we would move there until things resolved. The night before we were to join the camp, my mother baked a loaf of bread. The flour was not cheap, but she was intent on making something for her friends who had let us stay on their compound. She sang while she baked . . . *'Great is Thy faithfulness, great is Thy faithfulness, morning by morning new mercies I see. . . .'* When the bread was done, she sent Nzuzi and me next door to deliver it. I remember how warm it was in my hands, and how much I wanted to take a bite. It was the last time I craved bread.

"Nzuzi and I delivered the bread intact. The woman we

called Mama accepted it with a smile and offered us a bottle of Coke. I had not had Coke since Brazzaville. Nzuzi had never had it. I remember he looked up at me to see what I would say. Suddenly the boss, I put on my in-charge face, very serious, and was about to say no, thank you, when I found myself nodding like crazy. Nzuzi and I split a bottle of Coke. It was my last soda.

"When the gunfire started, I did not jump. Nzuzi stood next to me, holding my hand, and I remember his little fingers flinched, but just barely. We had grown used to it. By the time we got back to our room—"

. . .

. . .

Baz stared into the tiny flame of the candle, but something had changed. His eyes were expressionless even as tears filled them and spilled.

"They were dead."

. . .

At first I wondered how Baz had done it, thrown his voice like that. His lips hadn't even moved.

"Nsimba and Mother," he said, only again, it wasn't him. I turned, saw Nzuzi Kabongo looking at me, his voice cracking now. "They were dead. They had been killed."

I thought it likely that these words, the first I'd heard from Nzuzi's mouth, described the very incident that had made him stop speaking in the first place. And I found myself wishing for more time with him, more time to learn how to hear him say other things, things that weren't quite so hard and heavy.

There was more, I was sure—the Kabongos' story was a jar with no bottom, and so it could never be filled. But Baz was done. And so was Nzuzi. And I did not push.

"They were dead," repeated one of the Kabongo brothers. I honestly could not tell their voices apart.

* * *

At some point, I fell into uneasy sleep. When I woke up, I had to pee like a Super Racehorse. Mad and Nzuzi ate bread and cheese with unbridled gusto; Coco was still fast asleep across Baz's lap, and Baz quietly hummed a calming, gorgeous song. I did not know the melody, but I would have bet the house it was a hymn.

Baz stopped humming, handed me a piece of cheese. "Rise and shine, little man. We need to review the plan."

At three p.m. Margo Bonaparte would provide a distraction to clear the kitchen of employees and free us from the clutches of the grease trap for good. She would drop off Baz, Mad, and myself at the police station, then swing by Bergen Regional Medical Center to pick up Mad's grandmother, who, if Rachel had pulled it off, would be checked out under a false name and waiting in the front lobby. Margo would then take Nzuzi, Coco, and Jamma to St. Bart's, where Topher would be waiting.

"Father Raines said the God's Geese bus leaves precisely at four," said Baz.

Precision in time is a lost art. It was a hard detail to forget. There was no doubt what time that bus would start for Tampa.

Coco stirred in her sleep.

Baz lowered his voice, spoke now to Nzuzi. "Until further notice, Christopher is me. You understand? He is in charge until we get things sorted out." Baz reached into his back pocket and pulled out a thick envelope with the words

RENAISSANCE CABS written on it. I saw a couple of hundreds peeking out of the top. He handed it to his brother. "Make it last, Nzuzi. Also inside is a note for Christopher, explaining everything that has happened, including what to do with Mad's grandmother once you get to Tampa." He looked at Mad, put a hand on top of hers. "Remember what Father Raines said about those programs for the elderly. Until you can be with her, she will be taken care of. Okay?"

Mad nodded, wiping away tears.

"It helps if you say it, Madeline."

"Okay," said Mad.

Baz turned to me now. "I owe you an apology."

"You what?"

"We never completed your father's list."

"Baz, God. It's not your fault. You guys did so much for me, I just—" A thought occurred to me, and I went with it without thinking. "Mbemba Bahizire Kabongo," I said, feeling every bit the small boy, knowing I must have butchered the pronunciation, but seeing in Baz's eyes a certain amount of appreciation for trying. "Do you need help?"

Baz's smile grew into a dancing light. "Yes, I need help."

I considered those molecules of chance, those billion tiny happenings, all with a notion to push my plot, construct my setting, build my character.

"Did you hurt anyone?"

His smile grew into a cluster of stars, and he answered with a single word. "No."

"Okay then."

For a while, we discussed tactics. If-thens. We knew as soon as we stepped in the front door of the station, they would arrest Baz, but after that it was pretty up in the air. Again we challenged Baz about turning himself in at all, but he in-

sisted it was necessary. Innocent or not, he was wanted, and he wasn't about to jeopardize everyone's futures by skipping town. And there was the added benefit that once the police thought they'd got their man, they would call off the search, making it easier for the others to escape undetected. "Anyway, it is only temporary," he said. "I have faith in you and Mad."

I only wished I could harness an ounce of that faith for myself.

But hey.

At some point it was decided our stories should end no earlier than eight p.m., enough time to give the God's Geese bus about a four-hour head start, maybe more. The police could always call other states, put out an APB or whatever. The hope was that our escaping by bus wouldn't occur to them, or if it did, that the bus would have a big enough head start to make finding it near impossible. We considered leaving the bus out of our story altogether, but Baz put his foot down, insisting we avoid anything that could be construed as aiding and abetting.

"You must tell the whole truth," he said. "Which means stalling without lying."

"And how do we do that?" I asked.

"Diversion tactics, Vic. They will need time. And we must give it to them." He smiled down at my lap, where I held hands with Mad. "Like your parents, you now have a compass. Mad is east, you are west. You will have to talk, so talk. Tell them about all the girls you thought you loved, the ones from before."

It sounded like a complete sentence, but I knew better.

The ones from before . . . Mad.

It was silent for a moment, while I inside-smiled my heart out. Baz continued stroking Coco's hair, and just then he

struck me as such a father. Not in an overly protective way, but in a sort of deep-seated softness. "The police will make assumptions," he said, more to himself than to us. "Fine. Let them think what they want. But do not lie."

Coco stirred in Baz's lap and sat up, rubbing her eyes. "What are you guys talking about?"

Baz smiled at her. "How Coconuts like you belong in Florida."

. . .

"What's it like down there?" she asked, yawning. "Tell the truth."

Baz shrugged. "I've never been. But I hear they're on the verge of a Renaissance."

There were smiles (and inside-smiles), but no one laughed. I'm not sure it would have even been possible.

"Love you, Baz," said Coco.

Eyes wet, Baz whispered, "Love you, Coco."

From somewhere in the kitchen or dining area, a high-pitched ringing sounded, as if the love of Baz and Coco had set off literal alarms.

"Margo is here," said Baz.

Apparently her idea of a distraction was to pull the fire alarm, which meant we'd have precious few minutes to get out before the place was swarming with firefighters.

"You will take care of her?" asked Baz. He was speaking to me, and I didn't have to ask what he meant.

I squeezed Mad's hand, nodded. We'd suddenly run out of time. All these minutes stacked up under us were about to topple, and we knew it.

Mad leaned over and wrapped Coco in a tight hug. "Have fun in Florida," she said through tears. "I'll be down as soon as I can, okay?"

Now Coco was crying, silently, but so hard, her little body shook.

A hand was in front of me—Nzuzi's. I took it, shook it, and it was the best handshake of my young life.

"Good-bye, Nzuzi," I said.

He snapped twice, shook his head. I looked at Baz, who said, "He wants you to call him Zuz."

I am a Super Racehorse.

I held back the tears, said, "Good-bye, Zuz."

He released my hand, leaned across my lap, and hugged Mad. It didn't last long, but it was intense. She cried and whispered some things in his ear, things I would never know, never needed to know.

A single set of footsteps sounded just over our heads. There was no time to say the things I wanted to say. So instead I just looked at them. And I think maybe they were thinking the same thing, because no one said anything at all. We all just looked at one another.

It was quite momentous.

. . .

A swooshing sound: the kitchen mat being pulled back.

"And they called themselves the Kids of Appetite," said Coco. "And they lived and they laughed and they saw that it was good."

Zuz snapped once.

. . .

"And they saw that it was good," whispered Baz.

. . .

"And they saw that it was good," said Mad, her hand still in mine.

. . .

Everyone looked at me.

"You guys are the most beautiful run-on sentence I've ever heard," I said.

"We," said Mad.

"What?"

"*We* are the most beautiful run-on sentence you've ever heard."

We.

What a word.

The latch above our heads clicked; I looked up and whispered the words that simmered underneath, the words full of heart-sense, located somewhere between Somethingness and Nothingness. "And they saw that it was good."

We shielded our eyes as the hatch door swung open, and out of the violent light came the beaming face of Margo Bonaparte. *"Bonjour, mes petits gourmands!"*

ELEVEN

THINGS ARE DIFFERENT, THINGS ARE THE SAME
(or, The Biggest Thing Is Letting Go)

VIC

"Coming Up Roses" ends.

"Coming Up Roses" begins again.

The magic of Mad.

The wind hits my hair in a new way: short, sharp, staccato. I pull the blue hat out of my jacket pocket, slip it on. Mad sings into the nighttime ether while we sit on the curb in the parking lot across the street from the police station, a steady hum of traffic rolling by. Earlier this afternoon, Margo Bonaparte dropped us off in this exact spot, and I stood here with Mad and Baz, trying to build up the courage to walk inside.

Seems like weeks ago.

And Baz is still in there.

And like that—I understand why all the other Chapters gave more than a story. Baz had given me something. I couldn't define it, but it wasn't there before. It was something warm and real, something like what I had with Dad. They reminded me of each other, actually. And it was more than just their plans for the future, and their love of baseball. They understood the simmering underneath; their simmer-

ing bubbled up to the surface, burst through in the brightest of red lights.

"Okay, my turn to make a declaration," I say.

Mad smiles at me. "Do it."

"I, Bruno Victor Benucci III, being of sound mind and body, do hereby announce throughout the four corners of Bergen County—"

"Do we have four corners, though?"

"However many corners there are, let it be known that I commit to visiting the Hackensack Police Station on a daily basis, where I will annoy the ever-loving bejeezus out of anyone and everyone until they release Baz Kabongo."

. . .

. . .

Neither of us take our eyes off the police station. The declaration isn't enough, not by a long shot. Truth is, the minute it became clear they weren't immediately letting him go, I had a thought. It was an idea that would cost me something, sure, but not much when I compared it to what I'd gotten from Baz.

There were so few red lights left in my cluster. I'd already lost Dad; I couldn't afford to lose another.

"I'm serious," I say. "I have a plan."

"Good."

Even on a freeze-your-literal-thumbs-off night like this, Mad's up-closeness is undeniably warm. It makes me sad for the future, not knowing when or how often I'll see her. But it makes me glad for the now, because there she is. Right there. Next to me. Just being her.

. . .

. . .

"You sure he's gonna show?" she asks. No one had been

able to reach Mom all day, so before leaving the station, I had an officer call Frank to come get us. I flash back to Klint and Kory crooning atop their perches on my mother's dining room furniture while Frank took a knee, and I have to wonder the same thing—will he even show up?

"He'll be here," I say, hoping my voice sounds more confident than my brain.

"You think he could take me to the bus station?" asks Mad.

"Sure. As soon as we're done at the hospital."

"Hospital?"

I give her my best *Are you kidding me?* look. "Mad. You're injured. Probably, they'll put you on bed rest for weeks."

"Vic—"

"You don't wanna go to the hospital, fine. Don't come crying to me when your bones grow back at weird angles."

"You know I have to go, right?"

I swallow hard, avoid her eyes. "Sergeant Mendes told us not to leave town. You could get in serious trouble."

"I can't just abandon my grandmother down there. I have to go."

I stare at my boots. Suddenly I hate my boots. Fucking stupid boots. "Fine. I'm coming too, then."

"Vic."

"I am. I'm coming."

"What about your mom? And what about Baz? What about your plan? You leave town, who's gonna spread news through the four corners of Bergen County—"

"Or however many corners there are."

"Right, or however many corners there are. You can't leave, Vic. Not yet."

I want to kiss her really hard for that not yet. Like, really hard. But this is my problem, because that's basically how I

feel all the time around her. And a guy can't just go around kissing a girl really hard all the time.

I'm pretty sure about that anyway.

"So what then?" I say.

"I don't know."

"We just never see each other again?"

"Of course we'll see each other. And in the meantime, we can look at the same sunset."

I want to tell her she can shove her sunset; I want the sun itself.

But I don't.

". . . *and you're coming up roses everywhere you go.*"

While Mad sings, I rub the tiny scratch on my throat courtesy of the Self-Portrait Man. I can still feel the force of his arms around my shoulders, the heat of his breath on the back of my ear. He was strong; Zuz was stronger. I think about that photo of Coco's dad, Thomas Blythe, in the hospital. I may never know for sure what happened to him, but considering the ease with which Zuz dismantled the Self-Portrait Man, I can paint a fairly plausible picture. I hear Zuz's voice from the grease trap: *Nsimba and Mother,* he'd said. *They were dead. They had been killed.* And he was just a little kid at the time—I can't even imagine.

But I bet Zuz sees the vacant eyes of his mother and sister everywhere he goes.

"He was going to kill me," I say.

Mad stops singing.

"Your uncle was going to kill me. What Zuz and your grandmother did—it was self-defense."

Mad nods. "Self-defense."

I wonder how many times over the course of my life I'll remind myself of this. A lot, probably. Because no matter how

true a justification, it always rings of falsehood.

Mad pulls out a cigarette, lights it, inhales. "By the way, good work with the whole brothers-having-similar-DNA thing back there. Cracked the case, pretty much."

Frank's words from dinner last week cover me like a heavy quilt. *Genetically speaking, brothers are just as close in DNA to each other as they are to a parent.*

"Thanks," I say. "Guess all those crime shows finally paid off."

Tires screech, and an Acura sedan pulls into the parking lot behind us.

Speak of the poodle.

The door opens and out hops a gray suit. I almost expect a fountain of green beans to spill out behind him. Frank closes the gap between us in a few quick strides, and pulls me into an awkward hug. I could be wrong, but I'm fairly certain he's crying. After a couple of manly pats on the back, he steps away and studies me.

"New hat?"

"Yep."

"Nice," he says, wagging his nose. I didn't even know people could wag their noses, but that's Frank for you, constantly redefining the boundaries of humanity.

"Victor, where have you been?"

"Long story."

I wait for him to push, but he doesn't. Instead he says, "You smell awful."

"I know."

"I mean, *really* bad."

"Frank, where's Mom?"

He smiles a little, turns to Mad, offers a hand. "I'm Frank, Vic's . . . Well, I'm a friend of the family."

Mad shakes his hand, while I wonder why Frank avoided my question. He turns, opens the back door for us, but I don't move.

"Where is she?"

. . .

. . .

His shoulders drop. "She called a few days ago, let me know she's okay, then again last night. But she won't say where she is, just says she's out looking for you. Of course, she's not answering her cell."

The street fades, replaced by sand, replaced by waves, replaced by matching tattoos.

The swinging sign of the Parlour, newly inked.

The horizon of the Palisades immortalized.

The smoking bricks of first kisses, and the ill-wishing by wishing wells.

Mom saw me carry the urn from our house eight days ago—she must have. And she knew what was inside.

Drop me from the top of our rock.

"I think I know where she is."

* * *

According to the GPS in Frank's Super Racehorse of a luxury vehicle, we're about fifteen miles from Rockefeller Center. Mad fell asleep pretty much the minute her head hit the window. In the faint glow of the passing bridge lights, I flip through the first few pages of *The Outsiders*, and from the get-go, I understand the main character. He's a loner who wishes he looked more like Paul Newman.

I do not wish I looked more like Paul Newman. But I understand the sentiment.

I read a few more pages and find myself really getting into the flow of things. Flipping to the back, I read the final passage, which is, word for word, the same as the first. *The Hinton Vortex*: a simultaneous extreme opposite if ever there was one.

As we approach the city, I watch Mad sleep, wondering how our story ends. In a lot of ways, we aren't really from different worlds. We both know the pain of losing a parent (in her case, both parents). We both know what it's like to want more than what is offered us, to see an iron bell and feel the urge to ring it, to seek out the simmering underneath, to understand that none of us, for better or worse, are chained to our history.

Because history is history.

So I'll graduate high school. And, should Frank and Mom tie the knot, I'll show up for that, too. But after that, it's nothing but Super Racehorse 24-7. My future is my own. And considering Florida is sunny year-round, my future sounds momentously bright.

But first things first.

I take a deep breath, and reluctantly turn to face my only real idea, my grand plan, my last resort.

"So, Frank," I say. "You're a lawyer. Say the cops arrest an innocent man for murder."

There's a pause, then . . . "Okaaaaaay."

And I dive in. Using only broad terms and no names, I present Baz's case in a logical fashion, including his prior arrest and suspected charges. Frank confirms what Mendes said, that if the police find a closer DNA match, then that, along with the recorded accounts of two eyewitnesses, should be more than enough to clear him. He also confirms the part about being patient. "Unfortunately," he says, "this

stuff takes time, Vic. But if it would make you feel better, I could look into it, make sure this guy isn't in custody any longer than he has to be. I'd need his name, of course."

"That would be great. Thanks, Frank."

"Don't mention it."

I search Frank's eyes, unsure what I'm looking for. There's a definite resemblance between Frank and his kids, Klint and Kory, and for some reason—I really couldn't say why—I wonder what their mother looked like.

An image: Mom and Dad and I sit around the dinner table. Dad sets down his fork, moves his hand under the table in Mom's direction. (Those hands never got lost.) And then come the words. The I-have-cancers and the we're-going-to-beat-its and the tears and the sad smiles and the, and the, and the . . . And even though I know it will get bad, at first, I don't *feel* that it's bad. Because I can't see it yet. Dad looks the same, acts the same, goes to work early, comes home late, chomps his teeth when he chews pasta, watches the news while reading the paper, checks on me every night . . .

Hey, V. You need anything?

No, Dad.

You good?

Yeah, Dad.

All right then. Good night.

Night, Dad.

He's still Dad. In the beginning. But the end of cancer is what makes cancer cancer. In the end, Dad looks like a ghost. Like some kindergartner's drawing of my dad. And then, he isn't even that anymore.

And that is cancer.

That is the end.

After he died, Mom went to a support group. She wanted

me to go too, but I don't know—I just couldn't. Joining a group meant acknowledging the possibility that I wasn't alone in that particular boat. And I wasn't ready for that yet. But Mom was. She welcomed company in her boat, her arms wide open. For a few hours every Thursday she was my old mom again; those were the best nights. And she always said the same thing: "The doughnuts were awful, Vic, but the company was great."

I lean forward between the front seats, look up at the brown eyes in the rearview.

"Were the doughnuts really that bad, Frank?"

His eyes smile, fixed on the road. "Vic, they were fucking inedible."

I look out the window as we approach the city and, not for the last time, wonder what Baz is looking at right now.

* * *

The last time I saw Baz, Mad and I stood with him on the curb across from the police station, the three of us building up the courage to enter.

"Why Hackensack?" I asked.

"What do you mean?"

I needed an explanation for those chaotic, disastrous red lights. They had flickered and scattered and dwindled, and I desperately wanted someone, just once, to make a little sense of them.

"Coco's story," I said. "About seeing the TV ad—about Hackensack being on the verge of a Renaissance, and that's the reason you guys all moved here—I mean, it's bullshit, right?"

"There was an ad. And Coco was excited at the idea of moving here."

"But it wasn't really *her* idea."

Baz kept his eyes on the police station as he spoke. "Our first foster family in Syracuse had a child of their own. A son. Most people treated us like a commodity, or an exhibit in a museum. But he did not. I liked him immediately, and we grew quite close. Things happened, things I am not proud of, and Nzuzi and I had to move. At some point, I heard our foster brother had moved to Hackensack, so when we needed a place to go, we came here."

"Did you ever find him?" I asked.

"I did," said Baz. "You met him."

"Who?"

"Christopher."

. . .

"Topher," I said in a breath. I remembered the fierceness in their hug, and the shine in Topher's eyes when he spoke of the kids, and the speed with which he'd agreed to put his life on hold indefinitely to help the Kabongo brothers.

The red lights, it seemed, weren't always as chaotic as they appeared.

. . .

"This will definitely go in the book," said Baz, his eyes focused on the police station.

Mad pulled the edges of her knit cap down. "You think that thing's going to have a happy ending?"

"Happy in some ways," said Baz.

In the ensuing silence, Mad and I were left to consider the ways in which his book might have a tragic ending. There were, unfortunately, many possibilities.

"*'Do not be afraid of their faces, for I am with you to deliver you,' says the Lord.'*" Baz turned to face Mad and me. "I know what to call it now."

"You know what to call what?" asked Mad.

"The book. I have a title. It is quite long, which Dr. James L. Conroy advises against in his book. But I'm beginning to think Dr. James L. Conroy is full of shit."

"So, what is it?" I asked. "What's the title?"

Baz smiled, and his eyes clouded, and for once I knew exactly where he went: a place where he and his father watched movies in peace; where he rocked his baby sister to old hymns of great faithfulness and merciful mornings; where he and Zuz held quiet conversations well into the night; where he and his mother never had to write Chapters to begin with. In this land the only explosions were those of laughter, the only breaking was of bread, and the only shootings were of stars across the clear Brazzaville sky.

"*They Lived and They Laughed and They Saw That It Was Good*," said Baz.

He turned and walked across the street.

MAD

Manhattan is a great place to feel small. And I don't necessarily mean metaphorically, though considering the Ralph Laurens and Louboutins and Kate Spades, I suppose it works on that level too. I just mean, there are *so* many people, and *so* many cars, and *so* many structures, and structures *upon* structures, a vast expanse of hugeness the scope of which cannot be put into words except to say Manhattan is like a vertical ocean, and the sidewalk is the beach, and standing there, looking up instead of out, you think, *My God, where does it end?*

It is the infinite horizon.

Vic and I stand at the foot of Rockefeller Center. Frank found a spot to let us out, but apparently he can't park here. He rolls down the passenger-side window, hands Vic a cell phone, and a thin roll of cash. "Miss your cell?"

"Not really," says Vic, slipping the phone into his pocket. He thumbs through the money. "What's this for?"

"You're about to go to an observation deck atop a famous building in New York City during Christmas. This is called a perfect storm. And perfect storms get pricey."

Vic slips on his backpack, leans into the open passenger window. "You're not coming?"

"Parking's a nightmare. Listen, once you get up there, call me, okay? If you find her, I wanna know *immediately*. I'll just drive around till I hear from you."

Even with the knit cap, the cold is beginning to permeate my entire head. I pull out my pack of cigarettes and light up while Frank and Vic stare at each other, trying to figure out what to say next. It would almost be sweet if it weren't so painfully awkward.

Drag.

Blow.

Calm.

Vic clears his throat. "Umm, well, th—"

A car horn honks directly behind us. Frank honks back, then smiles at Vic. "You're welcome. Now go get our girl." He rolls up the window, pulls out into traffic, and disappears in the undertow.

Drag.

Blow.

Calm.

"He's nice," I say.

Vic turns from the street, faces me. "*You're* nice."

I laugh a little burst of smoke as he takes a step closer.

"I wish you wouldn't smoke," he says.

"You can't tell me what to do."

And now Vic is kissing me as waves of people crash all around, and I drop my cigarette, and he slips a hand up under my cap, his palm cold against the shaved side of my head. His other hand is on my back, and I can tell he's nervous, every move carefully calculated, but I don't mind—I love his math. His lips are cold and firm, and I keep my eyes open the entire time, knowing he can't close his, and we find sweetness in our mutual functionality. It's a wide-eyed, punked-up, open-mouthed, cold teeth, eager-tongued, asymmetrical feast.

The kiss ends as kisses do—it's done with us, even if we aren't done with it.

"Could you feel it?" asks Vic, a slightly smoky scent still hovering in the inches between us.

"What?"

"My smile. I wanted you to feel it."

I stand on my tiptoes and kiss his forehead, then his nose, then his lips, then his chin. "I felt it."

God, I love the sweet, sticky brine of Manhattan.

* * *

It's hard not to think in terms of necessity. If the KOA needed bread, we passed on ice cream. We rationed our Babushka's allotment, knowing it would only last so long. We made a habit of thinking in terms of usage over time and, in the process, discovered that frugality was not unlike a muscle: it strengthens with use.

So when Vic forked over sixty dollars for us to take an

elevator to the top of a motherfucking *building*, I snorted out loud. The employee behind the desk gave me a weird look, like I was the one with topsy-turvy perspective.

"Sorry," I say. "I'm sure your elevator ride is worth every penny."

We follow a line of people—rampant tourists, if the snacks and T-shirts and assorted knickknacks from the souvenir shop are any indication—to a set of elevators and climb aboard. Vic and I jostle into the back corner of the compartment as more people come out of nowhere. One little kid won't stop staring at Vic, and just when I'm about to say something, the doors close, and a number of things happen: first, the lights dim, which incites a chorus of screams; music begins as the elevator ascends, and I notice the ceiling is made of glass, so we can see the elevator shaft as we rise; the length of the channel is lined with bright-blue lights, so the whole thing actually *does* feel like a ride; a movie projects against the glass ceiling, some sort of Achievements of Human History video with cameos from Martin Luther King Jr., Neil Armstrong, and Richard Nixon (so okay, maybe not *achievements* so much as *milestones*), and it's all very bright and flashy and techno, until we reach the top, and the last frame flashes on Barack Obama's beaming face, and a robotic female voice says (I shit you not), *"Welcome to Top of the Rock,"* as if arriving at the top of this building is just one of the many Important Historical Things I might witness today, ranked slightly under Barack Obama's face.

Vic and I are the last ones off the elevator.

"Welcome," says Vic, a dreamy lilt in his voice, "to Top of the Rock."

I throw one arm out in wide-sweeping grandeur. "Where *all* your dreams come true."

We laugh, look around for where to go next. I'd expected the elevator to take us straight to the rooftop, but it only went so far as the highest floor of the building. There's another gift shop, and across the room, people in hats and coats are going up an escalator.

"There," I say, grabbing Vic's hand and starting in that direction.

"What's wrong with your face?"

Even though the voice is nearby, it seems to come out of nowhere, as if we'd had a third person with us this whole time who only now decided to speak up.

The kid is only a few feet away, holding his mother's hand in front of the gift shop window. It's the same kid from the elevator, the one with the staring problem. He's probably ten or eleven—old enough to know better. The mother says nothing, but I can tell she heard. Her face is beet red, even as she pretends to be window shopping. I'm about to tell them both off when Vic walks right up to the kid, bends down so he's eye to eye with him, and says, "Nothing."

The mother turns around now, if for no other reason than because a complete stranger is kneeling down, talking to her son. But she doesn't say anything. I think even she can sense the scary realness of what's happening.

The kid studies Vic's face from different angles, completely undeterred by their sudden proximity.

"Really?" he asks.

Vic points to the kid's head. "What color is your hair?"

"Brown."

"And your eyes?"

The kid smiles a kid-smile. "They're brown too."

For some reason, I start crying. I honestly don't know why.

Vic asks, "Do you like music?"

The kid nods.

"What kind?"

"The Ramones."

Vic looks at the mom, who shrugs, and I laugh through tears because the kid's answer reminds me so much of Coco.

"I like jazz," says Vic. "And a little opera."

The kid's mom smiles down at her son, and I think maybe she's smiling at Vic too.

"So you were born with brown hair and brown eyes," says Vic. "Some people have blue eyes and red hair, some have green eyes and no hair."

A small crowd of shoppers who'd been within earshot of the conversation now gathers around Vic and this kid. "Different skin colors, eye colors," says Vic, "different families and histories and ways to love. It's better that way. We get Joey Ramone *and* Miles Davis." The crowd chuckles quietly. "So you were born like that"—he points to the kid's face—"and I was born like this." He points to his own.

The kid nods and smiles up at his mom, and I think back to the first words I ever heard Vic say, on a snowy night by the USS *Ling*.

I hope you were right, he whispered into the jar. *I hope there's beauty in my asymmetry.*

I never got to meet Vic's dad, but I'm thinking he was a pretty smart guy.

* * *

At the bottom of the escalator, people zip up coats, and slip on hats and gloves as they ascend. Vic kneels over his backpack, pulls out his photos and the urn.

"Ready?" he asks.

But there's a subtext in his tone, in the way he's standing—

upright, feet together, the urn resting waist-high in both hands like he's about to walk it down the aisle and devote himself to it in sickness and in health.

"You go," I say, picking up his backpack and slinging it onto one shoulder. "I'll wait here."

"You sure?"

I motion over to the gift shop. "Yeah, I preordered one of those Obama Fatheads—gotta see if it's ready for pickup." Vic looks at me, and I know he's smiling. I smile back, hold up my index finger. "Might get a patriotic foam finger while I'm at it."

We sort of fall into the hug when it comes, and Vic speaks into my shoulder. "I understand why you have to go to Florida. I do. Just promise me, we'll figure something out, okay?"

"I promise."

"I'm serious, Mad. I want more than the . . . mother*frakking* sunset. I want a plaque on a park bench."

Under normal circumstances, the length of this hug would be way awkward. But these are not normal circumstances, and instead of pulling away, I pull closer. A big part of me is sad I'll have to leave Vic, but it's that very same part that is so happy to have found him. Vic's theory of simultaneous extreme opposites is starting to remind me of a certain goldfish I know: it just will not quit.

"I want a plaque too," I say. "And hey—it's not like I'm leaving this second."

"I know," he said, his words warm on my neck. "I may be stuck."

I smile, and we just stand there hugging, and it is entirely glorious. People are side-eyeing us, but fuck 'em. This isn't about them, and it's not even about me, not really—it's about Vic not wanting to go up those stairs. And I get it. If

I'd had a list of places Mom or Dad wanted to be scattered, places that reminded me of the way things used to be, of a love I was born into but somehow lost along the way, I'd prolong things too. In a way, the list resurrected Vic's father—as long as he had it, he had a piece of his dad. But its completion means acknowledging the end.

"So let's do this," I say, pulling out of the hug, looking him straight in the eye. "I'll tell you what you need to hear, not what you want to hear. Okay?"

"Okay."

I still don't know what the fuck I'm going to do with my life, but I know it'll turn out okay. Because Jamma and Baz and Zuz and Coco will always be my family, but they are my Alt. My Neu is gloriously asymmetrical.

"Vic."

"Yes?"

"The biggest thing is letting go."

VIC

The prospect of standing on an observation deck is quite exciting, a sort of mecca for a quiet observer such as myself.

An observation deck is a very literal place.

. . . up, up, up . . .

As the escalator rises, the temperature drops. Nearing the top, I shift the urn around and flip up my jacket collar, but it does very little to ward off the cold. The biting wind stings my eyes, but no matter how much I want to shield them, I can't.

Because: this view.

The entire deck is surrounded by tall glass partitions, each one separated by four or five inches. I walk right up to the edge. On the other side, New York City is spread out in all its bustling nighttime glory. Buildings on buildings on buildings, and lights everywhere. Parks and trees, cars and streets, people, people, people, buzzing about.

Thousands of tiny red lights, some dwindling, some just being born: the circle of light-life.

"Victor?"

Mom's voice is like recognizing a single grain of sand on the beach. I turn and see her standing next to a bench near the escalator. And now she's right in front of me, and now she's pulling me into a hug, and now she's crying. In my hands, the urn feels heavier. Like Dad gained weight.

Mom pulls away a little. "Where have you been, Vic?"

"You first."

For a minute neither of us speak. Answers are coming, but something about being up here with the whole world spread out before us messes with trivial matters like conversational timelines.

"This is where he brought me," she says, turning back to the view. "Your father proposed right here. Said he had little money and no ring, but plenty of plans. He always had plans."

I think about Dad's plans, how people might see the things he achieved—or *didn't* achieve—and assume he failed to see those plans through. But I know better. Because I was one of his plans. And so was Mom. And here we are, together, on top of the world.

Together.

What a word.

"We looked into bringing you up here once," says Mom.

"Show you the place it all started. But it got so expensive. Bruno planned to save it for a special occasion."

Considering the urn in my hands, the momentous nature of what I'd come up here to do, and the company I was currently keeping, I'd say Dad executed this plan to a T.

I set his urn between my feet, pull the photographs from my pocket, and stare at the first one—at Mom and Dad, my young parents in love, right here where we're standing, with New York City behind them—and think about everything that's happened between then and now.

Things are different: the Twin Towers are gone.

Things are the same: the city is alive.

Things are different: I am here.

Things are the same: Mom and Dad are here.

Things are different: Dad's in a jar.

Things are the same: we are, each of us, hopeless hopers.

All things revolve around simultaneous extreme opposites.

The second photo offers the ultimate origin story. Mom and Dad with their fresh tattoos: one east, one west. I look up at Mom, then down at Dad. Guess the tattoos worked. Even now he's compassing us in the right direction.

"Where did you get that?" Mom takes the photo in one hand, covers her mouth with the other.

I don't answer. She knows where it came from. The third photo I keep down by my side. That one's just for me. Maybe one day it will be my origin story. Maybe I'll have a kid with Mad, and they'll find that photo of their mom with no one else in it, and they'll see the same kind of east-to-west type love I see in my young parents.

Mom wipes her eyes, hands the photo back to me, and looks out at the view. "After you left, I was a wreck. Called the police, of course. It took me a while, but eventually, I realized something."

"What?"

"I know you. I knew you'd open the urn, find the list. I just knew. So I went to the Parlour, but by the time I got there, you'd already come and gone. I waited on our bench off the Palisades Parkway for a while, but there was no telling if you'd already been there or not. That's when I realized the only sure chance I had of catching you was skipping ahead. I got here four days ago. Found a cheap hotel nearby. Well. Cheap by city standards."

"You've been coming up here every day?"

Mom nods. "I pack lunch and dinner. Then I sit right there on that bench and wait until they kick me out at midnight."

I try not to think of how much money Mom has wasted.

A lot. It's a lot.

"You're everything, Vic. If you don't want me to marry Frank, I won't."

Her words take shape, float up into the ether, and I try to think with my heart. "I want you to be happy." It only gets me halfway there. "I just don't want to forget about Dad."

. . .

"We won't," she says. "I promise."

I stick the photos back into my pocket, pull out my cell phone.

"Expecting a call?" asks Mom.

"I was supposed to call Frank, let him know you're okay. But I don't have his number."

"Ah. Well, there's no reception up here anyway."

She's right. My phone has zero bars. Somewhere in my Land of Nothingness, I hear pieces of a conversation from earlier today.

"Leave a voice mail?"

"Tried. Her in-box is full."

At the time, this exchange between Sergeant Mendes and

Detective Ronald hit me heavy and hard. Not that her voice mail was full, but that the call went to voice mail in the first place.

"My first day up here," says Mom, "I realized how isolated I was. If they found you, I'd have no way of knowing. So every night, as soon as I got off the elevator and had cell service, I called Sergeant Mendes to see if there were any updates."

Every night for the last four nights she checks in by phone. Always just after midnight.

I stick my phone back into my pocket. "What about Frank?"

"What about him?" asks Mom. Her tone suggests she's as surprised as I am by the question.

. . .

"He's worried sick, Mom."

"I called him," she says. "Twice. Let him know I was okay. But all I could think was, he was the reason you left."

I pull back the edge of my KOA wristband, stare at my tiny paths going nowhere. The saddest of talismans, a different kind of tattoo. The soft fabric falls back in place, and I know—I'm done with that now. The tiny paths will fade, and there will be no more to come. Mad did more than sew together some metaphorical patch. It wasn't that she fixed me so much as she helped me fix myself.

She led me to Singapore.

"Mom, I think you should give Frank another shot."

She smiles sideways; I love it when she smiles sideways. "You think?"

"On one condition."

"What's that?"

"He has to read the collected works of Dostoyevsky before picking up another Churchill biography."

She laughs like a little bird, and I wonder if maybe I was part of a miraculous gaggle all along. "The man loves his Winston Churchill, doesn't he?"

"Yeah, what is that?"

Mom slips her hand in mine, nudges the urn with her toe. "Shall we?"

I kneel down, open the lid, and stick my hand inside. It's not nearly as full as it was a week ago, but I guess that's the point. I stand up with a fistful of ashes, the gap between the glass partitions just wide enough to wiggle my hand through.

Mom puts one hand on my shoulder.

I have Dad in my hand.

It is very complicated. But not bad. This is our family, the place our red lights have clustered and lingered.

"You okay?" asks Mom.

I nod, still holding the ashes safely in my closed fist. "I usually say something. Before I scatter him."

We stare into the ether of the New York City winter.

. . .

. . .

Mom says, "Memories are as infinite as the horizon."

It's strange and wonderful knowing we've been in the same places, learned the same lines, seen the same sights. All because of Dad's blueprint. Mom and Dad had gathered their love like kindling, burned it together. And now that love is being scattered all over the place.

My fist is my focus, the KOA wristband blurred in front, the city skyline blurred behind it.

"Till we're old-new," I say.

Mom cries through her smile. "Till we're old-new."

Now the city comes into focus, a view better than any Matisse, better even than "The Flower Duet." The view isn't

art at all. It's not a product of the rhythm or asymmetry. It's the opposite of the *Ling*. I can't say where this view came from or how it got here. It just is. And I am in it. And I don't want to be anywhere else. And I don't want to be anyone other than Victor Benucci, son of Bruno and Doris Benucci, sire and dam of the century, the superest of all racehorses. And maybe for the first time ever, I stop seeing the colors that are here, and focus on the ones that aren't.

And in the night sky, the soaring sopranos fly out over the city, guarding it with song, catching the souls of those rare, lovely heart-thinkers.

Catching their ashes.

. . .

. . .

I let go of Dad.

They Lived
and They Laughed
and They Saw
That It Was Good

(or, Kids of Appetite)

By Baz Kabongo

For my mother, my father, my sister

PROLOGUE

Dr. James L. Conroy does not approve of prologues (Conroy, v–vii). I imagine, should his eyes ever land on these pages, he will find a great many of my methods to be lackluster, and very possibly substandard. I am okay with this. His pages contain almost no luster at all. (More on this in a moment.) Notwithstanding the aforementioned, Dr. James L. Conroy does believe that good stories take time (Conroy, 18–154). I find this very encouraging. If the value of one's story is found in the amount of time one spends working on it, this will be a very good story.

For it has taken a very long time.

Truth be told, it's been a struggle. There are many things happening, many reasons not to write this book. My work in the church and at the local shelter takes up much of my time. My brother and I are seeing a therapist, which has been vital in helping us process our past, present, and future. When it comes to writing, I find myself repeating those four dangerous words: *I'll do it later.* And then—last night I had a conversation with my brother. This has become a habit of ours: we spend hours under a tiny tree behind our apartment in the Windy Palms apartment complex, talking long

into the night. Until recently there were four of us who participated in these late-night chats, but one of our number moved, and the other was adopted by a close friend. (Goodbyes are often bittersweet, I know, but these were more sweet than bitter.) So my brother and I usually devote a few minutes of our discussion to the past before moving on to the future. I find a great deal of luster in these conversations. They are, in fact, far above standard.

Last night my brother said, "You have spoken for long enough, Baz. It is time to write." (Since attending community college, he has grown somewhat big for his britches if you ask me. But okay, he was not wrong.)

So here I am. Writing.

Our mother used to say we were all part of the same story, and while we could not choose the setting or plot, we could choose what kind of character we wanted to be. (Dr. James L. Conroy says nothing of the sort, though I admit I have yet to finish his book, *Writers Who Write Right Write Right Now*. I do wonder if Dr. James L. Conroy had followed his own advice and gone with a shorter title [Conroy, 178–186], then perhaps the book itself would be less of a bore. I doubt it. It really is a heaping pile of excrement.) It is all, of course, one big metaphor, comparing life to a story, but it was the way we lived, Mother and I. Even today, I find enormous comfort in it.

So—my story has many Chapters. I had planned to write them sequentially, giving an account of my life, and the life of my family, from the time I was born to the time I sat down in this moderately comfortable chair in this moderately comfortable apartment in the Windy Palms apartment complex. But I recently listened to something, and am now convinced that my story should be told using a "nonlinear

narrative" (Conroy, 402–403, then again at 411–414, and also at 1, I suppose). I could—and will—tell the stories of my mother, the films of my father, the cries of my sister, the words of my brother. I will write of war and ruin, of a very long walk through hard lands, of a trip across an ocean, of finding family and losing it, of an orchard, a butcher shop, a restaurant, a tattoo parlor. I will write things that seem impossible; I will write places that seem improbable. I will write of death, whose presence makes itself known to all; of life, who got there first; of disappointments; of broken promises; of bad choices, some made by me, some made for me; of my many families, and how each of them, for better or worse, shaped me.

But first, I will begin (that is, Chapter One will begin) with two interviews, which were recorded one year ago this month. I recently acquired these interviews during my research, and upon hearing the audio knew exactly how to begin this nonlinear narrative of mine. It would begin not with plot or setting but with the most important aspect of story: character (Conroy, 209–222). And while it may not be the *best* story, I do hope it is a good one. I am optimistic. For it took a very long time.

It begins with my friends.

Baz Kabongo
Tampa, Florida
December 2

AUTHOR'S NOTE

While Vic is entirely fictional, Moebius syndrome is not. It is a rare congenital neurological disorder primarily manifesting itself in facial paralysis. Most individuals with Moebius cannot smile or frown, and many have respiratory problems, sleep disorders, difficulty swallowing, strabismus, speech and dental complications, clubfeet, and visual or hearing impairments. These conditions often lead to a variety of other issues, including prejudice and discrimination. Many teens with Moebius are ostracized and bullied by their peers, which can cause depression and low self-esteem; it is not uncommon for people with Moebius to be treated as though they lack intelligence.

> *I believe people with facial differences need to let others know we are just like everyone else. . . . I learned when I am stared at, instead of crawling under a rock, which I always felt like, that just opening my mouth and talking breaks the tension.*

The above quote was pulled (with permission) from one of many e-mails with Leslie Dhaseleer. I had the pleasure of hear-

ing Leslie's story, and the story of Roland Bienvenu, Daphne Honma, and Sheyenne Owens, each of whom have Moebius syndrome, and each of whom had a profound impact on the arc of Vic's character development. I owe them a tremendous amount of gratitude for sharing their stories, for patiently answering my many probing questions, and for reading various drafts of this manuscript along the way. Thanks, too, to Vicki McCarrell at the Moebius Syndrome Foundation, and to the Many Faces of Moebius Syndrome Facebook page, who, when I asked for help, eagerly gave it. Each of you showed me how to smile with my heart, and for that I am eternally grateful.

(For more information about Moebius syndrome, go to moebiussyndrome.org, or visit the supreme awesomeness that is the Many Faces of Moebius Syndrome Facebook page.)

Likewise, while the Kabongo brothers are a work of fiction, many of their experiences are based on historical events. From 1997 to 1999, the Second Republic of the Congo Civil War saw thousands of Congolese citizens killed or displaced—among the latter were the Kinzounzas.

For some years I had the privilege of working with Gigi Kinzounza, and while I knew she and her family were from the Republic of the Congo, devout Christians, and devoted teachers, I knew few details of their past. Until I asked. Through conversations, e-mails, and an in-home interview (which I will never forget), I heard their remarkable story. Baz and Nzuzi's exile from the Republic of the Congo, their time spent in the DRC refugee camps, and a few misconceptions of them here in the States are largely informed by my interviews with the Kinzounzas. I cannot thank them enough for their time, for answering my questions, for reading drafts of this manuscript, but most of all for having the courage to speak about something I could never begin

to truly understand. To Raymond, Gigi, Natey, Siama, and Kutia (Abigail)—my heartfelt thanks.

I would also like to thank Patrick Litanga, for valuable insight, and for sharing some of his own experiences with me; and Darko Mihaylovich and Colin Triplett at Catholic Charities for their time in helping me better understand the refugee resettlement process.

To each of you, I offer a resounding mountaintop *thank you*.

—David Arnold

ACKNOWLEDGMENTS

To my family, Arnolds and Wingates alike, you guys are seriously the bee's knees. So thanks for that. And everything, really.

Thanks to Ken Wright and Alex Ulyett at Viking, who, in addition to making me a better writer and person, are in fact magical unicorns of wisdom and benevolence. Thanks to my Penguin family: Elyse Marshall for generally ruling; Theresa Evangelista (cover design) and Yuschav Arly (illustration) for knocking this cover out of the park; Kate Renner (interior design); Dana Leydig; Jen Loja; Allan Winebarger; Tara Shanahan for the Hackensack knowledge; fabulous copyeditors Janet Pascal, Abigail Powers, Krista Ahlberg, and Kaitlin Severini; and John Dennany for being an excellent road companion and friend.

Thanks to my incredible agent, Dan Lazar (also a magical unicorn), and to everyone at Writers House who has had a hand in this story: Torie Doherty-Munro, James Munro, Soumeya Bendimerad Roberts, Cecilia de la Campa, and Angharad Kowal. Thanks to my film agent, Josie Freeman, and all at ICM.

Thanks to the following kids for having serious appe-

tite: Courtney Stevens, Ashley Schwartau, Erica Rodgers, Josh Bledsoe, Kristin O'Donnell Tubb, Sarah Brown, Lauren Thoman, Victoria Schwab, Ashley Blake, Nicki Yoon, Emery Lord, Kerry Kletter, Rae Ann Parker, Dhonielle Clayton, Jeff Zentner, Daniel Lee, Kurt Hampe, Kate Hattemer, Ruta Sepetys, Sabaa Tahir, Renée Ahdieh, Brooks Benjamin, Gwenda Bond, Sarah Combs, Megan Whitmer, and Dave Connis; Stephanie Appell and all at Parnassus Books in Nashville; Amanda Connor and Trish Murphy at Joseph-Beth Booksellers; Wyn Morris and all at the Morris Book Shop; everyone at the Carnegie Center for Literacy and Learning; my sister-in-law, Michelle, and Jennifer Heidgerd, for their racehorse expertise; everyone at North Lime Coffee and Donuts; Carl Meier and the good people at Black Abbey; Dan Garcia, for his vast knowledge of all things art; the dream factory otherwise known as the Society of Children's Book Writers and Illustrators (scbwi.org); Marge and all at the late, great Harley's Irish Pub in Hackensack; Meg, Perry, and Chris at Fresh & Fancy Farms in New Milford (fresh andfancyfarms.com); and a certain dormant submarine who sparked an early idea—you know who you are, you sexy thing, you.

Thanks to my beckminavidera kids: Jazzy Wargs, Becky "Just-Put-Down-the-Double-Stuf-and-No-One-Gets-Hurt" Albertalli, and Adam Silvera-Arnold. You guys save me every day. And I love you. (Romantically, I mean.)

Thanks to Sergeant Eric Hobson, Robbery/Homicide Unit, and Detective Billy Salyer, Forensic Services Unit, from the Lexington Police Department for lending their time and expertise.

Thanks to Gary Mac Smith and Bunny Welch, who (in addition to the respective publishers) graciously permitted me

the use of their son's work. Elliott Smith is one of my heroes if it wasn't pretty obvious, and I am beyond thrilled to have his lyrics included in my book.

Thanks to S. E. Hinton for getting me caught in the Vortex. I'm still there, actually.

Over the past year and a half, I've met countless librarians and booksellers who have absolutely leveled me with their knowledge of books, yes, but more importantly, with their ability to get the right books into the right hands at the right times. I would be aimlessly wandering the tall grass without you guys, and I think I speak for most authors when I say THANK YOU. A million times over.

I mentioned them in the author's note, but it never hurts to say thanks twice: Roland Bienvenu, Leslie Dhaseleer, Daphne Honma, Sheyenne Owens, Vicki McCarrell, everyone at the Moebius Syndrome Foundation, and the Many Faces of Moebius Syndrome Facebook page; the entire Kinzounza family—Gigi, Raymond, Natey, Siama, and Kutia (Abigail); Patrick Litanga; and Darko Mihaylovich and Colin Triplett at Catholic Charities—THANK YOU.

Lastly, thanks to Stephanie and Wingate. I'm a big believer in the power of words, but sometimes there are none. The only four that come close: I love you two.

KIDS OF APPETITE

Can you explain your choice to set Vic's story in Hackensack, New Jersey? What specifically about the city were you drawn to, and what about it made you realize it was where Vic's story should be told?

Shortly after *Mosquitoland* sold, I realized I hadn't ever taken a trip on a Greyhound bus. You write your first book assuming no one will ever read it, so it wasn't really a concern—but then once I realized people *would* be reading it, I knew I needed to experience a Greyhound firsthand while there was still time to make changes to the manuscript. Around this time, I had an idea for a second story that would end in New York City, but I knew the whole book wouldn't be set there. So I booked a Greyhound from Nashville to Newark, the ride up being research for *Mosquitoland* and the destination being research for what would become *Kids of Appetite*. I spent a week or so traveling around Newark, Hoboken, and Hackensack, and pretty quickly landed on Hackensack. It was the perfect location: a midsize city, very walkable, surrounded by a few quaint small towns (specifically New Milford, where I found the perfect orchard for the KOA), easy bus access to the Palisades Parkway, and the USS *Ling*, which really sealed the deal.

S. E. Hinton's perennial classic *The Outsiders* is mentioned several times during the novel. You have also said *Kids of Appetite* is, in a way, an homage to *The Outsiders*. How has *The Outsiders* inspired you as a writer, and how did that subsequently compel you to write *KOA*?

Writing a second novel was a huge struggle. It's not a unique problem; plenty of writers go through second-book syndrome. You pour everything into your first one and then feel strangely empty for round two. It was right around this time that I happened to reread *The Outsiders*. I was totally captivated by the pages of reckless abandon and youthful energy, kids doing kid things one minute only to jump into the fire of adulthood the next. It actually reminded me of one of my favorite bands, Arcade Fire. Not lyrically (though Arcade Fire does touch a little on the perils of kid-dom), but in the way their songs *feel*, the way the band performs like at any minute they might hurl their guitars into the audience and run down the street for an ice cream cone. I found myself wanting to write a book that *felt* like that. Youthful energy. Reckless abandon. Hurling guitars. Ice cream cones. So being a kid, basically.

Music is a huge influence in your life and your writing. What sort of music did you listen to while writing *Kids of Appetite* and how (if at all) did it differ from what you listened to while writing your first novel, *Mosquitoland*?

The music I listen to while writing is quite different from the music that inspires me to write. For example: I love Elliott Smith, Bowie, Sufjan Stevens, Daughter, Andrew Bird, The Antlers, M. Ward, Alex G, Courtney Summers,

Brooke Waggoner, The Centennial, and tons of others. These are artists that inspire me to write, and write well. But when it comes time to do the actual writing, I lean more toward film scores and instrumental music. Some favorites include Jon Brion, Zoë Keating, Max Richter, Yann Tiersen, Alexandre Desplat, and Jóhann Jóhannsson. For *Kids of Appetite* I did include some of the more ethereal Sigur Rós tracks, which hardly count as lyrical. Other than that it was mostly Desplat's score for the movie *Birth*, and Brion's score for the movie *Synecdoche, New York*.

Tell us a little about what inspired you to write a character with Moebius syndrome. Was it intimidating to research and write about a subject you had little prior exposure to? And how did your research end up affecting Vic's story in a way you hadn't originally planned?

I'd stumbled across this video online of a girl with Moebius syndrome who was sharing her experience and explaining how frustrating it was to be so misunderstood on a daily basis. I remember thinking, "This should be a character in a book," and then immediately deciding there was no way I could write it. It was just so entirely outside my own experience, I didn't feel like I could ever do that character (or community) justice. But the idea wouldn't go away, and eventually I decided I would try it only if I could find the right help. I emailed someone from the national Moebius Syndrome Foundation and was put in touch with two people, Roland Bienvenu and Leslie Dhaseleer, who were not only willing to help me write this character but eager to see someone in literature with Moebius. They graciously shared their experiences with me, how having Moebius syndrome

affected everything from bullying to dating to drinking from a cup to troubles sleeping to severe dry eye. For two years, I emailed with them while writing the book, and once I had something ready to read, I found two more individuals with Moebius who were willing to help, Daphne Honma and Sheyenne Owens. The four of them read the book before anyone, including my editors. I could go on for pages about the specific ways they breathed life into Vic, but the truth is I owe the whole book to them. Vic isn't just more accurate because of their contribution—he exists at all and only because of them.

(To learn more about Moebius syndrome visit moebius syndrome.org, and check out the Author's Note. And to hear directly from Roland, Leslie, Daphne, and Sheyenne, visit davidarnoldbooks.com and click on "videos" for an interview with all four of them.)

You also researched Congolese immigrants to write Baz and Nzuzi. What was that process like?

I used to teach preschool with a woman named Gigi Kinzounza whose family narrowly escaped the Congo during the Second Republic of the Congo Civil War. Again, I knew this wasn't a story to be taken lightly, or something I could write without help. Gigi and her husband, Raymond, were kind enough to respond to countless questions via email, read early drafts of the book along the way, and—in what ended up being a huge turning point in the life of the novel— host me for a living-room interview where they walked me through their family's experience fleeing their home in the Congo. They showed me maps online and video footage of a river they barely made it across. I recorded the interview and it very much informed everything about Baz and Nzuzi—

from their background to their names to their experiences coming to America. Again, this book would be a shell of a story without the Kinzounzas.

Coco's "Lettuce Rap" is one of the highlights of the book. Can you tell us how it evolved?

I actually wrote it as a joke. At one point earlier in the book, I'd mentioned something about Coco being an aspiring song-writer, and I thought, "It would be funny if she was working on a rap." So I wrote one and included it in the draft I sent to my critique partners, hoping it would be good for a laugh and that's that. But they all loved it and said I should keep it in. So then I thought, "Okay, I'll leave it there as a joke for my editors." But then they loved it too. So I guess the moral of the story here is: less with the jokes, more with the rapping.

Which of the Kids of Appetite do you relate to the most?

I honestly don't think I relate to any one character more than the others, which sounds like a cop-out, but it's the truth. There's a piece of me in all of them. I don't know if this helps to answer the question or not, but we're all equally Hufflepuff . . . ?

Where did you come up with some of the recurring expressions/adages, e.g., Super Racehorse, till we're old-new, sideways hugs, the inevitability of corresponding units, Venn diagrams, the Land of Nothingness, simmering underneath, simultaneous extreme opposites, to name a few.

Again—sounds like a cop-out—but I don't know where that stuff comes from. Ideas are funny like that. They just sort

of sprout up. The trick is knowing which ones to grab and which to ignore.

What did you learn from writing *Mosquitoland* that helped you write *Kids of Appetite*?

I'm working on book three right now, and I think I'm better at trusting the process than I used to be. I don't know if that's because I've done this twice, but it's nice knowing that being stuck now doesn't equate being stuck forever. I still panic a good bit, which is how I know I'm a writer. But now when it happens I can look around and be like, "Oh yeah—I've been here before."

**KEEP READING FOR AN EXCERPT
FROM DAVID ARNOLD'S
CRITICALLY ACCLAIMED DEBUT**

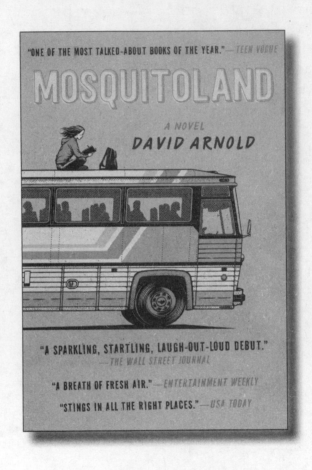

... *1* ...
A Thing's Not a Thing until You Say It Out Loud

I AM MARY Iris Malone, and I am not okay.

··· **2** ···
The Uncomfortable Nearness of Strangers

September 1—afternoon

Dear Isabel,

As a member of the family, you have a right to know what's going on. Dad agrees but says I should avoid "topics of substance and despair." When I asked how he propose I do this, seeing as our family Is prone to substantial desperation, he rolled his eyes and flared his nostrils, like he does. The thing Is, I'm incapable of fluff, so here goes. The straight dope, Mimstyle. Filled to the brim with "topics of substance and despair."

Just over a month ago, I moved from the greener pastures of Ashland, Ohio, to the dried-up wastelands of Jackson, Mississippi, with Dad and Kathy. During that time, it's possible I've gotten into some trouble at my new school. Not trouble with a capital *T*, you understand, but this is a subtle distinction for adults once they're determined to ruin a kid's youth. My new principal is just such a man. He scheduled a conference for ten a.m., in which the malfeasance of

Mim Malone would be the only point of order. Kathy switched her day shift at Denny's so she could join Dad as a parental representative. I was in algebra II, watching Mr. Harrow carry on a romantic relationship with his polynomials, when my name echoed down the coral-painted hallways.

"Mim Malone, please report to Principal Schwartz's office. Mim Malone to the principal's office."

(Suffice it to say, I didn't *want* to go, but the Loudspeaker summoned, and the Student responded, and 'twas always thus.)

The foyer leading into the principal's office was dank, a suffocating decor of rusty maroons and browns. Inspirational posters were plastered around the room, boasting one-word encouragements and eagles soaring over purple mountain majesties.

I threw up a little, swallowed it back down.

"You can go on back," said a secretary without looking up. "They're expecting you."

Beyond the secretary's desk, Principal Schwartz's heavy oak door was cracked open an inch. Nearing it, I heard low voices on the other side.

"What's her mother's name again?" asked Schwartz, his timbre muffled by that lustrous seventies mustache, a hold-over from the glory days no doubt.

"Eve," said Dad.

Schwartz: "Right, right. What a shame. Well, I hope Mim is grateful for your involvement, Kathy. Heaven knows she needs a mother figure right now."

Kathy: "We all just want Eve to get better, you know? And she will. She'll beat this disease. Eve's a fighter."

Just outside the door, I stood frozen—inside and out. *Disease?*

Schwartz: (Sigh.) "Does Mim know?"

Dad: (Different kind of sigh.) "No. The time just doesn't seem right. New school, new friends, lots of . . . new developments, as you can see."

. Schwartz: (Chuckle.) "Quite. Well, hopefully things will come together for Eve in . . . where did you say she was?"

Dad: "Cleveland. And thank you. We're hoping for the best."

(Every great character, Iz, be it on page or screen, is multidimensional. The good guys aren't all good, the bad guys aren't all bad, and any character wholly one or the other shouldn't exist at all. Remember this when I describe the antics that follow, for though I am not a villain, I am not immune to villainy.)

Our Heroine turns from the oak door, calmly exits the office, the school, the grounds. She walks in a daze, trying to put the pieces together. Across the football field, athletic meatheads sneer, but she hears them not. Her trusty Goodwill shoes carry her down the crumbling sidewalk while she considers the three-week drought of letters and phone calls from her mother. Our Heroine takes the shortcut behind the Taco Hole, ignoring its beefy bouquet. She walks the lonely streets of her new neighborhood, rounds the sky-scraping oak, and pauses for a moment in the shade of her

new residence. She checks the mailbox—empty. As always. Pulling out her phone, she dials her mother's number for the hundredth time, hears the same robotic lady for the hundredth time, is disheartened for the hundredth time.

We're sorry, this number has been disconnected.

She shuts her phone and looks up at this new house, a house bought for the low, low price of Everything She'd Ever Known to Be True. "*Glass and concrete and stone,*" she whispers, the chorus of one of her favorite songs. She smiles, pulls her hair back into a ponytail, and finishes the lyric. "*It is just a house, not a home.*"

Bursting through the front door, Our Heroine takes the steps three at a time. She ignores the new-house smell—a strange combination of sanitizer, tacos, and pigheaded denial—and sprints to her bedroom. Here, she repacks her trusty JanSport backpack with overnight provisions, a bottle of water, toiletries, extra clothes, meds, war paint, makeup remover, and a bag of potato chips. She dashes into her father and stepmother's bedroom and drops to her knees in front of the feminine dresser. Our Heroine reaches behind a neatly folded stack of Spanx in the bottom drawer and retrieves a coffee can labeled HILLS BROS. ORIGINAL BLEND. Popping the cap, she removes a thick wad of bills and counts by Andrew Jacksons to eight hundred eighty dollars. (Her evil stepmother had overestimated the secrecy of this hiding spot, for Our Heroine sees *all*.)

Adding the can of cash to her backpack, she bolts from her house-not-a-home, jogs a half mile to the bus stop, and

catches a metro line to the Jackson Greyhound terminal. She's known the where for a while now: Cleveland, Ohio, 947 miles away. But until today, she wasn't sure of the how or when.

The how: a bus. The when: pronto, posthaste, lickety-split. And . . . scene.

But you're a true Malone, and as such, this won't be enough for you. You'll need more than just wheres, whens, and hows—you'll need whys. You'll think *Why wouldn't Our Heroine just (insert brilliant solution here)?* The truth is, reasons are hard. I'm standing on a whole stack of them right now, with barely a notion of how I got up here.

So maybe that's what this will be, Iz: my Book of Reasons. I'll explain the whys behind my whats, and you can see for yourself how my Reasons stack up. Consider that little clandestine convo between Dad, Kathy, and Schwartz Reason #1. It's a long way to Cleveland, so I'll try and space the rest out, but for now, know this: my Reasons may be hard, but my Objectives are quite simple.

Get to Cleveland, get to Mom.

I salute myself.

I accept my mission.

Signing off,

Mary Iris Malone,

Mother-effing Mother-Saver

RETRACING THE STICK FIGURE on the front of this journal makes little difference. Stick figures are eternally anemic.

I pull my dark hair across one shoulder, slump my forehead against the window, and marvel at the outside world. Before Mississippi had her devilish way, my marvelings were wondrously unique. Recently they've become I-don't-know-what . . . middling. Tragically mediocre. To top it off, a rain of biblical proportions is absolutely punishing the earth right now, and I can't help feeling it deserves it. Stuffing my journal in my backpack, I grab my bottle of Abilitol. Tip, swallow, repeat daily: this is the habit, and habit is king, so says Dad. I swallow the pill, then shove the bottle back in my bag with attitude. Also part of the habit. So says I.

"Th'hell you doing in here, missy?"

I see the tuft first, a tall poke of hair towering over the front two seats. It's dripping wet, and crooked like the Leaning Tower of Pisa. The man—a Greyhound employee named Carl, according to the damp patch on his button-down—is huge. Lumbering, even. Still eyeballing me, he pulls a burrito out of nowhere, unwraps it, digs in.

Enchanté, Carl.

"This is the bus to Cleveland, right?" I rummage around in my bag. "I have a ticket."

"Missy," he says, his mouth full, "you could have Wonky's golden fuckin' ticket for all I care. We ain't started boarding yet."

In my head, a thousand tiny Mims shoot flaming arrows at Carl, burning his hair to the ground in a glorious blaze of tuft.

Before one of these metaphysical Mims gets me into trouble, I hear my mother's voice in my ear, echoing a toll, the chime of my childhood: *Kill him with kindness, Mary. Absolutely murder him with it.* I throw on a girlish smile and my mother's British accent. "Blimey, that's a lovely uniform, chap. Really accentuates your pectorals."

The Leaning Tower of Tuft calmly chews his burrito, turns, points to the open door. I throw on my backpack and ease down the aisle. "Seriously, old chap. Just dynamite pecs."

I'm out the door and into the squall before he can respond. I don't suppose that's what Mom would have meant by murdering with kindness, but honestly, just then, that was the only me I could be.

Flipping my hoodie over my head, I cross the station lot toward an awning, hopping a half-dozen rising puddles. Underneath the canopy, seven or eight people stand shoulder to shoulder, glancing at watches, rereading papers, anything to avoid acknowledging the uncomfortable nearness of strangers. I squeeze in next to a middle-aged man in a poncho and watch the water pour over the edge of the awning like a paper-thin waterfall.

"Is that you?" says Poncho Man, inches away.

Please don't let him be talking to me, please don't let him be talking to me.

"Excuse me," he says, nudging my JanSport. "I think your backpack is singing."

I sling my bag around and pull out my cell. The dulcet tones

of Stevie Wonder's "I Just Called to Say I Love You" echo off the walls of our little canvas-and-water prison. Stevie only croons when Kathy calls, altogether negating the sentiment of the lyrics.

"That's sweet," says Poncho Man. "Your boyfriend?"

"Stepmom," I whisper, staring at her name on the LCD screen. Kathy preloaded the song to be her "special ring." I've been meaning to change it to something more appropriate, like Darth Vader's "Imperial March" or that robotic voice that just yells *"Warning! Warning!"* over and over again.

"You guys must be close."

Singing phone in hand, I turn to face this guy. "What?"

"The song. Are you and your stepmother close?"

"Oh yeah, sure," I say, summoning every sarcastic bone in my body. Leaving the phone unanswered, I toss it in my bag. "We're tight."

He nods, smiling from ear to ear. "That's terrific."

I say nothing. My quota for conversations with a stranger has officially been met. For the decade.

"So where're you headed, hon?" he asks.

Well, that's that.

I take a deep breath, step through the mini-waterfall and into the rain. It's still falling in sheets, but I don't mind. It's the first rain of autumn, my favorite of the year. And maybe it's this, or the adrenaline of my day's decisions, but I'm feeling reckless—or honest, maybe. Sometimes, it's hard to tell the difference.

Turning toward Poncho Man, I notice his eyes are wet and

shiny, but it's not from crying or the rain. It's something else entirely. And for a split second, I have the peculiar sensation that everyone and everything around us has dissolved. It's just the two of us, cursed to face one another amid the ravenous elements of this bus station for all of forever.

"You know," I yell over the rain, breaking the curse. "I'm sixteen."

The other people under the awning are staring now, unable to ignore the uncomfortable nearness any longer.

"Okay," he says, nodding, still smiling with those glassy eyes.

I push a clump of sopping hair out of my face and pull the drawstrings of my hoodie tight around my head. "You really shouldn't talk to young girls. At bus stations. It's just creepy, man."

Soaked to the bone, pondering the madness of the world, I stomp through puddles to the doors of the Jackson Greyhound station. Next to Gate C, a short man in a tweed hat hands me a flyer.

LABOUR DAY SPECIAL

FOUR $DOLLAR-FIFTY GENERAL TSO CHICKEN

WHY U PAY MORE? DROP BY! WE FAMOUS!

The flyer is a domino, the first, tipping over a row of memories: a blank fortune knocks over Labor Day traditions, knocks over Elvis, knocks over fireworks, knocks over the way things used to be, knocks over, knocks over . . .

From a thousand miles away, I feel my mother needing me.

This is a thing that I know, and I know it harder, stronger, fuller than I've ever known any other thing.

Four days until Labor Day.

Ninety-six hours.

I can't be late.

D0468638

CONSIDER THIS: billions of people in the world, each with billions of *I ams*. I am a quiet observer, a champion wallflower. I am a lover of art, the Mets, the memory of Dad. I represent approximately one seven-billionth of the population; these are my momentous multitudes, and that's just for starters.